CRASHING
THROUGHTHE
WINDSHIELD

Kathryn Tatar Hardet

CRASHING THROUGHTHE WINDSHIELD

Kathryn Tokar Haidet

ARCHWAY PUBLISHING

This is a work of fiction. All of the characters, names, incidents, organizations, and dialogue in this novel are either the products of the author's imagination or are used fictitiously.

Archway Publishing books may be ordered through booksellers or by contacting:

Archway Publishing
1663 Liberty Drive
Bloomington, IN 47403
www.archwaypublishing.com
844-669-3957

Because of the dynamic nature of the Internet, any web addresses or links contained in this book may have changed since publication and may no longer be valid. The views expressed in this work are solely those of the author and do not necessarily reflect the views of the publisher, and the publisher hereby disclaims any responsibility for them.

Any people depicted in stock imagery provided by Getty Images are models, and such images are being used for illustrative purposes only. Certain stock imagery © Getty Images.

ISBN: 978-1-6657-3479-0 (sc)
ISBN: 978-1-6657-3480-6 (hc)
ISBN: 978-1-6657-3478-3 (e)

Library of Congress Control Number: 2022922592

Printed in United States of America.

Archway Publishing rev. date: 12/20/2022

For my husband,
Mark.
We are better together
than we ever could have been alone.

ACKNOWLEDGMENTS

No one goes through life alone. I certainly haven't. There were people who helped, guided, refined, encouraged, supported, and loved me, and those who didn't. All those people and the encounters I've had with them afforded me the life experiences I needed to write *Crashing through the Windshield.*

My parents, Hedwig and Stephen Tokar, were the offspring of Eastern European immigrants. Both struggled to find their place in a neighborhood that spanned two worlds, a neighborhood in the shadows of Cleveland's steel mills, a neighborhood in which I was born and raised. Although neither graduated from high school, each had a deep respect for education and the opportunities it provided. Together they were determined that their children would have a better life, and they sacrificed to ensure that my siblings and I were able to attend college. For that gift, I am deeply grateful.

My husband, Mark Haidet, and I have been together since our freshman year at Mount Union College (now the University of Mount Union). He has driven me across great swaths of the United States, sharing his knowledge of history and enjoying our mutual fascination with nature. I've seen more battlefields, forts, museums, historic sites, and state and national parks than most people. He's the love of my life and my best friend. Without him, this book would not exist. From discussing every aspect of the book, reading numerous drafts, cheering me on, and helping pick a publisher—he's been there for me. Thank you, Mark!

The author of a crime novel requires a general knowledge of the criminal justice system. I was neither a criminal nor was I in law enforcement. But I was blessed to know law enforcement personnel who were patient with my questions and generous with their time in answering them. A special shout-out to Patrick Clark, a man I never met in person but one who gave me the building blocks I needed to do the research to write *Crashing through the Windshield*. Thank you, Patrick, for your good will.

I always had the desire to write a novel. God gave me the talent to do so, and numerous people encouraged me, but I needed someone with credentials to nag me. How blessed I was to meet Nadia Christensen! She is a writer, educator, editor, Scandinavian translator, and Fulbright Scholar, and she has published more than twenty books. Better yet, she is my friend. Thank you, Nadia, for giving me confidence and for keeping me on task.

Mark and I have been blessed with three children: Jessica Hill, Jonathan Haidet, and Adam Haidet. Thank you, kids, for continuing to be there when I need you; thank you for keeping me young at heart. You have brought wonderful people into our family and have given us the most beautiful grandchildren. Such precious gifts are priceless!

I am also indebted to my two older sisters, Virginia Pirrotta and Susan Jarden, who saved me from succumbing to our childhood and have been my continuing emotional support.

In 1991, my friend Rosemary Spielmann bought me a sweatshirt from Universal Studios that had an image of a typewriter and the word "Writer." How often she told me, "You can do this!" Rosemary, it took over thirty years, but I'm wearing the sweatshirt now, and it feels great! Thank you for being there through my cancer diagnosis and treatment. Thank you for your caring, loving, generous spirit—you make the world a better place.

Thank you to those who ministered to my spiritual and emotional needs: Reverend Clarence Korgie, OFM; Reverend Francis R. Kittock; and Most Reverend Frederick F. Campbell, bishop emeritus of Columbus, Ohio. Yes, there were others over the years, but these three men were my teachers of life and the North Stars in it. I am eternally grateful.

Finally, to all those who were a positive force in my life, and there were many, thank you. To all those who read the drafts of my novel and offered suggestions, thank you. To Mark Haidet, Jessica Hill, and Virginia Pirrotta, who helped with the final galleys, thank you. To all those at Archway Press who brought my dream into reality, thank you. I couldn't have done this without you!

CHAPTER | 1

FRIDAY, SEPTEMBER 15

Elizabeth Edwards sat in the white wrought iron chair outside of Clementine's Creamery watching her two charges, Will and Emma Jurlik, jostle each other for the best position on the adjacent bench. Will, a big-for-his-age five-year-old, was loudly protesting Emma's coveted spot near the empty chair. Emma, a quiet ten-year-old, sat like a stone statue with arms crossed and eyes staring straight ahead. Elizabeth had met these children for the first time less than four hours ago. They were ignoring her.

The orange pink of the setting sun on the far horizon gave hope to the end of a wretchedly sweltering day and momentarily soothed her uneasiness. She mused that this day had not played out as she anticipated. She had thought that when Gloriann picked her up from the train station, they would spend a relaxing evening at home getting to know each other. But Gloriann had other plans—a picnic supper in Lafayette Park, a walk around the swan pond and fountain, time at the playground, then a quick jaunt to get "the best ice cream ever" at Clementine's.

The early evening held on to the day's heat. The temperature had hit ninety-one degrees, and although some relief came with the mellowing shades of darkness, Elizabeth was still uncomfortable.

"I want to sit there, Emma! It's my turn to sit next to Mommy. It's no fair," wailed Will.

"Will, your mother will be out in a minute," Elizabeth said as she got up to look through the shop window. Clementine's was crowded, but Elizabeth could see everyone waiting in the small store, and Gloriann wasn't among them. She looked for the stroller with the sleeping Martin but didn't see that either.

"OK, kiddos, let's go and help your mother with the ice cream."

Once inside, Elizabeth made her way to the counter and asked if a woman with a baby had ordered ice cream. Before the gal at the counter could answer, someone pointed to a side door and said, "She went out to the patio." Will and Emma ran out the door, with a relieved Elizabeth following close behind. Several couples were sitting in the horseshoe of park benches, and a family of four had claimed the only patio table.

"Where's Mommy?" Will asked as he scanned the people.

Elizabeth approached the family. "Excuse me, have you seen a woman with a baby in a stroller?"

"Ah, yeah. She left," the man said, pointing at the gate that led out to the street.

Emma, Will, and Elizabeth walked out, stood on the sidewalk, and looked in each direction. Gloriann was not in sight. They walked around the wood fence that enclosed the patio and eyeballed the adjoining parking lot. There were only two cars and just a few empty spaces. Since the parking lot was adjacent to an alley, Emma bolted ahead to see if her mother was hidden by the nearest garage. As Elizabeth and Will caught up to her, she turned to face them, alarm overtaking her face.

"Don't worry. Your mother must be around here. I'll call her. She has got to be here someplace," Elizabeth said, fumbling for her cell phone. When Gloriann didn't answer, Elizabeth swallowed down her panic and began to search the phone for walking directions back to the house. She really did not know where she was in relation to Gloriann's house or if they would have to walk back through the now-dark park. Then Will sat down on the ground and curled up in a ball; Emma stood ramrod straight, tears rolling down her cheeks; a befuddled Elizabeth called 911.

Elizabeth coaxed the children into reclaiming their spots on the wrought iron chairs in front of Clementine's. There was no fighting now as Will and Emma molded into one slumping mass, shielding themselves from Elizabeth. "Don't worry. It will all be OK. The police will come and help get us home. Maybe your mother is already there. If not, we can at least call your father. He'll know what to do. Look, I know we just met today but, Emma and Will, it's going to be OK," said Elizabeth.

Emma looked up with a squint of hope in her eyes. Will's body relaxed a bit. Neither one of them spoke.

It was about 7:30 p.m. when the white squad car pulled up to the curb with its rack of lights flashing. Both children sat up, and Elizabeth stood. She hesitated, wondering what she should do with her hands, remembering the recent police shootings that dominated the news. As the officer opened the squad door, Elizabeth tentatively approached with her arms held out at her sides, hands visible with palms showing. Standing several feet in front of the officer, she stated clearly, "I called nine-one-one. My name is Elizabeth Edwards, and I want to report a missing person."

The officer looked at the sixty-something woman, stole a quick glance to the left at the children, who appeared to be waiting for Elizabeth, and then to the right at the small gathering of onlookers.

"I am Officer Brian Vickter. Are those two with you?" he asked, pointing with his head toward Emma and Will.

"Yes, Officer."

He looked again to his right and then asked, "So who is missing?"

"Gloriann, the children's mother, and her baby, Martin. So there are two missing persons. They were here with us, and now they seem to have disappeared. I called her cell phone, but she didn't answer. I don't know what happened to her, and, well, I'm new in town. I just met Gloriann and the kids today, and frankly, I just don't know what to do."

Emma and Will began to approach Officer Vickter. Smiling in their direction, he whispered to Elizabeth, "Their names?"

"Emma and Will Jurlik," answered Elizabeth.

"Is there a father?" Officer Vickter continued.

"He's back in Tucson on some kind of FBI assignment."

"FBI?"

"Yes, he's an FBI agent and went back to Tucson for a week. They are originally from Tucson but are here in St. Louis for a couple of years on assignment. I guess he had to go back for some reason."

"Have you called him?"

"No. I've never even met him! I asked Emma if she knew his phone number, but she said she didn't. She said her mom has it in her phone, and it's written on the wall at home," Elizabeth replied, trying to keep frustration and upset from overtaking her.

"OK. All right. Tell me what happened."

As Elizabeth related their evening, beginning from when she met Gloriann and ending with the ice-cream stop, Will began whining, "Where's Mommy? I'm hot. I don't feel good. I want Mommy."

Officer Vickter asked him, "Would you like to sit in the back of my squad car? We'll get you some ice cream, and you can eat it in there. Would that make you feel better?"

Will considered this and decided it would. "Can we eat in your car? Mommy doesn't let us eat ice cream in hers."

"No problem, Will. If you make a mess, I can just hose it out," explained Officer Vickter.

"Really?" Emma was doubtful.

"Yes. Really."

When the two children were settled in the back, examining their new plastic police badges, Officer Vickter sent Elizabeth into Clementine's to get the ice cream while he questioned onlookers and customers. After identifying who might have seen anything and obtaining their contact information and answers to a few questions, he returned to the squad and told Elizabeth that he had contacted another squad to check the park and surrounding area. Then he drove them back to Gloriann's house.

"You do know where it is?" asked Officer Vickter.

"Well, it's on Park Avenue across from the entrance to the park. I have the address in my phone." Elizabeth began scrolling through her contacts. "I'm not sure I'd recognize it, especially in the dark. Remember, I just got here; I've never been here before." She gave Officer Vickter the address.

"I know what my house looks like," came the flat voice of Emma, who was sitting next to Elizabeth.

Elizabeth looked at the two tired children. She felt sorry for them, and she felt sorry for herself. How did they ever end up in this situation? It was craziness! And where were Gloriann and Martin? Why had Gloriann been so eager to go to the park and Clementine's, when all Elizabeth had wanted to do was spend a quiet evening before tomorrow's full day? She closed her eyes and sighed, then opened them and looked out the window. There had to be a logical explanation.

In the dark, the house looked scornful with its unyielding stone facade looming over them as they mounted the steps to the front door. There was a light in the downstairs front window, and Elizabeth hoped beyond hope that Gloriann was home. When no one answered the doorbell, Officer Vickter asked, "Does anyone have a key?"

Elizabeth looked at the children and then said to Officer Vickter, "No. Can you do something to open the door?"

"Oh, no, ma'am. We're not allowed to open a locked residence unless we have a warrant or there are exigent circumstances, like a crime being committed or someone in danger," said Officer Vickter.

As they stood there looking at each other, Will piped up, "Emma, tell them about the key."

"No, Will. Be quiet," an irritated Emma responded.

Officer Vickter asked Emma, "Do you have a key?"

"No."

"Why did Will ask you to tell us about a key?"

"I don't know."

"Emma, if for some reason, you know about a key, please tell us. Right now, we should be looking for your mother and talking to your father. To do that, we need to get into the house. If not, we probably will have to go down to the police station and find out how to contact your father. That's going to take a while. The faster we get into the house, the faster we can get some answers. Emma, please," said Elizabeth.

"Well, there is a key in a secret hiding place in case we get locked out," offered Emma. "I can go get it, but I'll need a flashlight." When no one moved or said anything, Emma continued, "It's under a rock next door."

"Next door?" Elizabeth asked.

"Yes, Mom said that if we hide the key next door and someone finds it, they'll think it is for that house, not ours."

Officer Vickter accompanied Emma to the narrow space between the two houses, retrieved the key, and soon they gained entrance to Gloriann's front foyer. Will started to run into the house, but Officer Vickter gently grabbed his arm to stop him, saying "Wait a minute, Will. I want to make sure everything is OK."

Elizabeth wanted to say, "So now you have an exigent circumstance?" but remained silent, for she felt her skin begin to crawl with a feeling of trepidation as she looked at the shadows created by the light coming from the parlor. The parlor was to the right of the front door, with two large mahogany pocket doors that were three-fourths open. To the left, opposite the parlor, was a granite fireplace with an oak mantel. Directly facing the front door, an arched stairway led to the second floor; it was flanked by a hallway offering passage to the kitchen. A large gold and white hurricane glass chandelier hung from the ceiling. The house was eerily quiet.

This was an old house, built at the end of the nineteenth century, with over four thousand square feet, three stories, a basement, and several roof porches. If Gloriann was there, she could be anywhere, Elizabeth thought. Officer Vickter must have read her mind because he again contacted dispatch, this time for backup.

"Let's just wait here until another uniform shows up," Officer Vickter said.

"Why do you need another uniform?" asked Emma.

"Did you make a mess in your uniform?" Will said with a smirk. He put his hand over his mouth and began to giggle.

"Oh, gosh no." Officer Vickter was taken aback. "No, when I said another uniform would show up, I meant another police officer."

"Well, that's silly. Why do you call police officers uniforms?" Emma asked.

"Yeah," said Will. "They're not uniforms; they're people."

Officer Vickter tried to explain, but the children were having a hard time grasping the concept. Finally, his shoulder radio squawked, and he felt an overwhelming sense of relief to end their conversation. "OK, everybody. The other squad is close. He'll be here any minute. He will check out the house. When he's done, we'll go into the kitchen to look for the phone numbers. You know where they are, Emma, right?"

Emma nodded. She kept looking around the foyer and up at the ceiling, listening for movement coming from upstairs. Only the furnace fan cycling the air-conditioning produced any sound.

Officer Vickter heard footsteps on the porch, opened the door, and explained his plan to the responding officer. When that officer cleared the kitchen, Officer Vickter said, "OK, Emma, show me where the phone numbers are." They all followed Emma as she led them to a list of names posted on the side of the refrigerator. Officer Vickter looked at the names. "Mom" was at the top of the list, followed by "Dad." "Emma, what is your father's name?" Officer Vickter asked as he tapped the numbers on the kitchen phone.

"Jack Jurlik."

When the landline number of his St. Louis house displayed on his cell phone, Jack smiled and quickly answered. He was surprised to hear a man's voice, a police officer who began informing Jack of the disappearance of his wife and infant son. At first, Jack thought it was a prank call, a scam, something other than what the officer was telling him. When Officer Vickter told him that Will and Emma were all right and that they were with Elizabeth, Jack shook his head. "Who?"

"Elizabeth Edwards. She was with the children at the ice-cream shop."

"I don't know anyone named Elizabeth Edwards."

"Your wife picked her up from the train station, and she's staying here overnight. She was the one who called for help."

"Tell her that I never heard of her."

When Officer Vickter repeated Jack's assertion, Elizabeth stiffened. "Oh, for pity's sake! Tell him I'm Helen's cousin from

Minnesota. I'm here for a writers' conference. Helen, his mother-in-law, is my first cousin! Helen wanted me to meet Gloriann, and Gloriann invited me to stay tonight."

Jack was lodging with his in-laws, Helen and Stan Novak, because he and Gloriann had rented out their house when they moved to St. Louis. He asked Officer Vickter to hang on while he checked with Helen. When he returned to the phone, he told Officer Vickter that Elizabeth was indeed Helen's first cousin. They had reconnected on Facebook a few years ago and visited with each other in person briefly in February. He added, "I don't know anything about her. She might be fine and her visit just a coincidence, but don't leave her alone with my kids."

"Understood," Officer Vickter said, transmitting a concerned look to Elizabeth.

"I'll call someone from the agency to come over," Jack continued.

"Listen, that's not necessary. St. Louis PD—"

"I know," Jack interrupted. "I understand. I am only sending a friend from the agency to stay with the kids. I do not want you taking them to social services. Someone will be there within a half hour. Just check creds."

"All right," Officer Vickter agreed.

"I'll get a flight as soon as I can. It's about 6:30 p.m. here, 8:30 p.m. your time; I should be able to be there before you see the sun rise," Jack said, thinking out loud. "Please stay in touch with me. Keep me posted if anything should develop. I'll work things on my end. I'll talk to her parents, her sister," Jack said as he was already throwing clothes in his suitcase. "As soon as the detective gets on the scene, have him call me. Thanks, Officer Vickter," Jack said and disconnected.

This can't be, Jack thought. *What is happening?* He told himself to calm down and began to make a mental list of what he needed to do: call Lou at the agency; call Greg and Glenn to schedule a flight;

talk to Helen and Stan; call Mel. Even if this were some sort of misunderstanding, some minor incident, he'd better get back to St. Louis and handle it all. If this were an abduction—no, he couldn't think of that now. He had to stay focused. "Stuff the emotions. Do what you do best, Jack," he told himself as he made his first call.

Lou Esposito would stay with Emma and Will. The kids had met her several times, so she would not be a stranger to them, and Jack trusted her. She assured Jack that although she could not be there in an official FBI capacity, she would guard the kids and keep abreast of the investigation until he arrived. "Don't worry, Jack. I am dressed for the job. Nothing is going to happen to Emma and Will. At least you can rest your mind about that."

Jack dialed his friend Greg. "Hey, Greg? Jack. Look, I need your help. Something has happened to Gloriann, and I better get back to St. Louis as soon as possible. Can I get a flight out tonight?"

"What happened Jack?"

"I'll explain later. Do you think you can get me a flight?"

Greg could hear the tension in Jack's voice. "Yeah. Sure. I can work something out. Let me call Glenn and see what we can do."

"OK, thanks. I really appreciate it." Jack sighed and walked out of the guest room and down the hall to talk to Helen and Stan.

Helen and Stan were both seventy-five years old, retired for the last ten years, and doting grandparents. They were active and in good health, so Gloriann and Jack felt they could relocate to St. Louis for two years and not have to worry about them. Of course, Helen and Stan were not happy with the move, but they realized that Jack would have to travel for his job, and he had been lucky that this was his first long-term, out-of-state assignment. Still, they mourned the loss of not having their grandchildren nearby. They had been to St. Louis for Christmas and again in July to help Gloriann after Martin was born, and they were delighted to have Jack stay with them now.

They were looking forward to having everyone back in Tucson by the end of the year.

Helen and Stan were in the living room, sitting rigid in their matching rust-colored La-Z-Boys, solemnly waiting for Jack to come back and tell them what was happening. He did not want to alarm them; he didn't want to lie to them; he didn't want to tell them that their beloved Gloriann and almost-three-month-old Martin were missing. He spoke quietly and matter-of-factly, telling them exactly what Officer Vickter had told him. They absorbed the news too calmly, not as people who did not understand the gravity of the situation but as people who knew that if they surrendered to their emotions, they would lose all control.

Stan spoke first. "What do you think happened, Jack?"

"Stan, I honestly don't know. That's why I need to leave soon, so I can get a flight back tonight."

Helen asked, "Jack, do you think they were kidnapped? Do you think it has to do with your work? I mean, even when you were here with Border Patrol, you were working drugs and human trafficking."

"I don't know how that could be. I really don't. Let's not start creating scenarios in which we have no proof. I need to get back, take care of Emma and Will, find out what the police know. I'll contact you as soon as I know anything."

"What can we do to help? We need to do something, Jack," Stan said.

"Right now, don't say anything to anyone except Mel. It's too early. We need to figure things out. You can pray. You can contact the prayer teams with a special intention. That would be a huge help. I've got to get to the airport now. Tell Mel I'll call her as soon as I can," Jack said as he stood and hugged first Helen, then Stan.

He heard them begin sobbing as he closed the front door. He walked fast, wanting to flee to the car away from the pain, but the pain was inside him, lodged below his breastbone with unrelenting burning. He threw his work duffel and suitcase on the front passenger seat, tapped the Glock nestled in his shoulder holster, got behind the wheel of the rental, took a deep breath, then started the car. He felt guilty leaving Helen and Stan the way he just did. He felt guilty for leaving his family behind in St. Louis. He had lied to Gloriann. He didn't have to come back to Tucson for a week. He hadn't been ordered to do it. He had orchestrated the trip because he needed to get away from Gloriann and Martin to clear his head and come to a decision. Now they were both gone! "Oh, God, let them be all right. Please help me find them," Jack pleaded.

CHAPTER | 2

As Jack left the Catalina Foothills and turned right onto Tanque Verde, he was driving on autopilot. Movies of memories played in his mind; puzzle pieces of thoughts begged for composition; regrets and anger and fear took turns tightening the muscles of his neck. When he saw the neon sign of G & G Aviation, he was astonished that he was already at the airport. He didn't even remember the drive. Glenn was walking toward him.

"Greg is waiting for us inside," Glenn told Jack, clapping him on the back and bringing him back to the present.

"You're both here?" Jack was incredulous.

"Hey, Jack. You said something happened to Gloriann. Of course, we'd both be here. We're your pilots for tonight."

Jack nodded and turned his head so Glenn wouldn't see him blinking hard. Jack had met Glenn and Greg in 1998 when he began working at the Tucson Air Branch of US Customs and Border Patrol (CBP). They were seasoned Air Interdiction agents who left the CBP in 2001 and began flying charters for a private Fixed-Base Operator (FBO). When Greg became heir to a large inheritance in 2003, he bought the company, took Glenn as a business partner, and renamed the business G & G Aviation. That was fourteen years ago, and they became one of the more popular FBOs at the Tucson Airport. When

Jack married Gloriann twelve years ago, Greg and Glenn and Jack's two brothers stood as groomsmen. Glenn and Greg had shared so much of his life; they were always there for him, and they were there again for him tonight.

In the FBO terminal, Greg came up and gave Jack a quick half hug. He wanted to interrogate him about what was happening but held back. Jack would tell him when he was ready. "We're taking you out in our newest acquisition. Oh, Jack, she's a beauty! Top-of-the-line Cessna Citation CJ4," Greg told him. "Let's get going. We're ready to take off in fifteen minutes."

"What's this costing you, Greg? I can—"

Greg cut Jack off. "Hey! Don't worry about it. I already talked to Al in St. Louis, and he has some clients looking for empty-leg flights to Tucson. We'll fly you in, refuel, pick up a few fares, and fly back. No problem."

Greg completed the walk around and boarded the jet first. When he got to the top of the stairs, he turned and smiled at Jack. "Welcome aboard. It is a beautiful night for flying. We should be arriving in St. Louis in a little over three hours." After Jack boarded, Glenn entered and then closed and locked the door.

Jack stowed his gear and took the couch seat in the cabin behind the copilot. Greg was already in the left captain's seat when Glenn closed the cockpit door. Jack knew they would not open it until they reached cruising altitude, as they did not want any distractions or the glare from the cabin lights.

He missed flying. He closed his eyes and imagined Glenn saying, "Your aircraft," and Greg responding, "My aircraft." Soon, they would be cleared to start engines. They would check instruments; with engines spinning, they'd call ground for clearance to taxi. Jack had heard the engines start up and opened his eyes. He was bumping along, looking out the window as the scenery passed. Then the jet stopped. He knew they were holding short of the runway until cleared for takeoff. The engines started to whine, then roar, the sound growing louder and higher pitched. The jet began to vibrate; they were picking up speed. He guessed they were past V1 and knew they hit V2 when the nose tilted up and they started climbing out. His ears popped. It was a clear night, and soon the lights of the city were replaced by the beauty of the stars.

He realized they were past ten thousand feet when Glenn slid open the cockpit door. "You OK back there, Jack?"

Jack knew this was Glenn's subtle invitation to tell them about Gloriann. He did.

Greg mused, "They are both missing? Gloriann and the baby? But not the other kids? Hmmm."

"What are you thinking, Greg?" Jack asked.

"Well, I can't say. It just seems odd. Odd that they literally disappeared while the other two kids and this Elizabeth were sitting in front of the store. Maybe I saw too much human trafficking in my day—Gloriann is a looker, and the baby, well, you know. I mean they could have been abducted. But no one saw what happened? No one heard anything? Humph."

"Maybe she has postpartum depression and decided to ditch the kids for the night since Elizabeth was there. She'd have to take the baby. She's nursing, right? Maybe that's all it is, Jack, and she'll show up in the morning," Glenn said. "Heck, I remember when my sister had postpartum depression. She waffled between being supermom, wanting to throw the kid out the window, and running away from home. Her doctor helped her get a handle on it. Thankfully, she got over it."

Jack sighed. "I don't want to think about abduction. There are people capable. I know that. I just can't go there until I have more information. Maybe she does have postpartum depression. She hasn't been herself lately. She was on an emotional roller coaster during the pregnancy. And I know doing this stint in St. Louis has been hard on her. I've been so busy, and it's not like back home where she had her folks and friends. I put in a lot of hours with the Bureau; there's a higher expectation, more pressure."

"Well, you can always come back to the CBP. They are begging for people. With Trump tightening up the border, they'd welcome you back in a heartbeat. You were their golden boy, Jack," Greg said.

"I don't know about that. No gold here tonight."

Greg and Glenn changed the conversation, updating Jack on their lives and the business. They talked sports and news. When they exhausted their talking, and Jack did not break the silence, Glenn closed the cockpit door. Jack left the couch for one of the club seats, put on his seat belt, reclined, and tried to catch some sleep before they landed.

He drifted in and out of sleep, only becoming totally alert as the jet was touching down in St. Louis. He pulled the seat up, rotated his neck, and stretched his arms. The jet came to a stop, and Glenn opened the door to the cockpit. "Did you get any sleep?"

"Yeah, thanks. I did," Jack said as he stood up and collected his things.

When all three men were outside standing near the jet, Greg said, "Listen, Jack, if you need anything—anything at all—just call. Keep us posted if you can."

"I don't know how to thank you guys."

"You can buy us a beer when this is all over," Glenn said. "How are you getting home?"

"The car's in long-term parking. I'll shuttle over there."

"OK then," Greg said with two hands on Jack's shoulders. Glenn shook Jack's hand and slapped him on the shoulder with the other. It was half past two in the morning when Jack finally got behind the wheel of his car.

As he was nearing his neighborhood, he could hear sirens in the distance. He began to drive faster. Approaching his house, he noted there were two cars parked in front but no squads. Lou's car was across the street, under the trees outside the park. He drove around the corner to his alley. He hit the garage door opener and watched the door slowly rise, revealing first the tires, then the back, then the roof of Gloriann's van. He took the flashlight out of his glove compartment and shone it through the van's windows. Martin's car seat and Will's booster were still in the back. He closed his eyes, took a deep breath, and walked to the back door of the house.

Jack knocked, making his presence known before inserting the key. Lou was at the door even before Jack could open it. Her face was like a fast-forwarded movie, changing from relief, to worry, to deep concern, and finally pausing on a neutral expression. Jack looked from Lou to a man he didn't recognize. Lou said, "Jack, this is Detective Allen Klein."

The two men shook hands, and Jack waited for Klein to take the lead. He did. "Jack, are you carrying?" Klein could see the bulge in Jack's jacket. "I'd like you to give the gun to Lou." Jack hesitated. He had every right to keep his gun, but he handed it to Lou with a question in his eyes. Klein continued, "We're in the kitchen. Detective Wyatt Guilder and I will bring you up to speed."

"I want to see my kids first. I need to see them," Jack said.

"They are OK, Jack. They're sleeping," Lou assured him.

"And Elizabeth?" Jack asked.

"She's in the guest room. I'm not sure if she is sleeping or not. But I think she might be." Lou was restrained in her response.

Klein was rigid, his gaze intense. He motioned for Jack to head to the kitchen. Jack acquiesced. He entered the kitchen, met Guilder, and took a seat at the kitchen table. "OK, here's where the investigation stands," began Klein. "We took a quick look at the house and garage and didn't notice anyone or anything suspicious. Did a quick canvass of your neighbors. Didn't find out much, but we'll continue in the morning. Canvassed the park—nothing.

Found Gloriann's cell phone under one of the cars in the parking lot by Clementine's."

Jack moaned. "Her cell phone under a car? Does it work? Where is it?"

"We've got it in an evidence bag," answered Klein. "Put out a BOLO and activated the Emergency Alert System. Got photos from your friend Lou. Elizabeth was able to tell us what Gloriann and Martin were wearing. Sent a missing person's report to Tucson and Phoenix." Klein paused and looked at Jack. "And we got a search warrant for your house and garage."

"What?" Jack exclaimed, shooting a look at Lou, who raised her eyebrows and gave him a tight smile.

Klein continued, "You know the drill, Jack. We've got a woman missing under suspicious circumstances and an at-risk minor. You know the time frame on this."

Jack knew, but he wanted to scream, "Why didn't you call me? Why didn't you keep me posted like I asked?" He felt his neck getting red, but he checked the emotion before the color crept onto his face. He was steady when he asked, "OK. Anything of help?"

That's when Detective Guilder stood up and asked, "Do you want some coffee or tea or something?"

Jack stared at him. This was Jack's kitchen. Jack's coffee. Jack's tea. Jack's house. Jack's family. "What are you trying to tell me?" Jack asked.

"Looks like Gloriann's clothes are missing. Suitcases are still in the closet, but there are a lot of empty hangers. Either she didn't have a lot of underwear or …. Baby's things are missing too—no diapers or wipes; we believe clothes are gone. We'd like you to have a look to confirm. You know we couldn't ask the kids without you being present."

Jack looked again at Lou. She slowly nodded her head in agreement. Guilder and Jack went up to the bedrooms. Jack checked the closets, the dresser, the bathrooms. He checked Martin's room. The sight of Martin's empty crib with the smiling forest animal mobile gave him a gut punch that made it hard for him to maintain his composure.

"You're right. Gloriann's things are gone. So are Martin's. This doesn't make sense. None of this makes any sense," Jack said.

"No. Of course not, Jack," agreed Guilder. Then he added, "Do you know the password to her phone and computer? We are going to have forensics search those. It would be easier for us if—"

Jack interrupted, "Yes. I know them. I'll give them to you."

"Do you think she is capable of hurting Martin?" Guilder probed.

"No! She'd never hurt him. Gloriann wouldn't hurt anyone. She wouldn't leave like this. Something is wrong. They must be in danger. I want to call my supervisor," Jack responded.

"For now, we are assuming that Gloriann is at risk, and she has Martin with her. We'll do everything we can to find her. We have a search warrant for your phone and computer, too, Jack. You understand."

Jack did understand. He knew that over half of all female homicides were committed by a man intimately connected to the woman. He knew that "look to the husband first" was part of investigative thinking. He could not blame Detective Guilder; Jack himself had acted on that same philosophy. He had questioned husbands, boyfriends, and former lovers, considering them suspects until he could prove otherwise. He ignored their protestations and sometimes raw, hurting emotions. Did they feel what Jack now felt? Unjustly accused; frustrated over wasted time not looking for the real perpetrator; angry and hurt for even suggesting that he could have harmed his wife and child? And scared? Jack was so scared for Gloriann and Martin. No, he knew that it would be best to cooperate and aid the St. Louis PD as best he could. They all had the same goal, and so far, the police had acted quickly and efficiently.

"Yes. I understand, Detective Guilder. I know how the investigation must go. Let me just call my supervisor. The FBI can start things on their end, seeing if there is any connection with my work. Then can I talk with Elizabeth?"

"Call your supervisor. But, no, better we talk to you first before you talk to Elizabeth. We plan to interview her more extensively in the morning," Guilder said. After Jack made the call, and the three men resumed their seats at the kitchen table, Lou went to lie down in one of the unoccupied beds.

"OK, Jack, let's just get to it," said Detective Guilder as he put the voice recorder on the table.

After it was established that Jack did not know of any plans for Gloriann to leave; that she did not have his permission to take Martin; that she was not on any kind of drugs or medication; and that he had neither met Elizabeth Edwards nor knew that she would be staying at his house, Detective Guilder let silence hang in the room. Jack knew that Guilder and Klein were giving him time to ponder what was coming next and to observe his facial expressions and body language. Jack could wait them out.

Klein then began the next round of questions. "Has Gloriann ever gone missing before?"

"No," Jack responded, shaking his head.

"Do you think she would have left you and the older kids?"

"No. That would be totally out of character for her. She's not that type of person. She'd never leave us. I can't explain why her clothes and Martin's things are missing. That's why I told you it doesn't make sense."

Klein continued, "How would you describe her emotional state lately? Was she unhappy with the move to St. Louis? How was she after the birth of your son?"

Jack thought for a while and then responded, "I think the move was harder on her than she let on. She lost her extended support system and didn't engage with people here. When the excitement of the move wore off, she was a bit down but didn't complain. After Martin was born, Gloriann seemed preoccupied, a bit tired, maybe a little withdrawn, but I thought it was just the baby blues—a bit of postpartum depression. We are going back to Tucson at the end of this year, so I wasn't worried. It wasn't that long to wait."

"Did she want to come to St. Louis?"

"Absolutely. I wanted her to stay in Tucson, and I'd fly home when I could—that way no one else would be disrupted—but she wanted an adventure. Said she was ready to do something different. Plus, she wanted us all to be together, so we rented out our house in Tucson and moved here."

"OK, so what you are telling us is that there is no reason to believe that Gloriann would harm herself or the baby or leave voluntarily?" reiterated Klein.

"That's correct. No reason at all," Jack affirmed.

Detective Guilder rejoined the interview. "Jack, why were you back in Tucson? Were you sent there by the FBI?"

"It was part of my work for the FBI, but it was my decision to go now."

Guilder looked momentarily surprised, then continued. "And why was that?"

Jack didn't hesitate, but he was careful in his answer. Careful with his facial expression, his body language, his eye contact. Not too careful, because that could sometimes be a tell that someone was lying. He knew how to do this; he had been trained well. "I needed time away. I knew that the move to St. Louis didn't work out the way Gloriann had thought, and I wanted some distance to think about the future of my career and how it might affect the family, especially now that we have Martin."

"Did Gloriann know that you needed space to think about the future?"

"No. We didn't discuss it."

"You didn't discuss it? Jack, there are loose ends here. You go back to Tucson; Elizabeth Edwards shows up, a woman neither you nor Gloriann have met before; and Gloriann and Martin go missing without a trace. Doesn't this all seem a bit too coincidental? What's your take on it?"

Now Jack allowed himself to show irritation. "I know what you are thinking—that I have something to do with my wife's disappearance and that I was in Tucson for an alibi. Listen to me: I did not have anything to do with Gloriann's and Martin's disappearance. I do not believe that Gloriann left of her own accord. I have no idea about Elizabeth Edwards. I do not know what has happened. I want my wife and son back! Do what you must to satisfy yourself that I had nothing to do with this and move on, boys. Like you said, time is not on our side."

Detective Guilder studied Jack and then said, "We'll continue to check you out. In the meantime, we'll need a list of Gloriann's family, friends, anyone who might have an idea of her whereabouts. We will need to interview the kids. We'll check out Elizabeth Edwards. If there is anything else that you think we need to know, make sure I get it. I'll work with your boss to see if this is in any way related to what you've been doing with the FBI."

Jack nodded.

"That's it for now. We'll hit the street—people should be home on a Saturday morning. We'll be back at 1:00 p.m. to interview Elizabeth and the kids. I will give you an update then. Let us know if anything changes," Klein said as he gathered his things and started for the door.

Jack watched them go. He stood in the foyer, exhausted but anxious. He knew he had to catch a few hours of sleep, but first he had to do his own search of the house. He had to know. He did not want anyone to see him searching—not Lou, not Elizabeth, not the kids. He would do it quickly and quietly, and then he'd lie down on the couch so he could hear if anyone descended the stairs. He would not hinder the investigation, but he also didn't want the truth to come out. He chuckled to himself. "I can't believe that now I'm looking at the law from the other side." Then his mood darkened, thinking, *Withholding evidence? No. It is none of their damned business. It's nobody's damned business.*

| 3

SATURDAY, SEPTEMBER 16

It was almost five o'clock in the morning when Jack finally dropped on the couch and closed his eyes. He hoped the kids would follow their usual Saturday routine and sleep late. He had found what he was looking for. It didn't surprise him that the police hadn't found it, but he knew that their first search was quick and looked for the obvious. They might search again more extensively, but there was nothing left of any interest to them. He found Gloriann's diary, a spiral-bound yellow notebook with a bouquet of white, purple, and yellow pansies pictured on the cover. It was in an empty waffle-iron box in the top cupboard. He knew that Gloriann kept a diary and would hide it. She had forgotten it once. He saw it lying on the kitchen counter and was tempted to read it, but he forced himself to walk away. He respected her privacy. Now he had it and would read it later when he could do so without the threat of being observed. He knew it was evidence. If there was something that would help the investigation, he would turn it over to the police. If not, they would never see it. Her private life, and his, would not be part of the official case record.

At 8:30 a.m., Jack heard someone coming down the stairs. When he came into the foyer, he saw an older woman who was already dressed for the day and assumed it was Elizabeth. He smelled coffee coming from the kitchen. Lou must have snuck down without waking him.

"Elizabeth?" Jack asked.

"Yes. And you are Jack?"

He nodded.

"Jack, I'm so sorry that we are meeting under these circumstances. I can't believe that this is all happening," Elizabeth said with tears coming to her eyes. "I'm, I'm, I don't even know what to say or do."

"Come on into the kitchen. We can get something to eat," Jack offered.

Lou was sitting at the kitchen counter, eating a bagel and drinking a cup of coffee. She looked at them with a smile of encouragement. Her eyes mirrored theirs—tired and concerned. When Jack and Elizabeth had settled in with their bagels, Jack told Elizabeth that the police would be back at 1:00 p.m. to interview her. Jack noticed the defeated, resigned look on her face as she said, "OK."

"Elizabeth, would you mind if I asked you a few questions?" Jack asked.

"No. Go right ahead."

"How is it that you ended up here in St. Louis and at my house?"

Elizabeth sighed. "Jack, again, I'm sorry that Gloriann and Martin are missing. I'll try to explain everything to you, and I'll make it short. I am Helen's first cousin. Her mother and my mother were sisters. I am the youngest of the cousins, as my mother was the youngest in her family. We all grew up in Cleveland. Helen left for Arizona when I was thirteen. I never saw her again. I moved to Minneapolis forty-one years ago. A few years back, Helen and I became friends on Facebook. Last winter, my husband, Carl, and I spent February in Tucson, and Helen and I reconnected. When she learned that I would be in St. Louis for a writers' conference, she suggested that I meet Gloriann. Gloriann emailed me, and we worked it out."

"So Gloriann emailed you?" Jack was surprised.

"Yes. Because the conference starts today with a luncheon, and the fact that I took the train from Chicago, Gloriann offered to have me stay here for one night, and then she was going to take me to the hotel near the Arch. I have a room there booked for three nights. Carl is driving down on Monday. He's in Chicago, giving a lecture on WWI and food conservation. Then we were going to take a small vacation."

"You are going to miss the luncheon," Jack said.

"I know. I'll help you in any way I can, but if you don't need me, I would like to go to the hotel after the police interview. I'm too shook up right now to even think about attending a conference, but I don't want to stay here either. No offense, Jack. I'm just ill at ease. I'm sorry. That sounds selfish. I just don't know what I can do."

Jack looked at Elizabeth as if he were seeing her for the first time. She was in her sixties, dark brown hair with a few gray streaks, blue intelligent eyes, maroon wire-rimmed glasses. She was dressed in blue jeans, a purple and blue plaid shirt, and black loafers. He considered her predicament. Here she was in a house of strangers, thrown into a missing person's case, in an unfamiliar city, and missing a conference for which she obviously spent a decent amount of money. His opinion of her softened.

Lou spoke up. "Jack, I took some of my personal time off to help you. I can take care of the kids. Do whatever."

"Oh, Lou. Personal time? I can't let you."

"What are you going to do, Jack? Think about it. You are between a rock and a hard place." Lou crossed her arms and shook her head.

Jack nodded. "Yeah, you're right. Thanks." Then he looked again at Elizabeth. "I know that you never met Gloriann before, but how did she seem yesterday?"

"Well, she was cordial to me. Picked me up at the station. I was tired, and it was so hot. When she suggested that we go to the park, eat outside, and walk to the ice-cream shop, I tried to dissuade her. I didn't want to go. I don't do well in the heat. I wanted to stay in the air-conditioning. But she was persistent, so what else could I do? When we got to the park, she seemed a bit intense, like she was on some sort of mission. And I thought it odd that she wanted to go inside to get the ice cream and take the baby with her. I didn't argue. Good thing you had a small umbrella stroller, or it wouldn't have even fit through that door."

Elizabeth paused, looked down at her hands, then up at Jack. She searched his eyes. "I replayed this in my mind several times last night, and I might be totally wrong, and I don't want to upset you, but I think she orchestrated all of this. She obviously never told you I was coming. You were in Tucson. I was here—someone to leave the kids with. I think she left you and took the baby with her. I just can't figure out why she would leave Emma and Will. Someone must have been waiting for her in that parking lot. How else could she have gotten away so quickly?"

Jack took a deep breath, laid his palms flat on the counter, and spread his fingers. "It looks that way to you. But it can't be. *You* don't know Gloriann. This is not something she would do." Before he could say anything else, Emma and Will bounded into the room. They ran to Jack, and he wrapped them both in his arms. Lou and Elizabeth looked at each other, got up from the counter, put their dishes in the sink, and went upstairs.

"Did Mom come home?" Emma was the first to ask.

"No. Not yet," Jack told her.

"Where's Mommy? Where's the baby?" Will asked his father.

Jack felt the joy of seeing his children being overshadowed by the heavy darkness that was bearing down on his shoulders. How was he going to handle telling the kids? He didn't want to scare them, yet he knew that if he lied to them and things didn't work out well, they would never trust him. They were too young to grasp the difference between a sliver of hope and a positive presumption. He would have to stay in their realm of not knowing and be their buffer from reality.

"We still don't know where Mom and Martin are. The police were here for a very long time last night. In fact, they only left early this morning. There are a lot of people trying to figure out what happened to Mom and Martin. They are doing their best. We are just going to have to wait," Jack explained. "Detective Wyatt Guilder will be here after lunch to ask you a few questions. I'll be with you too. Make sure you tell him everything he wants to know."

Emma looked worried, but Will brightened and ran out of the room.

"Hey, Will, where are you going?" Jack called after him.

"To see if the BOLO is still here."

Jack and Emma ran after him. Will was trying to open the front door. Jack put his hand on the top of the door and looked down at his son. "You're looking for a BOLO?"

"Yes. I heard the policeman tell Lou that he had put out a BOLO. I want to see if it's still on the porch. I want to see what a BOLO looks like."

Jack smiled. He wanted to release the laugh that was beginning to explode inside him. He looked down at Will's earnest little face, then answered evenly, "Will, BOLO is short for *be on the lookout*. It's something police do to help find a missing person. They emailed a copy of Mom's and Martin's pictures to lots of police officers so that these officers know whom to look for."

"Oh." Will sounded disappointed. "So there's nothing on the porch? I can't have the BOLO?"

"No. Here, have a look," Jack said, opening the door.

Will peeked around the doorframe and then was off to the kitchen. "I'm hungry."

Jack made the kids breakfast, glad for this bit of normalcy. Lou had showered and changed, and now she and Elizabeth rejoined Jack and the kids in the kitchen. Jack told them that he needed to make calls to work, to Gloriann's parents and sister, and to his own family.

"Hey, Jack, before you do, can I talk to you in the other room?" asked Lou.

When they were away from the others, Lou began to tell him about the riots. "I didn't want to pile too much on you when you came in this morning, but yesterday, a judge found that White, former St. Louis police officer not guilty of first-degree murder in the death of a Black man. All hell's broken loose in the Central West End. Riots into the night and more protests planned for today. My guess is that the PD is stretched thin right now."

Jack ran his hands through his hair. "Damn it. I wondered why I didn't see more of a uniformed presence around here. What else is going to happen? We've got to find Gloriann and Martin. Can you do something with the kids? I've got to make these calls, Lou."

"Yeah, Jack, don't worry. You do what you have to do."

Will began jumping up and down with excitement at Lou's suggestion to go play in the park, but Emma balked at the idea. "I don't want to go to the park. I want to stay home," Emma said. She looked unhappy. It took almost ten minutes of negotiating before it was decided that Lou would take Will to the park, and Emma would stay with Elizabeth and play fashion plates.

Emma brought her fashion plate kit, colored pencils, and sketchbook down to the kitchen since Jack wanted privacy in the upstairs den. She began to show Elizabeth the outfits that she had drawn. "I've named my models. This one is Iris, and this one is

Daisy." Flipping the page, she continued, "Here's Violet, and here's Rose. I've also got Marigold, Lily, and Amaryllis."

"Amaryllis? How do you know that name?" asked Elizabeth.

Emma smiled proudly. "I learned it from watching *The Music Man.* Mom told me that it was a flower name."

"I like the outfits you designed, Emma. They fit the models' names. Rose looks so sophisticated in her gown, and Daisy is adorable in her yellow blouse and print skirt," complimented Elizabeth.

"When I get married and have kids, I want to name all my daughters after flowers. Do you think my mother and Martin are OK?"

"I think they are, Emma. I don't know where they are, but I think they are OK," said Elizabeth.

"Are you sure?"

"No. I'm not sure. But I still think they are OK," Elizabeth answered.

They fell silent as they traced the fashion plates, Elizabeth using paper taken from the printer, and Emma choosing a new page in her sketchbook.

Jack ended his call to the office and hit the number for Mel.

"Jack? How are you? What's happening?" Mel asked before Jack even said a word.

"Mel, I'm sorry that I couldn't call you sooner. It's been crazy. How are the folks?"

"They're worried but OK. I'm here in Tucson. I drove down last night to be with them. They told me what they knew, but that wasn't much. Anything changed?"

Melanie was Gloriann's older sister, her only sibling. She lived in Phoenix and worked as a senior digital signal processor architect and system engineer for an aerospace and defense contractor. She and Gloriann were as different as night and day. Mel was a tall, athletic brunette whose looks favored her father, while Gloriann was a petite five-four, blue-eyed blonde who looked like her mother. Mel was single and career oriented and traveled quite a bit for her work. Gloriann stuck close to home, taking care of the kids and Jack, volunteering at church and school.

When Jack told Mel that some of Gloriann's and Martin's clothes were missing and that Elizabeth thought Gloriann had left him, Mel snickered. "Are you kidding me? Gloriann? Sure, I'd like to think she took Martin and left you, because then I'd know they are safe, but come on, Jack. Gloriann?"

"The FBI is working on a possible abduction related to my work, but the missing clothes just don't fit the picture. OK, Mel, let's pretend she really did leave. Help me figure out why and where she might go."

Mel thought for a while, then answered, "Jack, you know Gloriann and I have never been close, so it's hard for me to say for sure. Here's what I think though: Gloriann is intelligent but also a bit too emotional. And she is naïve. Gosh, she is naïve! Mom and Dad coddled her something terrible. If she got in over her head, she looked for someone to help her out. I think she saw too many Disney movies where the princess is saved by the knight on a white horse, if you know what I mean."

Jack did, but he always fathomed that he was her knight.

"Mom told me that Gloriann wasn't happy in St. Louis. She was out of her element, felt guilty that she insisted on coming along but didn't think she could come back sooner than planned, missed home and all."

Jack said, "OK, well where do you think she might have gone if she left?"

"I'd guess she'd come back home to Tucson. Maybe she had a friend pick her up, and she's driving back. I know it is all dramatic, but who knows? Maybe she figured if she mysteriously disappeared, you'd appreciate her more, and there would be a romantic reunion scene at the end."

"Do you really think so, Mel?" asked a hopeful Jack.

"Jack, you told me to pretend. That's all I'm doing. Too many maybes."

"You're right, Mel. I'm grasping at straws," Jack said wryly. "That's what desperate people do. Listen, I'll try to keep you posted as best I can. Will you be my Arizona point person? Keep people updated but filter out what you don't think the folks or others should know. Keep Glenn and Greg updated. Handle the information chain the same way you handle questions about your job. You may even have to deal with the press."

"Well, Jack, you know I can do that!"

Jack did know. Mel had a high security clearance and the ability to talk about her job in such a way that no one was sure of what she did or where she traveled. She could make people feel special and enlightened without divulging sensitive information. She'd smile and be gracious, and it was only after she left that people realized she never answered their questions.

"Is there anyone else who can keep me in the loop if I can't get a hold of you?" Mel asked.

"I'll text you Louise Esposito's cell number. Call her Lou. She's an agent in my office here in St. Louis and is helping me with the kids right now." After catching up on a few more details, especially with regard to the press, Jack ended the call. He was relieved that Mel would handle details on her end. He looked at the time on his phone. It was almost noon! He went down to the kitchen to find Elizabeth and Emma setting the table for lunch. There was a bowl of canned peaches in the center of the table, along with a pitcher of ice water.

Elizabeth said, "Lunch is on me today. I called the local sandwich shop, and they should be here any minute. Why don't you call Lou and have her bring Will home? I figured we should eat before that one o'clock interview."

The sandwiches, Lou, and Will arrived in the foyer within seconds of one another. The sandwiches smelled of fresh bread and cold cuts. Lou and Will gave off a more humid, salty aroma, which reminded Elizabeth of how canvas sneakers smelled after wearing them without socks on a hot day. They took their seats at the table, and Jack blessed himself to begin grace before meals. They all joined in, Elizabeth and Lou raising their eyes to look at each other as they both made the sign of the cross. After they finished eating, Jack said he had time to give Will a quick bath. Lou decided on a second shower, and Elizabeth and Emma tidied up the kitchen.

When Detectives Klein and Guilder arrived, Jack led them into the living room, where the kids were already seated on the couch. Emma sat straight-backed, feet on the floor, hands folded in her lap. Will slumped next to her. Jack did not intervene to try to get the kids to relax; he knew the detectives would put them at ease. Soon the kids were eagerly answering questions.

"Did you see your mom packing clothes?" Detective Guilder asked.

"She didn't pack them. She put them in garbage bags!" Will exclaimed.

"Was she going to throw them out?"

"No!" Will squealed and started to bounce on the couch. Jack had to stop himself from giving Will a "settle down" look. He did not want the detectives to think he was trying to influence Will's answers.

Emma interjected, "She was going to donate them. Sometimes Mom donates things to the poor. She puts them in a black garbage bag, then writes a name on a white card and tapes it to the bag. Then she puts the bag on the porch, and a truck comes to take it to the poor."

"So you saw her put clothes in the black garbage bags and put them on the porch?"

Emma and Will both nodded.

"When did she put them on the porch?"

"Yesterday morning before we left for school," Emma answered.

"And were the bags there when you got home from school?"

"No," answered Emma.

Jack put his hand over his mouth as he processed this information. Gloriann packed the clothes, put them on the porch, and someone picked them up. Why would she act like this? Why would she donate the clothes? Was someone working with her? He had to find a link, something he could follow. He was adrift.

Detective Guilder asked him for permission for Lou to sit in on the rest of the interview in his stead. Jack agreed. He knew that they would ask his children if they felt safe, if their parents argued, if there was any violence in the home. They had to explore the possibility that Jack was an abusive husband, and Gloriann ran away to a safe house with the intention of eventually having someone bring Emma and Will to her. Jack knew they would not get anywhere with that line of reasoning, but his worries about the children's safety increased.

After the interviews with the children and Elizabeth were over, Guilder and Klein met with Jack privately. "We've gathered a lot of information since this morning, and we want to give you an update," Klein said. He told Jack that they would not be investigating Elizabeth any further. Jack learned that Elizabeth had no criminal history, no driving violations, and nothing in her background that was suspicious. In fact, she had worked as a teaching assistant in special education in an elementary school for six years and then as a church secretary for fourteen years. She and her husband, Carl, were crime-watch block captains and helped organize National Night Out every year. Carl was retired from the Minnesota Historical

Society, where he had a stellar career as a historian and director of development. They had a good credit rating and were not in debt. There was nothing that would connect either of them to a possible abduction. They believed Elizabeth was just a victim of circumstance.

What the children had revealed about the clothes in the garbage bags lined up with what one of the neighbors told them about seeing a white panel van picking up black plastic bags from the porch. The van did not have any markings indicating a charity. The neighbor could not give a definite description of the man who made the pickup other than that he wore jeans, white athletic shoes, a black nylon windbreaker, a black baseball cap, and black gloves. His face and hair were obscured by the cap. The neighbor did not notice a license plate.

As for Jack, they did not believe that he was suspect in his wife's and son's disappearances based on earlier talks with the FBI. They also believed that Gloriann left of her own accord and took the baby with her. The FBI was pursuing their own investigation into a possible dual abduction and would currently be taking the lead. Right now, with unrest in the city due to the court ruling over the police shooting and everyone putting in overtime, St. Louis PD was grateful for the FBI's help. Since the FBI was taking the lead, Detectives Klein and Guilder would only contact Jack if they had something to report; otherwise, he should work with the Bureau until further notice.

Jack told them that he was worried about Emma's and Will's safety and that he would not have the children return to school or live in the house until he was assured they were not in danger.

"That might be a bit paranoid, Jack, but I'm not going to second-guess you. Are you going to make other arrangements for their education?" Klein asked.

"Yes. They are not going to be truants if that's what you mean. I'll let you know what I decide."

"OK. Let us know where you'll be staying if you're not going to be at this address. You might want to get a security system for the house," Guilder added.

"You do know that we don't own the house; we're renting it. It was furnished. We only brought our personal belongings. Nothing of consequence. I'll let the owners know of your suggestion though, and they can add one if they want," Jack said. As he walked the two detectives to the door, his mind began processing algorithms that would ensure the safety of the children while giving him the freedom to look for Gloriann and Martin. By the time he joined Lou and the kids, he had churned out a scenario that he felt would work.

Lou agreed to keep the kids at her place in Chesterfield until Monday or Tuesday, when Jack could make permanent arrangements for them.

"Why can't Lou just stay here with us while you go to work?" Emma asked. "I don't want to miss school."

"I don't want to miss B week! We'll be on B, and we get to play with bats and balls and balloons! That's why I wanted the BOLO. BOLO begins with B. I wanted to bring the BOLO." Will began to cry.

Jack was thinking, *No, we skipped to C week: crying, craziness, and catastrophe*, but he soothed Will, saying, "It's OK, Will. You'll get to play with balls and balloons another time. Emma, I'll call the school and get your assignments; they will understand. Lou will help you, and you'll have fun. It will be like school with a vacation."

"What about Elizabeth? Will she come too? Will she stay with us?" Emma was pleading.

Lou looked at Elizabeth and said, "Why don't you? I have a three-bedroom townhome, so we'd all fit. It's probably too late to cancel your room for tonight, but you could cancel the other two nights."

"But my husband is coming in on Monday, and…"

"He can stay too. I've got the room, Elizabeth." Lou was hoping Elizabeth would stay and help her with the kids; she was starting to feel overwhelmed. Elizabeth was unsure, but she also was afraid to be by herself in an unfamiliar city that was dealing with riots.

"OK, thanks. I'd like to stay at your place. Are you close to a Catholic church? I want to go to Mass this weekend."

"That's no problem. We can all go to my church either tonight or tomorrow," said a relieved Lou.

"OK, kids, let's get packing so your father can get to work finding your mother and brother," Elizabeth said as she clapped her hands together. Emma and Will jumped up and ran to their rooms. Lou looked relieved.

"Hey, Lou, is there a pool around you?" Elizabeth called down the hall.

"Yep. In my complex."

"Emma and Will, pack your swimsuits! And your church clothes. I'll come check your suitcases when you're done," Elizabeth said, taking charge.

Jack was finally alone. He leaned back on his pillow and stretched out his legs. He held Gloriann's diary in both hands, pondering if he would find the information he was looking for. Most of the diary was an account of the touristy places they had all visited and innocuous notes about the kids, but there were others that filled Jack with a deep sense of regret and foreboding:

Wednesday, August 17, 2016
I've been born and died and born.
I died again today.

It happened while washing dishes,
washing memories,
rinsing them both with tears.

Joyous faces in glistening plates.
His, hers; no not mine—theirs.
Reflections of another time,
stacked in the cupboard drying.

Thanksgiving, November 24, 2016
Roasting a 14-lb. turkey, making homemade stuffing and gravy, and cooking the cranberries are no longer worth the effort.

Thursday, August 24, 2017
"It's as important to marry the right life as it is the right person."
—*Mrs. Miniver* by Jan Struther

Tuesday, September 12, 2017
Took Martin mall walking after the kids left for school. As I made my way around the shoppers and looked in the store windows, it struck me that in one hundred years, we will all be dead, and other people will be living in our homes.

Twenty-four hours ago, Jack was in Tucson. Twenty-four hours ago, when his phone rang, he thought it was Gloriann calling. Now, what he had fled to Tucson to ponder had morphed into a situation he never believed possible. He would protect Emma and Will. He would find Gloriann. He would find Martin. He would find his answers.

4

SUNDAY, SEPTEMBER 17

Sunday morning broke hazy and humid. Jack put up the car windows and turned on the air-conditioning when his shirt started to stick to his back and the exhaust from the bus in front of him made him lightheaded. He should have eaten breakfast, but he was anxious to get to the office to meet with his boss. Being the first one in, he flipped on the lights and started the coffee, inhaling the fresh aroma of the beans. Agent Rose Washington arrived next, wearing slim-fitting khakis and a white blouse. Her smile was bright as she held up a white bakery bag. Special Agent Dave Harlan strode in, jacket and tie, right hand in his suit pants pocket, jiggling his keys.

While Jack and Agent Washington put their orange and cranberry scones on napkins, Special Agent Harlan got right to the point. "Jack, it looks like Gloriann left of her own accord, taking your son without permission. But since there are peculiar circumstances surrounding their disappearance, we need to be confident that this is in no way tied to our drug investigation. I should pull you off this investigation immediately, but it's better that you stay and help in this first phase. So I want you and Agent Washington to use the informants you've established and determine if there is a connection. Let's reevaluate once we have that information. Right now, we are out of leads. I also want to think about press releases. If we can get information to the media tonight, it will hit the web immediately and the papers tomorrow. Your wife is either a victim or a criminal. Figure it out, Jack."

Of the three informants, Rose worked exclusively with one, Jack with the other, and one was known to both. Armed with photos of Gloriann and Martin, they each went their separate ways, with plans to reconnect as soon as possible. They didn't get back to the office until well into the afternoon. Neither one of the first two informants knew anything about Gloriann or Martin.

Rose said, "Looks like we've got one shot left. I guess we'll be buying some vinyl. I'll need to change. I've got a sundress and sandals here in the office. It'll only take me a minute."

"OK. As soon as you are ready, let's hit the road," Jack said.

They drove down to Cherokee street and parked the car in front of Raheel's Records, a narrow, two-story brick building sandwiched between an antique shop and a women's boutique. Rose looked in the boutique's window, then raised her head to Jack. "Honey, do you like that hat?"

"I do. Do you want to go in and try it on?" Jack opened the door, and Rose walked in. Fifteen minutes later, Rose carried the pink Betty's Boutique bag into Raheel's Records. Cool air banished the outside humidity. Tan brick walls, black tin ceiling, and unwaxed wood plank floors had a calming, almost reverent effect. The soft blues of B.B. King were barely audible. Thousands of records, shelved like library books, hugged the walls. Discounted records tucked into black plastic milk crates stood beckoning on tables. Priceless records stared out from behind the glass of the sales counter. In the very back, through the arch, was an area displaying turntables, needles, and accessories. A repair workshop was in the far-right corner.

Three other customers were in the store. One was looking at the record index on a desktop computer nestled inside an oak roll top desk; the other two were flipping through the records in the milk crates. Jack and Rose slowed to a stop at the discount table.

"Oh, honey, do you think we'd find Brel? There's a certain rendition of *Jacque Brel is Alive and Well and Living in Paris* that I would love to have. I can't find it anywhere," Rose said, looking at Jack, eyes wide, breath sighing.

"Mmm… Rosie my girl, you have a one-track mind. It's always Brel. Let's find Raheel. Maybe he can help us," Jack said, tilting his head toward the back room.

Raheel saw them before they could move. "Well, well, well. If it isn't Jumpin' Jack and Ramblin' Rose! Haven't seen you salt and pepper for a while. What's your pleasure today?"

"Well, I need a replacement stylus for a Shure M55 cartridge, and Rosie is still looking for that particular Brel."

"Come on back then and bring your better half. Raheel's always happy to help."

While Raheel rummaged through some stock boxes on the shelf behind the counter, Jack whispered, "We've got pictures."

"Give me a minute to find that stylus. Don't you be getting anxious, Jack. You know I'll find it. Ah, got it!"

Raheel put the package on the counter. While Jack inspected it, Rose angled her body to block the other customers' views and laid the snapshots of Gloriann and Martin on the counter. Raheel took a quick look before Rose dropped them into the boutique bag.

"You know, Rosie, I've seen that Brel record at the Chesterfield Mall. Went out there for a vintage record show. Talked to a guy, name escapes me right now, but he said he sells his wares on eBay. High prices online. Cheaper in person. Seemed like a ladies' man. You could probably talk him down. Told me he eats often at that winery restaurant. Check him out there."

"Well, thanks, Raheel. But without a name, how will I know whom I'm looking for?" Rose asked, hands on hips, feet spread, shoulders back.

"Oh, you'd pick him out. Tall guy, dark hair, good build. I've seen him there a couple of times with a cute little blonde who had a bun in the oven. Last time, that love child made a threesome. You'd find him," Raheel said with a smile. Then Raheel turned to Jack. "That'll be twenty bucks."

Jack laid the twenty on the counter, picked up the bag with the stylus, and gave Raheel an empty look and tight smile. "Thanks, Raheel. See you around."

"You take care now, Jumpin' Jack. Don't you go rambling, Rose. You let me know if you get that record," Raheel called after them as they headed for the door.

As they rounded the car, Rose said, "Give me the keys. I'll drive."

Jack got in the passenger seat, clicked on his seat belt, took a deep breath, and said, "I don't understand. I knew she had something on her mind, maybe depressed, but what the hell is going on? This isn't Gloriann. It just isn't."

"Jack, I'm driving to the restaurant. They must have tapes. Raheel seems to think we won't have any trouble spotting them. Martin is your infant, right?"

"Two and a half months, almost three."

"What time of day would she have been at the mall?"

"It would have to be midday. The kids would be in school. Gloriann's always been home in the evenings."

"All right. So, let's say eleven to two."

"Martin was born July first. Her folks came up for two weeks. I kept close to the house for the next two weeks. Kids went back to school mid-August. She wouldn't have had her six-week check until mid-August," Jack reasoned.

"OK. We'll check September weekdays minus Labor Day. Jack, I think we'll find them. You'd better call in. Tell Harlan what we are doing."

They arrived at the restaurant as the dinner rush was in full swing and asked to talk to the manager. When he saw their badges, he quit breathing and stared at them. As they explained their mission, he exhaled, shoulders relaxing, mouth curving upward.

"Yes, of course, I can help you—more than willing. Let's go to my office." Once there, he boasted, "We have an integrated security system: CCTV with DVD recorders, intrusion detection, environment monitoring. I can see the tapes. So can our monitoring company. I've got cameras at all the entrance and exit doors, the kitchen, the bar, cash register, tables. You know with employee theft, liabilities with food prep issues or overserving at the bar, and now with sexual harassment claims, the insurance this system provides is well worth the cost. Some places, I've got the dome cameras; others, I've got the box. What do you want to see?"

"Can we look at the tables from the beginning of September during lunch, eleven to two?" asked Jack.

"Sure. Let me pull that up for you. I've got to call my assistant manager down on the floor. Then I'll help you if you need it," he said, pulling out his cell phone.

Rose said, "Let's look for Martin. He'd be the easiest to spot."

It didn't take long to find the infant car seat holder adjacent to one of the tables. "That's Martin," Jack said. "That's the blanket my mother made." They had a clear view of the table and food but limited view of Gloriann and her tablemate. They could see some of his face, his dark, wavy hair, and that he was wearing a pale-yellow golf shirt with a blue logo on the pocket.

"We'll catch him on the entrance video," Rose said, her heart racing.

Jack did not share her enthusiasm. On the tape, Gloriann looked like she was enjoying her lunch. She didn't look coerced. Jack knew she was naïve, but how naïve was she? Victim or criminal? Jack found it hard to normalize his breathing.

The manager pulled up the entrance videos and gave control of the computer back to Rose. Since Rose and Jack already had the day and time, the dark-haired stranger in the yellow shirt was not hard to find. "OK. Stop it there!" Jack said to Rose "Get a close-up on his face."

"That's a clear shot, Jack," Rose said, sitting back from the computer and contemplating the face on the screen.

Jack called the manager back over. "Can you print this for us? I've got a flash drive. Can we take a copy of this file and the earlier table shot?"

"Sure, no problem," the manager said. "Do you want me to do a printout for my employees to ask them if they know the guy?"

"No," Rose and Jack answered in unison. Rose continued, "No. We need to do some internal investigating first, so we need you to keep this in confidence. Do you understand?"

"Sure. I'll keep it to myself." The manager hesitated, then nodded.

"You don't have to worry," Jack said. "If you do see this man, though, don't approach him. You can call us. Here's my card. If we think you need to know more, we'll call you. We appreciate all your help tonight. It has been invaluable. Thank you."

When Rose and Jack got back to the car, it was Rose who again slipped behind the wheel. "Let's go back to the office and run a probe through IPS face recognition," Rose said.

"Yeah, but we won't get a hit with the Interstate Photo System if he doesn't have a mug shot. Although I don't want him to have a criminal record. I just ..." Jack fell into silence.

Rose kept her eyes on the road, not saying anything. She knew Jack was vacillating between wanting Gloriann to be a victim, because if Gloriann was a victim, she didn't leave him of her own accord, but if she was involved in the abduction, then she and Martin were probably safe. Rose didn't know what to say to Jack. She only knew that she wanted to find an answer so that everyone would know what they were dealing with. Rose felt any answer would help jolt Jack out of his misery and into action.

Back at the office, they ran the photo through IPS and within seconds received a candidate list of fifteen photos. None of them were Gloriann's mystery man. "We'll submit it to FACE," Rose said as she pulled up the image-search request form. FACE was the acronym for the Facial Analysis, Comparison, and Evaluation Services Unit, a twenty-four-seven operation at the FBI's Criminal Justice Information Services Division (CJIS) near Clarksburg, West Virginia. "You know, my husband is from Marietta, Ohio, and would like to move closer to his folks. Clarksburg is less than a two-hour drive from Marietta. I've put in an application. Waiting to hear if I get the needed clearance. We'd like to start a family; I'm not getting any younger, and the center has an on-site day care center. I don't want to leave the Bureau. I just don't want to do field work anymore." Rose finished the request form and hit send.

Jack sat back in his chair and studied Rose. She was almost thirty years old, capable, intelligent, and a good field agent. He couldn't imagine her sitting behind a desk. "Do you really want to go to Clarksburg, or is this your husband's idea?"

"No. I really do want to move on. Clarksburg is an exciting place, Jack! Three thousand people work there. It's huge, almost on a thousand acres. I know what you are thinking—that I'll miss the field work. Yeah, it is a paradigm switch, but this way I can still work at something I'm passionate about and be there for whatever kids I might have. I want a family, Jack. That is important to me. You know I never really had one."

Jack was silent. He pondered his own life. He was passionate about his work, and he loved his family. He wasn't always available to them—how could he be? He was the breadwinner. He and Gloriann were partners. They were in sync before the move to St. Louis. "Rose, how long do you think it will be before we get an answer back from FACE?"

"If mystery man is part of an ongoing investigation, I'd say fifteen minutes. After the automated face recognition is complete, then it's manually reviewed by a biometric image specialist to see if there are any likely matches to the probe photo we submitted. We should be high up on the queue—I indicated that we are dealing with an abducted child."

At 8:45 p.m., the report from FACE came back, with one of the photos indicating a high-percentage match, providing an investigative lead and analysis. Jack and Rose studied the photo and agreed that Rodney Wilter was their mystery man. Then Jack took over control of the computer and began searching FBI indices to see if there were any open cases involving Rodney. He discovered a recently initiated file with a case number beginning with the digits 318, which indicated financial fraud. Rodney Wilter, forty-three years of age, was being investigated by the Phoenix field office for running a Ponzi scheme.

As Rose went to answer her ringing cell phone, he opened the background information available in the Ponzi scheme file. The information was brief, and as he read it, he leaned forward, eyes widening, jaw dropping open. Then he sat up and closed the screen as fast as a guilty teenager hoping his mother did not catch a glimpse of his online browsing. Wilter had graduated from the same high school as Gloriann! Jack swiveled his head, stealing a glance at Rose. She hadn't seen the screen.

Misinterpreting Jack's body language, Rose said, "Jack, we won't be able to contact the Phoenix fraud unit until tomorrow morning. And I mean *me*, not you, Jack; Harlan will pull you off this case."

"I know, but I think Harlan should wait with the press until we find out more about Rodney Wilter. I don't think Martin is in danger with Gloriann. You saw the tapes; she didn't look coerced. Let's call it a night. I've got to contact Lou; she's got my kids. We are just not ready for a media release," Jack said, rubbing the back of his neck. Then he stood up, put his right arm up and behind his back, and with his left hand pushed down on his elbow to stretch. Releasing his arm, he said, "Let's go."

CHAPTER | 5

As soon as Jack was alone in his car, he activated Bluetooth on the dash. He knew he needed to touch base with Lou and the kids, but he said, "Call Mel." When she answered, he asked her if she knew a man named Rodney Wilter.

"Yeah, I knew Rodney Wilter. We went to the same high school. He was a freshman when I was a senior. Why?"

"I need to know everything you can tell me about him. This is important, Mel." She could hear the tension in his voice.

"OK. Well, we were both in the band. He was in drumline with me. When he was a senior, he became the drum major."

"Were you good friends?" Jack pressed.

"Oh, no. I put up with him. That's about the sum of it."

"What do you mean?"

"Rod was full of himself. Popular with the shallow crowd. He was a player. Good-looking—the girls used to call him 'Bod.' He could be all things to all people—a schmoozer who knew how to get what he wanted; intelligent but slippery. He was an accomplished liar, but I could see through him even if others couldn't. I didn't have any time for him," Mel concluded.

"Would he have known Gloriann?" Jack asked.

"She's ten years younger than me, Jack. She would have been in second grade! He might have seen her when the folks brought her to the band shows, but no, he wouldn't have known her otherwise. He was a fourteen- or fifteen-year-old boy with raging hormones, eyes for the girls in the freshman click, and quite successful in having his fun with them, I might add. I don't think he would have given an eight-year-old a second look."

"What else do you know about him?"

"Not much. He had an older brother who was a year ahead of me, but he was a quiet guy who kept to himself. I think he eventually went to Mexico. I know they had a mother. Never heard anything about a father. Jack, why are you so interested in Rod?"

"I believe Gloriann is with this Rodney."

There was a prolonged silence. Jack waited. Finally, he heard, "What? Wait. Why?"

"Following some leads, we got them on surveillance tapes at a restaurant here and were able to identify Wilter and Gloriann. She had Martin with her. The three of them were having a cordial lunch. He even picked up Martin and was holding him. I'm trying to get my head around it, Mel. I think she left me and the kids," Jack finally admitted.

"OK. OK, let's think this through," Mel said.

"Do you think she knew him in Tucson? I mean lately," Jack said.

"No. No. They must have met in St. Louis, Jack. Come on. Before you guys went to St. Louis, she was fine. You know that. She wasn't looking elsewhere. She wouldn't have even had the time to be with Rod Wilter."

"Well, she obviously had time now," Jack said quietly to himself.

Mel heard him. "That's because she didn't know anybody there. Back home, she had the folks and her friends. She was busy with the kids and the church. She volunteered. No, she had to have met him in St. Louis. Maybe she was having postpartum depression, and truthfully, Jack, you've been so busy with work. Maybe she met him after Martin was born, and he played her," Mel explained.

Jack was silent. He didn't tell her that he knew that Gloriann was meeting Rodney even before Martin was born. He couldn't tell her what Raheel had said. He knew Mel did not know all the details of Gloriann's disappearance, and he wasn't prepared to tell her.

Mel continued, "Although, Jack, something's still not right about this. Gloriann wouldn't leave Emma and Will. Plus, if she was going to run away with Rod, why didn't she just take all the kids, leave you a note, and go? People do get divorced. She was a good mother; she'd probably get custody of the kids. Not that you weren't a good father, Jack. But you weren't home all that much."

"I don't know if this is helping, Mel," Jack said.

"Jack, I'm just trying to figure out her reasoning. Of course, the way I reason, and the way Gloriann reasons are night and day. And when you throw Rod Wilter into the mix, well, all reasoning goes out the window. If she is with him, you can bet it was his idea. He conned her; she fell for him and then got caught up in a situation that got out of hand. That's what had to have happened. Find her and get her out of this mess, Jack." There was silence on the phone. "Jack? Are you still there?"

"I'm going to find her, Mel. I'm going to find her and Martin, and when I do, nothing is going to help Rodney Wilter. Mel, I'm at Lou's townhouse. Gotta go. I'll keep you posted."

Jack called Lou on her cell phone and told her he was by her front door. He didn't want to chance ringing the doorbell and possibly waking up the kids. After Lou led him into the kitchen and made him a sandwich, he gave her and Elizabeth a redacted version of the day's happenings. He finished by announcing that he wanted Emma and Will to go to Green Bay to stay with his brother Joe while he looked for Gloriann and Martin.

Lou asked, "Why Joe in Green Bay?"

Jack explained that his brother Joe and wife, Tessa, had three boys, ages nine, six, and three. Tessa was a stay-at-home mom, and Joe was a police detective. Plus, Jack's parents and youngest brother also lived in Green Bay and could help with the kids.

Lou continued to question Jack's decision. "Don't you think going back home to Tucson would be easier on the kids? Not so disruptive?"

Jack sighed. "Moving to Green Bay will be disruptive, but I think Will and Emma will be safest with my brother. Joe and Tessa are set up for kids. Plus, my folks are ten years younger than Gloriann's parents. I know I can count on Joe to protect Emma and Will. I just need to figure out the best way to get them there."

Lou said, "I can fly with them, Jack, but it has to be soon."

"My husband will be here tomorrow, and we can drive whatever you need to Green Bay," Elizabeth added.

Jack was pleased. "Thank you. Lou, see what flight you can get. Here's my credit card. Elizabeth, I'm grateful for your help. You've been so understanding with all of this."

Looking up from her phone, Lou said, "I can get a flight on Delta tomorrow. Leaves 7:49 p.m. and arrives in Green Bay at 11:00 p.m. There's a short layover in Minneapolis. I can get a return flight at 6:30 a.m. on Tuesday and be back here before 11:00 a.m."

"Go for it," Jack said.

"Wow. That was quick! I'll call Carl and see if he can leave Chicago earlier. It will take him about five hours to get here. If we left no later than six, we could at least get two hours of driving in before stopping for the night. I'll give him your address, Jack. Is that all right? Will that give you enough time to get to the airport?"

"That will be fine, Elizabeth."

"OK. I'll make the arrangements, and then I'm going to bed. I have to get more sleep before tomorrow," Elizabeth said, heading for her room.

When Elizabeth closed her door, Lou moved closer to Jack. "There's more to this than you've told us."

"Lou, I've got to call my brother and parents. It would be better if you stayed tomorrow night at the folks' house in Green Bay. They have the room, and it will be a madhouse at Joe's with the kids and all. I'll see you tomorrow back at my rental," Jack said as he headed for the door. "Call me when everyone's up and ready to leave so I make sure I'm home. I'll see Emma and Will then and help them pack. Thanks."

Lou sighed and shook her head. "No problem, Jack," she said to his back.

Monday, September 18

Jack arrived at his office early Monday morning. His supervisor, Special Agent Dave Harlan, walked past his desk, saying "Glad you're here, Jack. You're first on my docket for today. Let's meet in ten minutes." During the ensuing conversation, Harlan told Jack that Rose would be back on the drug investigation, Lou was slated to return Wednesday, and that agents other than Jack would be leading Martin's kidnapping case. Jack knew that it was standard procedure to remove agents from cases in which they or their families were personally involved. He wasn't upset because he had already made his decision the night before.

"I'm requesting a leave of absence without pay, Dave. There's no way that I can focus when my mind is on Gloriann and Martin, and I have Emma and Will to worry about," Jack said.

"Understandable. What's your plan?"

"I'm going to find them," Jack said.

"Jack, I'd do the same thing, but I caution you to stay within the law. Remember that once you go on leave, you cannot use FBI resources or personnel. You know that, don't you?"

"I know. But I can still interview people on my own, provided they know I am a private citizen. Look, Dave, I want to find my wife and son. I know the law. I want to be able to come back to the Bureau. If I find out what you need to know, I'll share. You'll keep me updated?"

"Of course, just like for anybody else. When do you want to begin this leave?" Special Agent Harlan asked.

"Now," Jack said, placing his creds and Glock 19M on Harlan's desk.

"You are ready to do that now?" Harlan's eyes were wide.

Jack had already contacted the Phoenix fraud unit and found out where Rodney lived and worked. He knew Rodney's license plate number and make of car. He knew Gloriann's friends. He knew journalists who owed him and a few private detectives who would help him out if he needed it. And he was personally licensed to carry his Sig Sauer P 320 in several states, translating to most states because of reciprocity laws. "Yes. After I sign whatever paperwork, I plan to leave," Jack said.

His phone rang while he was driving home. Lou's number appeared on the dash's screen. "Jack, we're ready to hit the road. Are you home?" Lou asked.

"Almost there. How are the kids?"

"Not sure. They're a bit overwhelmed, but Elizabeth has kept them moving. You know she used to work in an elementary school." Lou's voice suddenly became distant. "Kids, are you locked in?" Then her voice was clear once more. "All right, Jack. We're rolling."

Jack entered the house and had just laid his keys on the kitchen counter when he heard the slam of car doors and Will yelling, "Last one in is a rotten egg." Jack met them at the door, and as soon as he opened it, both Emma and Will clung to him. Neither of the kids spoke. Jack hugged them both, but when he realized that they were blocking Lou's and Elizabeth's entrance, he backed up with Emma still holding him tight and Will standing on Jack's shoes, hanging on for the ride.

"Is Mommy home? Where's the baby?" Will asked.

"Do you know where they are? Have you heard from them?" Emma talked over her brother.

Jack sat down on the floor and pulled the children to him. "No, they are not home. No, I don't know where they are. No, I haven't heard from them. *But* don't worry. I'm going to find them. I promise."

"Why are you sending us away?" Emma said.

"I'm not sending you away," Jack immediately said. Emma narrowed her eyes and pursed her lips. Will tried to mimic her by scrounging up his face and crossing his arms. "OK. You are going to stay with Uncle Joe and Aunt Tessa, but it is not because I want to send you away."

"If we have to go somewhere else, we want to go back to Tucson." Emma stiffened.

"Yeah, we want to go back to Tucson," Will echoed.

"There's no one there who can look after you. Aunt Mel works, so she can't. Grandma Helen and Papa Stan are in an old folks' area where kids can visit but not live. You like Uncle Joe and Aunt Tessa. Plus, there's Grandma Sophie and Papa Pete and Uncle Teddy. And you like your little cousins, Andy, Ben, and Charlie." Jack could see Emma was considering his explanation, while Will looked confused, focusing on Emma, trying to figure out what she was going to do.

"That's what Lou and Elizabeth told us," Emma conceded. "How long are we going to stay? Are we going to go to school? Are you going to be there?" Emma now wanted reassurance and specifics. Will put his head in his hands and slumped against Jack.

Jack again wrapped his arms around his two children and held them against his chest. His voice was thicker than it was before. "I don't know how long you'll be staying. Yes, you will go to school. You'll go to St. Nicholas, the same school where Andy and Ben go."

"What if the school won't take us?" Emma asked.

Jack chuckled. "Oh, they'll take you. They took me and my brothers!"

"Is your teacher still there, Daddy?" asked Will.

"No, not anymore. But the teachers who are there are nice. The school is very close to Uncle Joe's house. It is going to be fine. Don't worry," Jack soothed. "And, Will, you'll probably be in class with Ben."

Will was beaming, as if he had won a prize. Emma, however, was shaking her head. Then she stopped, looked up at her father, and said, "I don't want to go! I don't want to do anything! I just want to sit here and wait until Mom and Martin get back." She started to cry. In between sobs, she said, "This all stinks! Why did Mom leave us?" Will's rising good mood vanished, and he again slumped against Jack.

Jack wanted to punch the wall. He wanted to scream at Gloriann. Anger and frustration taunted him. He closed his eyes until his raging emotions dissipated. Then he opened them and looked down at the heads of his children. He felt their pain, but he knew that if he gave them too much sympathy, they would all fall down the proverbial rabbit hole. The situation was untenable.

Jack helped Emma and Will to their feet. "OK, look. I know we all miss Mom and Martin. I know none of us are happy right now. But we can't just give up. Come on! Let's pull ourselves together. We're a team, yes? My job is to find Mom and Martin. Your job is to go to Green Bay and be good for Uncle Joe and Aunt Tessa. Don't be whiners and complainers. I know it is not going to be easy, but you can do it. I know you can. Right now, things are hard, but little by little, things are going to get better. You've got to believe that. So, are we all on the same team?"

Emma and Will nodded. Jack saw both resignation and determination in Emma's face. Will would follow his sister's lead. Now Jack knew that his plan would work. "Let's make the best of a bad situation. We need to pack you two to be ready to fly out tonight. Take just what you need for a few days. Elizabeth and her husband will drive up to Green Bay and bring the rest. It must fit in their back seat, so you can't take everything. Bring your warmer clothes. You'll need them. I'll be upstairs in a minute," Jack said as the children headed for the stairs.

When Elizabeth and Lou heard the kids run up the stairs, they came out of the kitchen to follow them. "Elizabeth," Jack called. She turned to look at him. "Will you help Emma? I'll get Will packed," Jack said. "Lou, could you throw out all the fresh food in the fridge? I'm flying to Phoenix tomorrow and don't want to have a mess to clean when I get back."

"Phoenix, Jack?" Lou asked as she came back down the stairs.

"Yeah. I need to pack too. I'll be flying out on the same plane. We go our separate ways in Minneapolis when we switch planes. I'll be in Phoenix at 11:30 p.m. even though I'll be in the air a lot longer."

Lou looked puzzled. "I'm not connecting the dots, Jack."

"It's the time change that makes the difference, Lou."

"I know that. Why are you going to Phoenix?"

"Press release is going out sometime today. Kidnapping unit is getting it ready. It will have Gloriann's and Martin's photos and a picture of a guy named Rodney Wilter, who we believe is traveling with her. Wilter lives and works in Phoenix. Hasn't been in work for a week—was using vacation days. So that's why I'm going to Phoenix ... Wait," Jack said as he spotted his briefcase and began to rifle through it. "Here's some paperwork to give to Joe. Medical permission, privacy instructions for the school."

"You really think Gloriann is going to abduct Will and Emma?" Lou asked.

"Heck if I know! Everything is on the table right now, Lou. I want to make sure that the school does not give out any information about the kids, no photos or even first names on the internet. I don't even want them to say, 'Can't answer your question due to student privacy laws.' I want them to say, 'We have no students like that here.' Same for the church. I don't want any mention of the kids in the Sunday bulletin. No photos. I don't care if the photos are taken in a public place. You know how easy it is to track someone on the net."

"So, you think Gloriann is with Rodney Wilter?"

"I do," Jack said as he opened the cupboard and handed Lou a box of garbage bags. "As soon as we are all ready, I'll get take-out for lunch." Then he headed for the stairs.

By 12:30 p.m., Elizabeth, Lou, Emma, and Will were back in the kitchen, waiting for Jack to arrive with lunch. The luggage was in the foyer, as was a mound of black plastic garbage bags containing what would go with Elizabeth to Green Bay. It was decided that the bags would be easier to mold onto the back seat and floor of Carl's Camry, easier to fit them around Carl's and Elizabeth's suitcases in the trunk.

Jack returned with potato salad, fruit salad, and rotisserie chicken from the deli, as well as rolls, single-serve chocolate milk for the kids, and coffees for the adults. After lunch, Jack took the kids to the park, while Lou and Elizabeth watched a show on cable. Carl arrived around 3:00 p.m., and by 5:00 p.m., everyone was saying their goodbyes.

Elizabeth hugged the two children and kissed the top of their heads. "See you in Green Bay!" she said as she got in the passenger's seat.

Will was jumping up and down yelling, "Go, Packers!"

Carl slipped out from behind the wheel, stood on the floor of the car, looked over the top, pumped his arm in the air, and cheered, "Go, Vikes!"

CHAPTER 6

Jack drove the rental from the airport to his sister-in-law Mel's condo. The apartment was spacious: 1,600 square feet, two bedrooms, two baths, with a fourth-floor balcony overlooking a golf course. It had an outdoor pool and a large indoor workout room and game center. There were restaurants, shops, and an upscale grocery on the street level. It was resort living without the resort. She buzzed him in, gave him a warm but short welcome, a spare key, and an inventory of available food, then left him alone. That's what Jack liked about Mel. She understood that right now he did not want to sit and visit or be interrogated about Gloriann. He just wanted to be.

TUESDAY, SEPTEMBER 19

At 8:40 a.m. the next morning, Jack was in the lobby of Pronghorn Financial Services, a company consisting of independent financial advisers and brokers. He asked the receptionist if Rodney Wilter was in his office.

"Rod Wilter is no longer working here. Can someone else help you?" the twenty-something with long red hair and large hoop earrings asked.

Jack opened the front section of the *Arizona Republic,* to the page that had the article and photos of Rodney, Gloriann, and Martin. He pointed to the latter two. "This is my wife and son. I need to find them. I need to talk to someone who knew Rodney Wilter." He looked at the young woman who had stood up and leaned over the counter to read the article. "What is your name?" Jack asked.

"Destiny."

"Destiny, did you know Rodney Wilter?"

"Aren't you a cop or something? Says here you work for the FBI," Destiny asked, her finger holding her place in the article.

"Not currently. I'm on leave. I'm just a private citizen who is trying to track down my missing wife and son." Jack's eyes were pleading. "I need to find out more about Rodney. Anything would be of help."

"Well, he worked closely with Billy White. Billy's a good guy. Rod was mentoring him. They hung out together. Billy is probably in. Usually comes in early. You know, the time in New York and all. I just started ten minutes ago. I'll ring his office."

"Thank you, Destiny." Jack gave her a shy smile.

Billy White came down to the lobby to meet Jack. Here was another redhead, except, unlike Destiny, he was unremarkable. His hair was lighter and cropped short. His skin was not that of a typical suntanned Arizonan. He had pale blue eyes. He wasn't handsome, but he wasn't ugly. He was washed out, and he faded into the background like a chameleon. The two men shook hands, and Billy led Jack to the elevator. When the doors opened on the third floor, Billy instructed, "My office is to the right."

Billy's office was almost as small as a jail cell, with only a desk, two chairs, phone, and laptop. He had a window that looked out over the street. Papers on his desk were strewn about as if he had been looking for something but didn't find it. Several books were stacked in a pile on the floor in the corner of the room. He had a gold-plated nameplate identifying him as "William W. White."

"Have a seat," Billy said as he sat behind his desk and silently observed Jack.

Jack took the lead. "Billy, my wife, Gloriann, and my son, Martin, are missing. I don't know where they are, but I have reason to believe they are with Rodney Wilter. You've seen the paper?"

Billy nodded.

Jack continued, "I am an FBI agent, but I took a leave of absence to find them. So you don't have to help me or answer any of my questions. But I'm hoping you will. I understand that you know Rodney, and I need information about him."

"What kind of information?" Billy asked, a bit breathless. He was jiggling his knee up and down.

"Well ..." Jack sighed and, for the second time this morning, consciously looked vulnerable, "I ... I just want to, in a sense, get to know Rodney so I know if Gloriann is in danger and where they might be."

"OK," Billy said.

Jack could see that Billy was not going to offer anything without being asked. "Billy, how did you meet Rodney?"

"I met him a couple years ago at my first accounting job. We got to know each other, and he encouraged me to strike out on my own. He helped me get set up here."

"How long have you been here?" Jack asked.

"About three years, since 2014."

Billy looked young to Jack. "When was your first accounting job?"

"Right after graduation. I graduated in 2012. I worked at a package carrier, and they helped pay tuition. I went to school part-time. So I'm probably older than you think." Billy smiled.

Jack smiled and raised his eyebrows.

"I'm thirty. Just had a birthday." Billy was relaxing.

"Wow, that's great!" Jack said. Billy's knee was now motionless. "So tell me about Rodney. He was in St. Louis; did you know that?"

The knee started up again. "Well, yes. He often went to St. Louis. He had clients all over, so sometimes he would go visit them. He was actively trying to expand his client base, and he felt Phoenix, even Tucson, was drying up, so he'd travel. We're self-employed in a sense. It's not like we're punching a time clock." Billy was defending him.

"Have you heard from him lately?" Jack asked.

"No. I haven't heard from him for a week."

"Is that unusual?"

"Yes. We talk almost every day." Billy looked uncomfortable. He regretted giving Jack that information.

Jack did not show surprise. He acted as if he hadn't noticed. "Do you have a cell phone number for him?"

"It doesn't work. I've tried calling him."

"Did he ever mention Gloriann or that he had a girl in St. Louis?"

Billy laughed. "Rod had girls in every city. He even fixed me up with dates a few times. Oh, sorry. I didn't mean that your wife …"

"It's OK. I know what you mean. If he was going to run away with someone's wife and kid—mine, for example-—where do you think he'd go?"

"Geez, I'm not sure. Rod is not the family-man type."

"Let's say for some reason he decided he wanted to play house. Where do you think he'd go?"

"South of the border?" Billy guessed. "Rod is fluent in Spanish."

"Well, that makes sense. But do you think he'd really leave the country?"

"Oh, I don't know. Maybe, because that would be dramatic. Rod is like that. Hiding out in someplace like Kansas wouldn't be exciting enough. No, not for Rod. He likes to live large."

Jack was thinking. Maybe Billy was right. Gloriann was also fluent in Spanish. She received her elementary teaching certificate first through eighth grade with a bilingual endorsement. Would Gloriann leave the country? Suddenly, Jack's stomach tightened as he thought about his work with border patrol. He thought about human trafficking. He was in his own world now.

"Jack? Mr. Jurlik?"

"Oh, sorry. I was just thinking."

Billy took charge and changed subjects. "If your wife really is with Rod, will you keep me posted? I know you are worried about your wife, but I'm worried about Rod. I can't imagine why I can't get a hold of him. Doesn't seem right." He was pressing Jack now. "Here's my business card so you can contact me."

Jack took a Post-it note from Billy's desk and wrote down his own cell number. "Call me if you hear from him or think of anything else."

"You don't have a business card?" Billy looked doubtful.

"Well, I have one from the FBI, but I'm not here as an agent, remember? Can you give me Rodney's address?"

"He's not there."

"No, but maybe a neighbor can help me."

Billy wrote down the address and handed it to Jack. It was the same address that Jack had seen in the FBI file.

"Thanks, Billy. I'll be in touch."

When Jack left, Billy rocked back on his chair and thought, *Maybe my luck is changing. Maybe Jack Jurlik, on-leave FBI agent, can lead me to Rodney-frickin-Wilter.*

When Jack got back down to the lobby, Destiny asked, "Was Billy able to help you?"

"Yes, he was. Do you know where he lives?"

"If you wanted to know where Billy lives, why didn't you just ask him?" Destiny said, crossing her arms over her chest.

"Honestly, I didn't think about it until I got down here. He gave me Rod's address but says he's not there. If I had Billy's address, maybe I could find out if anyone has seen Rod lurking around or something." Jack knew it was a feeble excuse, but he thought he'd try it to save himself time researching Billy's address. He wanted to know more about Billy. When Destiny remained silent, Jack said, "I can go back up and ask him," and turned to the elevators.

"Wait. I have it," Destiny said and pulled out her cell phone. "I picked him up once when he needed a ride to the airport," she explained as she scrolled through her contacts. "Here it is."

"Thanks, Destiny."

"Is your wife a nice person?" Destiny was trying to read Jack's face.

Jack looked surprised. "Yes, she's very nice. Why do you ask?"

"I just wondered that's all. I hope you find her and the baby."

Jack nodded and turned for the door. A feeling of dread came over him, and for the first time, he wasn't so sure he would find Gloriann. He looked at the paper, which was growing damp in his hand, then punched Rodney's address into his cell phone. Rodney lived ten minutes away in Midtown, Phoenix.

When Jack arrived at the apartment building on Central, he noticed the black SUVs parked in front. Jack parked the car and walked into the foyer. He found Rodney's apartment number on the listing and pressed the button on the intercom. No one spoke over the open-line static, so he announced his name and who he was into the speaker. He heard the buzzer and pushed open the door.

FBI agents were searching Rodney's apartment with slow precision. Their actions did not correspond with the state of the apartment. It looked as if a haboob had gone through it—not that it was full of dust and dirt, but it looked as if the wind had had its way. Drawers were open; couch cushions lay on the floor; papers and magazines were in disarray; pillows were torn open. The agents were wearing nitrile gloves and disposable shoe covers. One was dusting for fingerprints, another putting an item in a plastic bag.

"Do you think my wife was here with Rodney?" Jack asked from the doorway.

"Nothing to suggest that. Someone got here before we did and cleaned the place. There's no files, no phones, no computer. Nothing to help our fraud investigation," said the lead investigator, "and nothing to indicate anything to do with kidnapping."

"Any ideas who might have done this?"

"Nothing we can say. I'll save you the time—neighbors didn't notice anything unusual. Better tread lightly, Jack. Do you know something we don't?"

"No. I was just curious." Jack didn't mention his meeting with Billy White. He knew the fraud unit would have preliminary information on Billy. His next stop would be Billy's place, which was southeast of Rodney's, about twenty-five minutes away, on the other side of the Salt River.

Billy lived in a quiet residential neighborhood, probably developed sometime in the early 1990s. His contemporary, ranch-style house was mauve-tinted stucco with a matching clay tile roof. The front yard was tan pea pebbles. A mature African sumac tree and clump of blooming Angelita daisies broke up the monotony of the landscape. There was a two-car garage with a three-car, cement driveway. The house and yard were meticulously kept.

Jack sat in his car across the street and a few houses away. He had the windows up and the air-conditioning running. He turned the radio down low and studied Billy's house. Jack was pondering why Billy White would live there. It didn't look like the house of a thirty-year-old man. "This has got to be his parents' house!" Jack said out loud.

He put the car in drive and pulled away from the curb, taking a last look around. He drove north over the Salt River on the South Sixteenth Street Bridge. The Salt River in September was no more than a stream, which dried into randomly situated large puddles.

The riverbed was sand and stone, with sage brush dotting its course. It was nothing like the mighty Mississippi that teemed with boats and barges and people on water skis in St. Louis. Jack thought about Gloriann. Where would she have gone? She didn't take her phone; she hadn't used any credit cards. *Did she come back to Arizona where she has lived her whole life? But Rodney wouldn't want to come back here, not if he was guilty of running a Ponzi scheme out of Phoenix. Are they still somewhere in St. Louis?* "Gloriann, where are you?" Jack cried out loud.

He stopped to pick up a chicken salad at the local fast-food restaurant, then headed back to Mel's apartment. He ate while he worked on his laptop. He searched both national and local news sites covering the disappearance of Rodney, Gloriann, and Martin. He read some of the comments that readers made—nothing helpful there. Several of the sites had already updated the story. Jack chose the best ones and subscribed to their eEditions.

The Phoenix paper's website had a new headline added "12 minutes ago": "Missing man allegedly bilked investors." Jack knew that now the FBI would be inundated with calls from Rodney's clients who believed they were victims of Rodney's Ponzi scheme. One of these victims must have called a reporter when he recognized Rodney's photo in the morning paper. It was too early for the FBI to have given fraud information to the press. The agents were only in the initial stages of their investigation, gathering records and checks and reviewing bank records or boxes of seized documents. Fraud cases moved slowly, only beginning in earnest once the scheme collapsed. The pace was slower because there was little risk of violence. Things would change now with the oncoming feeding frenzy of phone-in tips and information. The urgency and speed of both the kidnapping and fraud investigations would grow exponentially.

Jack was confident that the FBI would tell him when they had any credible leads regarding Gloriann and Martin. It was standard practice when working with families of missing children. He was sure, too, that his fellow agents, whom he had worked with for years, would keep him in the loop as best they could. He began searching the internet for the highest-rated professional investigative database. The one to which he subscribed was comprehensive, offering people search, lists of relatives and neighbors, reverse lookup, email, social network presence, property records, criminal records, bankruptcies, liens, judgments, and lawsuits. It also enabled Jack to remain anonymous, using a proxy to keep his IP address hidden.

He looked up Billy White first. Jack was right. Billy lived with his parents. He had an older sister who was married and had two children. She and her husband lived in Tempe. Billy's record was clean.

Rodney's record showed a citation for underage drinking and a class 1 misdemeanor for driving while under the influence. Both were during his college years. He had a few extra points added to his Arizona driving record for speeding. Jack searched further. Miquel Wilter was listed as his brother; no location indicated. There was no location for his mother, Francesca. His father, Michael, had died the year after Rodney was born. The cause of death was listed as industrial accident. Rodney had a business website. Jack clicked on the link and came to a "Rod Wilter Independent Financial Adviser" page, listing services, glowing testimonials, and contact information. Jack tried the phone number. It had been disconnected. He tried the email address and immediately received a "permanent error" response from mailer-daemon.

Jack wanted to check Facebook and Twitter for any information on Rodney and Billy, but he needed to keep his IP address hidden. He subscribed to a virtual private network; initiated a Gmail account using an obscure address; then went to howmanyofme.com to choose a popular name. According to the site, there were 47,295 John Smiths in the United States. He took the chance that there would be dozens of John Smiths on Facebook. He downloaded a public domain photo of mountains from Wikimedia to use as his profile picture for both Facebook and Twitter. Then he set up his two bogus accounts and became an official Facebook and Twitter stalker.

Jack could not find any accounts for Rodney. If he had them, he must have deactivated them. *Prudent*, Jack thought. *Wouldn't want the ex-girlfriends or irate clients posting nasty comments.* Billy White did not have a Twitter account, and Jack soon discovered that there were more Billy Whites and William Whites on Facebook than there were John Smiths listed. He kept scrolling down, looking for Billy in the profile photos. When he didn't find him, he went through the list again, clicking on every profile that didn't have a personal photo. He finally found him. Billy used a photo of mountains for his profile picture. Jack chuckled and shook his head. Billy had 106 friends, and if Jack "wanted to see what Billy shares with friends," he would have to "send Billy a friend request." Jack could see some of Billy's prior profile photos: a gutted deer; a large catch dangling from a fishing pole; a new car; Billy at a baseball stadium. Although Billy had hidden his photo album, Jack could browse through his list of friends. Most of them appeared to be relatives or school friends. Destiny was listed. None of them looked out of the ordinary. Jack could come back to the list later if he needed.

When Mel walked into the apartment, Jack looked up from the screen. His shoulders felt stiff. He stood up and asked Mel about her day. When he realized that she had not heard about Rodney and the Ponzi scheme, he said, "Mel, let's get take-out for supper. We can eat and talk. We'll save time and have privacy."

"Why don't you go downstairs to Vincenzo's and get something while I change? They're quick, and the food is excellent."

Later, Mel said, "Jack, two things: One, I can't believe the information that is available on the internet! There is no privacy anymore. I'm going to want to use your account to see what there is about me. I don't have anything to hide, but still. What if you were divorced at one time and didn't want people to know? Or you just didn't want people snooping around your personal information? It's sick, you know that?"

"What's the second thing, Mel?"

"I'm going to have to go see the folks. I'm so busy at work right now, but I'll have to take time off. They aren't going to be able to handle this. Gloriann running away with a possible criminal?" Now Mel was pacing.

"No. I'll go. I'll go early tomorrow morning. I was planning to go to Tucson anyway. Check in at the office. They'll probably have some sort of lead soon. Call the folks tonight and explain what is happening. Tell them I'll stay with them. I know they haven't talked to reporters. Emphasize that it's best they give 'no comment.' Kids are safe with my brother in Green Bay; let them know that too. Thanks, Mel."

PART II

CHAPTER 7

SATURDAY, SEPTEMBER 16

Gloriann wakened to Martin's cries. At first, she didn't know where she was, having slept the sleep of the dead. Then she remembered. She went to the portable crib and picked up Martin. He was wet and hungry. She looked over at Rod, who was now sitting up in bed grinning at her, his mustache still in place.

She handed him the baby. "Will you change him while I use the bathroom?"

As she sat on the toilet, she looked at the plastic trash bag next to the stool. She could see strands of her blonde hair, stained gloves, empty plastic bottles, the crushed "Nice N Easy Light Radiant Auburn" box. She washed her hands and studied herself in the mirror. Her long blonde hair was now cut in a short bob with bangs. She liked the shorter cut; it made her look younger. She would have to get used to the color and the bangs.

She could hear Rod shushing the baby and softly singing to him, "Lily, Lily, Lily, don't be silly. You're no longer wet, so please don't fret. Ah, here's Mommy *Kimmy* just in time."

Gloriann chuckled and shook her head when she saw Martin. Rod had dressed him in a pink, one-piece bodysuit with a rose applique and matching headband placed around his brown, soft curls. Martin started to wriggle and cry when he saw her. Rod handed her the baby. "Thank you, Daddy *Larry*," she said.

"I'll run down and get breakfast to bring back to the room," Rod said as he zipped up his jeans and pulled a T-shirt over his head.

Gloriann sat on the easy chair by the window. As she nursed the baby, she watched men getting into two white trucks in the parking lot below. They were from a tree-trimming service, "Serving Iowa City, Coralville, and Surrounding Area" according to the advertisement painted on the sides. Both trucks had cherry pickers, and one had a trailer with cut logs. She thought it odd that she was looking down at them. She didn't remember going up stairs or taking the elevator last night. She and Rod had driven from St. Louis to Coralville, Iowa, and had gotten in around midnight. Rod paid cash for the room and presented his Larry Jackson driver's license. It was Rodney's idea to dress Martin as a girl, and Gloriann chose the name Lily. She had always liked that name, but now looking at Martin in his pink outfit made her think of Emma and her penchant for flower-named girls. Martin would get a new name in Minneapolis, and right now, Gloriann did not want to think about Emma and Will.

When Rod came back into the room juggling a tray laden with juice, coffee, two hard-boiled eggs, sweet rolls, yogurt, and bananas, Gloriann was thrilled. "Oh, that looks so good! I am starving! Larry, I don't remember taking the elevator last night, but we can't be on the first floor."

"No. The hotel is a walkout. Say, we have about seven hours of driving today. How about if we eat and get moving? I'd like to be out of here by eight thirty. Pack that bag of trash from the bathroom and put it in the diaper bag. Wear the black wig until we get to Minneapolis. I'll take care of packing the car. It you top off Lily before we head out, maybe we can get in two hours of straight driving."

"Rod, I'm nervous. Do you think we will really be able to pull this off?" Gloriann searched his face.

"Hey, *Kim*, of course we will. You know I'll protect you and the baby. It is all going to work out. You have to remember to use our new names though when we talk. Yeah?" He bent over and kissed Gloriann, then took Martin, put him up on his shoulder, and began to gently pat his back. "How about if we eat, shower, and get going?"

When they were finally in the car, Gloriann opened the glove compartment and took out the Garmin. She remembered how important it was to use it, as it gave an alert every time there was a camera at a traffic light. She and Rod laughed about how many times they had to look down during last night's getaway.

Once they got on the freeway, Gloriann asked, "What do you think Jack is doing today?"

"He's probably scratching his head trying to figure out where you are." Rod snickered. "Let's not think about him though. We've got to stay focused on what we must do to get through the next few days. Remember, Jack is with the FBI, which puts us at a disadvantage. But if we play it smart, we'll soon be scot-free."

Gloriann leaned to the left in her seat and turned her head to look back at the infant car seat mirror. Martin was sleeping. She rubbed Rod's shoulder; he looked at her and smiled. Gazing out the window, she thought about Will and Emma. She had hated to leave them, especially in the manner she did, but she felt she had no other choice. Everything fell apart when Jack moved the family to St. Louis. He was hardly ever home. The kids were needier than before. She was exhausted and felt defeated. Jack was too busy to notice what was happening; she was invisible. Then she met Rod, and her life miraculously changed. She was free! She could be mom and wife when she was home and get the attention she craved when she was with Rod. It was a perfect solution. Then she got pregnant, and Rod was thrilled. She knew then her life had changed, and there was no going back. Her marriage was over. She knew everyone would be shocked and disapproving. This was the only way out. She couldn't take all the kids now; she'd get them once she and Rod were settled.

By 9:15 a.m., she could see the skyline of Cedar Rapids with its white and tan buildings baking in the sun. Continuing north on 380, she spotted the tallest building, Alliant Energy, out her window. Quaker Oats had a large complex with a row of tightly packed white silos just west of the highway. It wasn't long before they left the city and were driving through calendar-photo scenery—a patchwork quilt of tidy farmsteads, green grass dotted with black cows, ribbons of dirt roads leading to homes nestled in the rolling hills. Then came the corn greeting them from both sides of the road.

"I don't think I've ever seen this much corn!" Gloriann said to Rod. "There's nothing else out here. It's like the desert! Of course, it's not as hot, but it's flat and sort of monotonous. Instead of sand, they have corn."

Rod pointed out the front window. "See those big blue silos over there? They are Harvestores. Can always tell if a farmer has money by how many Harvestores he has. A guy who sells general obligation bonds once told me that if you want to know how much money a farm town has, just drive around and count the Harvestores."

"Well, you could do the same thing, Larry. Then you'd know where all the good investment prospects are."

"Nah. Those farmers are shrewd. They invest but only with the local boys. You've heard that tune from *The Music Man*." Rod began singing, "We can stand touchin' noses for a week at a time and never see eye to eye."

Gloriann laughed. "Oh, come on, Larry, 'you really ought to give Iowa a try.'"

By 10:45 a.m., Martin was starting to fuss. Gloriann looked at Rod. He said, "I know, I know. We need to stop. Check the Garmin for places to eat."

Gloriann began reading the list of restaurants. When she got to Casey's in Lime Springs, Iowa, Rodney said, "That's good. Let's go to Casey's. We'll get gas and pick up some food. Maybe there is a park around where we can eat. We can't eat in one of those small-town cafés. Everybody knows everybody, and we'll stand out."

"Are you worried people will recognize us?" Gloriann asked.

"*Kim*, we have to be careful. There was nothing on the internet last night. I checked at the hotel. But now we don't have access, so we don't know if there are photos or alerts."

Martin's protests were getting louder. Gloriann unlocked her seat belt and stretched over the front console to put a pacifier in Martin's mouth. She rubbed his head gently, and he quieted. When Gloriann was sitting back down and buckled in, Rod looked in the rearview mirror. He smiled at Martin furiously sucking on the pacifier. "That's not going to hold her for long." Returning his focus to the road, he said, "Oh, good. Here's Lime Springs."

When the car pulled into the parking lot and stopped, Martin spit out the pacifier and began to wail. Gloriann said, "I'll nurse Lily first. Why don't you go in and get the food?" Rod nodded and got out of the car.

By the time Gloriann put Martin to the breast, he was frantic. His swallowing was fast and audible, as if he were chugging a beer. His big eyes looked up at her—accusingly, she thought. His little body was tense. When she switched him to her other side, he sucked slower, and his body relaxed. She smiled at his emerging playfulness. She cuddled him every time he stopped and smiled up at her. "Oh, my pumpkin pie, my little sweetie peetie," she cooed as his little legs started to wriggle. She studied Martin in his pink playsuit. "Oh, baby, you make such a pretty girl!" That was the thing about infants. Sex was so often inferred by the clothes they wore. Dress a baby in pink and frills, and she had to be a girl; in a slugger T-shirt and baseball cap, and he had to be a boy. She could never figure out why parents who dressed their baby in unisex clothes were offended when someone guessed the wrong gender. At three months, there was no other outward clue.

Rod was at the window. "How about if you put Lily back in the car seat and go use the restroom? There's a little park and pavilion just down Merrill Street," he said as he pointed in its direction. "We can eat there, and Lily can lie on a blanket to stretch out. I'll gas up." Then he added quietly, "Remember to keep your head down."

At the park, Gloriann put Martin down on a blanket and changed him but did not put his legs back in the playsuit. "It is too hot for her, Larry. I'd put her in shorts, but she'd get cold in the car with the air on. It is so humid; everything is sticking to me. Boy, it's true what they say: it's not the heat but the humidity." Gloriann sat on the blanket next to Martin and played with him while she ate her sandwich. Rod sat at the picnic table, eating and looking at a map. Gloriann looked up at him. "We really are old-school, Larry. I don't know the last time I used a map."

"We'll go Sixty-three to Fifty-two to Ninety-four. Finished? We've still got a lot of driving. I'm guessing about two and a half hours to Minneapolis. I've got to meet our contact at three o'clock sharp. We can make a stop for you to feed Lily. When we get in the car, I'll give you an address for the Garmin," Rod said, folding the map and standing up.

They didn't drive long before Gloriann saw the "Welcome to Minnesota" sign. "Have you ever been to Minnesota before, Larry?"

"Yeah, a couple of times. I was even here in the winter once when the actual temperature was twenty-five degrees below zero and the windchill was minus fifty. It was so cold that the mucus in my nose froze, and my teeth hurt. You know, the next Super Bowl is up here. They're promoting the Twin Cities as the 'Bold North.' The 'Cold North' would have been more like it."

"You are scaring me, Rod—I mean Larry."

"Don't worry, Kimmy. You'll get used to it. How come you never came to Minnesota?"

"I don't know. When we would visit Jack's family in Green Bay, we'd stay there or go up to Door County. Jack's been in Minnesota. He'd fly up to go with his dad to a football game. Jack's family is crazy for the Packers. Their whole rec room is done up in green and gold. His dad even likes to tell people that he's an owner of the Packers. I think he has one share!" Gloriann thought about Jack's family and all the good times they had together. Rod made a comment about the Vikings and Packers and something about how odd it was that Elizabeth was from Minnesota.

Gloriann no longer heard him. She turned her face to her window. Flashbacks of last year's family reunion at Bay Beach Amusement Park in Green Bay drifted in and out of her consciousness. She was standing next to Jack, watching Emma and Will on the kiddie helicopter ride. Up and down they went, taking turns to push and pull the command bar. Jack's father was taking pictures, and his mother waving each time the kids circled around. Now, she imagined herself walking away while Jack was still looking up. Her shorts and tank top morphed into a long white cotton dress that blew in the wind as she entered a far-off cornfield. She looked back over her shoulder. The scene had not changed except for her absence. She closed her eyes and fell asleep.

"Kimmy." Rod was shaking her shoulder. "Gloriann, wake up!"

Gloriann sat up from her slump toward the door. The right side of her neck hurt from the shoulder harness, and the left side from being stretched by the heaviness of her drooping head. She rubbed her neck and yawned. Her chin felt crusty. She must have been sleeping with her mouth open; she had to swallow several times to rehydrate her throat. "Oh, Rrr-Larry, I really knocked out," she said as she yawned again. "Where are we?"

"We are going to be coming into St. Paul soon. I noticed a Walmart sign up ahead. I thought that would be a good place to take care of Lily and get something to drink. Then we'll drive straight to our meeting, take care of business, and be on our way."

Rod parked the car beneath a tree in the far corner of the parking lot and let it run to keep the air-conditioning on. He mentally prepared for his meeting while Gloriann nursed Martin. He pulled out his wallet from his right front pocket and flipped through the bills. Putting it back, he then felt his left front pocket and checked the right back pocket. Everything was in place.

Gloriann opened the door so she could lay Martin on the seat to change him. The air outside felt heavy like the inside of the bathroom when she took a hot shower but forgot to run the vent fan. "I'll put Lily in the short romper so she doesn't get too hot. Would you hand me that receiving blanket from the back just in case it is cold in the store?" Gloriann asked Rod.

"Welcome to Walmart!" the smiling, white-haired man in the bright blue vest said as they walked into the store. "What a beautiful little princess!"

"Thank you," Rod and Gloriann responded in unison as Rod cuddled the baby and picked up a blue plastic basket.

"Why don't you freshen up while I pick up some juice smoothies and cereal bars?" Rod suggested to Gloriann.

She used the restroom and replaced her nursing pads. After washing her hands, she rubbed her face and neck with cold water and looked in the mirror. Her wig hadn't moved. She'd be glad when she could take it off and shake out her own hair, which felt matted as if under a too-tight winter hat.

Rod was standing in an aisle where she could see him when she exited the restroom. "Are you ready?" she asked.

"Yep. Why don't you wait outside with Lily while I check out? It'll only be a minute."

"I can wait with you, Larry."

"No need, honey. I'll only be a minute."

When they were walking to the car, Gloriann asked him, "Why didn't you want us to check out with you?"

"Cameras, Kim," was his only answer.

CHAPTER | 8

As they continued their drive, Gloriann could feel Rod's tension escalate. The calm of the morning evaporated as an invisible uneasiness filled the car. Even Martin was awake and waving his arm to make noise with his monkey-shaped wrist rattle.

Gloriann put on the radio and pushed the "seek" button. She pushed it again when she heard something about the air quality: "An air advisory is in effect until eight o'clock tonight. Smoke, warm temperatures, slowly rising ozone layer coming from the south, and particulates from the wildfires out west can adversely affect infants, elderly, and asthma patients. Caution is advised. High pollen levels are adding to the discomfort."

She glanced over at Rod, who sat rigidly upright, arms tight, white knuckles rimming the steering wheel. She concentrated again on the radio station, whose disc jockey was talking about the Minnesota State Fair. Niall Horan would play at the grandstand on the fair's opening night. She thought, *Slow Hands*, and smiled. Reaching over to Rod, she put her hand on his shoulder to massage it, singing quietly, "Yeah, I already know that there ain't no stopping your plans."

Rod jerked his head and stared at her. His eyes were cold, his jaw set. Gloriann startled but for only a moment. Rod's face quickly softened to a warm glow. He slid his hand over the console and squeezed her upper thigh. "No, sweetheart, you can't stop my plans," he said, his eyes glistening and his hand moving closer to her belly.

"Rodney!" she said, laughing, and batted his hand away.

"The state fair starts in three hundred and forty-one days." WCCO was wrapping up the news. Gloriann shut the radio off. Traffic buzzed around them. Increasing numbers of cars and trucks sped down the entrance ramps. Rodney maneuvered the car to blend in with the flow. Coming down a hill, Gloriann could see the dome of the Minnesota State Capitol. Then they were crossing the Mississippi and another bridge that ran perpendicular below them. Orange engines led a long, snaking train on the north side of the river. A black helicopter flew low over the buildings in the distance. Now they were being squeezed between two concrete walls as they first descended then drove back up to take the Minneapolis 94 West exit. A large yellow construction crane hung its head over what looked like the beginnings of a huge roller coaster off the Snelling exit. "Look at that, Rod. What do you think that is?" Gloriann asked.

Rod said, "We have to watch for exit 235B, Huron Street. Gloriann, let's just go over what we talked about. I'm going to park the car. If you see anyone approaching you, call me. I've got my phone on vibrate. Remember, we are tourists from Iowa and heard about the grain elevators. Wanted to see them before they are gone. Stopped so you could feed the baby. That's all you have to say. I'll take care of the rest."

"Do you think we are going to have a problem?"

"No. No problems as long as you do what I say. Just stay calm, Gloriann," Rod cautioned.

"I'm OK. I can do this," Gloriann said, hoping that no one would approach the car. Gloriann was alarmed as they drove down Huron to Twenty-fifth. She thought it would be a more secluded area. At least that's how she had interpreted the paper map. But instead, the area was full of apartment buildings. Light-rail tracks ran in both directions. A University of Minnesota athletic field was adjacent to the grain elevator. There was no place to park on the street. In fact, they could not turn right or left. "Do Not Enter" and "Buses and Emergency Vehicles ONLY" signs were on both sides of the T in the road. Rodney drove straight onto the gravel drive directly in front of them, ignoring the "Keep Out" and "Private Property" signs. Then he quickly turned right and nestled the car between the grain elevator and an old brick building whose windows were broken or partly covered with plywood.

"This place is creepy," Gloriann said. "Are you really going in there?"

"You know I am. Keep the air on so you don't have to open the windows. Keep the doors locked. This won't take long."

"How long, Rod?"

"Ten minutes," Rodney said as he pulled out a pair of vinyl gloves from his left front pocket and put them on.

"Why the gloves?"

"This guy is an identity theft broker. I'm not leaving prints for him to use," Rod said and got out of the car.

Gloriann looked at her watch, then at the rearview mirror. She saw Rod disappear between the athletic field fence and the grain elevator.

Rodney walked quickly on the gravel, touching his right back pocket and scanning his surroundings. He spotted an opening at the base of the far tower. He was glad that Idman had sent him a diagram, or he would not have found it. Inside, the smell of urine and feces made him gag. He swallowed hard and looked around. There was a steel mesh staircase to one side of the concrete room. Walls were covered with graffiti; litter, several inches high, shielded the floor. Sun coming through exterior cutouts splashed white rectangles on the floor. The interior was a hellish study of light and shadow. Idman was standing at what looked like an old store counter.

"Hey," Idman said, sizing up Rod.

Rod looked around nervously. "Are we alone?"

"Yeah, dude. Don't worry."

"I've never done this before." Rod's voice was uncertain.

"It's cool. You got the money?"

"Yes. Yes, I do."

"All right. Let's see it."

Rod pulled out the bulging wallet from his front pocket. He took the stack of hundred-dollar bills and held them up so Idman could see them. Idman studied Rod, then took the backpack off his shoulder and unzipped the top. Rod stiffened as he watched Idman put his hand inside the backpack and begin to pull something out. It was a large envelope. Rod let out a long breath. Idman held out the envelope with his left hand, while his right hand gestured for the money.

He grabbed the money at the same time as he shoved the envelope into Rod's chest. Rod could feel something flat and hard. He opened the top of the envelope and retrieved two Minnesota license plates and a smaller envelope that contained two Minnesota driver's licenses, two passports, and two birth certificates. He walked past Idman's side of the counter so he could stand in one of the rectangles of light to inspect what he had just purchased. He looked back at Idman with a nod and smile.

"Good stuff, eh? I only deal with the best. Get what you pay for. None of that Chinese shit."

"Yeah, thanks. Wow. This stuff is great. I can't tell you how much we appreciate this." Rod was gushing.

"No problem. It sucks that you have to be running from your old lady's ex. A cop that beat her, and now he's stalking her? Well, good thing you hooked up with me. Guess that was your lucky day,"

Idman said and turned to walk back to a ten-speed bike that was propped against a pillar. Rod waited until he saw Idman begin to swing his leg over the crossbar. Then he made his move.

He took the garrote out of his back pocket and ran toward Idman. Crossing his arms at his wrists, Rodney threw the paracord over Idman's head and around his neck. Then he pulled his arms out and back, tightening the cord while he wrenched Idman from the bike. Idman lost his balance; his hands flew to his neck but then dropped. He went limp. Rodney held the cord taut until he counted to sixty. He wanted to make sure Idman wasn't going to come back to life.

This guy really is dead weight, Rod thought as he dragged the body to a dark corner. He reached into the man's pocket and reclaimed his wad of cash. He rifled through the backpack but found nothing problematic. Then he compacted the body, molding it into a fetal position, and partially covered it with debris, hoping that it would not be discovered for at least a few days. He looked at the bike, trying to decide what to do with it. Picking it up, he climbed the stairs to the second level and left it there. Anyone venturing to the second level would probably steal it.

When he was back on the first floor, he kicked around the litter so that there was no discernable path. He took a few deep breaths to compose himself, straightened his posture, and brought a shining countenance to his face as he imagined a fashion model might do. Then he retraced his steps to the car.

Opening the car door, he handed Gloriann the envelope. "Here. Put this under your seat. And put Duluth in the Garmin." Taking off the gloves and stuffing them back in his pocket, he looked at Martin, who was in his car seat sleeping, and then over at Gloriann to make sure she was buckled in. He backed out slowly, then maneuvered the car so that he could exit the complex driving straight over two sets of light-rail tracks until he got to University Avenue, where he turned left.

"How'd it go?" Gloriann asked.

"OK. All right. We got everything we need. I just have to figure out a place to stop to change the license plates. We gotta change them before we get to Duluth."

"Do the pictures look like us?"

"Well, yeah, Gloriann. I sent him the photos of us. He did a good job of changing your hair color to red and making it look shorter. Yeah, they look just like us."

"What names do we have?"

"Honestly, I didn't even read the names. I just wanted to get in and out of there."

"Rod, do you think we are safe? I mean, do you think he'll tell someone or report us?"

"Oh, honey, don't worry about that. The man's a professional. There is no way that he is going to say anything to anybody. I promise you."

"Is United Crushers part of ADM?" asked Gloriann.

"What?"

"United Crushers. It was in big block white letters at the very top of those concrete silos. And ADM was faded out below. Didn't you see that?"

Rodney chuckled. "Oh, that's graffiti, Gloriann. The 'United Crushers' is graffiti. Why did you think it was part of ADM?"

"Well, I thought that maybe they crushed the grain and then stored it."

"Hmm," Rodney said. "I can see why you might think that. Things definitely got stored in those silos."

They were through the city now, and traffic started to fade away the farther north they traveled. The sumac was beginning to change color, with tips flashing a rusty red. Trees were still green but looked exhausted in the heat. Some had patches of dull yellow leaves. The landscape was untamed, wild with a few interspersed cornfields. Tall straw-colored grasses bent gently in the wind.

"Here's Hinckley. Let's see if there is somewhere we can change those plates," Rod said to Gloriann as he put on the blinker and took the Fire Museum exit. Hardees, a Holiday gas station, and Days Inn were at the top of the ramp. They passed the Whistle Stop Café, which advertised "Homemade Pies." Another café was closed and vacant; the Firestorm Café boasted "50-cent coffee."

"Let's try farther down the road. There's no place here to make the switch," Rod said.

"We need to find someplace soon. I've got to use the bathroom, and Martin is getting hungry again. I am too."

"I know, Gloriann. Believe me, I know. We'll stop at the next town. We are bound to find a spot."

Rod took the Sandstone exit and followed the signs to Robinson Park. Driving down Old Wagon Road, Rod said, "Now, this looks promising. I think we'll be OK here." He parked the car in a secluded lot next to the Kettle River. "Gloriann, take off your wig and put it in the diaper bag. Then do whatever you have to do. I'm going to change the plates right now," Rodney said as he gingerly pulled the moustache from his upper lip.

"You don't want to be from Iowa anymore?" Gloriann laughed.

"No. Now we are Minne-sow-tans. Don't cha know."

After Rod finished attaching the Minnesota plates to the car, he took the Iowa plates and, using his foot, bent them in half. He wrapped them in some newspaper and put them in a dark plastic bag. Then he took the wig and moustache, put them in a brown paper bag, and crumpled it up. The only thing left to do was to cut up their Larry and Kim licenses as well as the Rodney and Gloriann ones. "We won't use the trash containers here. Too risky," Rod said. "We'll get rid of the stuff bit by bit as we go."

Gloriann was busy finishing taking care of Martin. "Let's see who we are. Gosh, I hope I like the names."

Rod retrieved the passports, licenses, and birth certificates from the envelope. "Who do you want to know first?"

"Martin's. Who is Martin going to be?"

"Good. Idman picked a non-gender-specific name just like I asked and gave us two certificates covering both sexes."

"Well, what is it?" Gloriann was eager.

"Sydney Johnson."

Gloriann smiled. "I like Sydney! That's a good name. I like the Vicar Sidney on *Grantchester*. What's Martin's middle name?

"Doesn't have one. He or she is just Sydney Johnson."

"OK. Who am I?" Gloriann was holding her breath.

"You're Carol Mae, and I'm James Russell."

"Those aren't bad. How do you think he picked these?"

"I'm pretty sure Johnson is one of the more popular surnames in Minnesota. Our first names are those of people who no longer exist. He has access to records, I guess."

"Well, Jim—you do want Jim?"

"Yeah, I'm not a James."

Gloriann was looking at their new licenses. "Rod, these are really good! So are the passports and the birth certificates. How did you find Idman?"

Rod paused, thinking of his contact on the dark web, then looked at Gloriann. "I found him. That's all you need to know, Gloriann. It's better that way."

Gloriann stared at Rod but nodded her head. She was solemn.

Rod tried to perk her up. "OK, from now on, we are who we are. I'm Jim. You're Carol, and Martin is Sydney. We begin anew. Right here. Right now. The Johnson family from Minneapolis is on the move."

"To Jim and Sydney and Carol," Gloriann said, raising an invisible glass for a toast.

CHAPTER | 9

Back on the road, Jim said to Carol, "Let's look for another gas station where we can pick up a sandwich or something."

"Oh, Jim, can't we stop and eat at a sit-down restaurant? I'm starting to feel sick. I got to get out of the car for a while."

"We'd be taking a big chance, Carol."

"Oh, come on. We're new people now, aren't we? Have we been in the news or something that I don't know about, Jim? I mean, we have burner phones and haven't even used them for anything other than calling each other. You've paid cash for everything. I can't take it anymore. I need a break," Carol said and started to cry.

Jim took a deep breath. "OK, just tonight. That's it until we get well past Duluth. All right? Watch the signs for someplace to stop."

Carol wiped her eyes and stared out the window. A large gray cloud began to crowd out the sun, and a light drizzle dotted the windshield. She turned down the air-conditioning and laid one of Sydney's receiving blankets over her chest and shoulders. "There— there's a sign for a sports bar in Sturgeon Lake," she said as she pointed out the window.

It was sixty-four degrees and misting when they pulled into the parking lot and opened the car doors. The scent of pine hung in the air. Carol remained seated while Jim opened the trunk and took out jackets for them and a change of clothes for Sydney. They wrapped Sydney in a heavier blanket and walked quickly to the restaurant. The inside mirrored the rustic exterior. A mounted buck looked down on them from above an oval mural that depicted a summer scene on its left and a winter scene on its right. Tin signs sported logos of the Vikings, Twins, and Minnesota Wild.

They were immediately seated by a window overlooking the parking lot. Carol was grateful for the big bowl of chicken noodle soup. Jim had fries and a Hermann the German sandwich of roast beef, green peppers, onions, sauerkraut, and pepper jack cheese.

"Who's Hermann the German?" Carol asked, taking some of Jim's fries.

"I don't know, but I'm not going to ask. Minnesotans must know who he is," Jim whispered.

When they had finished eating, Carol put her hand on top of Jim's. "Thanks for eating here. The soup was just what I needed."

"Good. I'm glad you're better. We should be in Duluth in less than an hour and can hunker down." Jim started to laugh. "Funny. We are staying in Hermantown."

"Who is Hermann?" Carol was now also laughing.

Jim shook his head, stood up, and kissed Carol on the cheek. "Let's go."

They had only driven a few miles when the light mist turned into a light fog. A semitruck hauling logs was now in front of them. "Don't be behind that truck. Please don't be behind that truck. Pull over or something," Carol said, putting her heels on the edge of the seat and pulling her knees toward her.

Jim looked at her, not understanding. "What?"

"Pull over. Please, just pull over."

Jim had never seen Carol like this before. "OK, OK. Calm down. I'm pulling over."

When another car passed them, Carol said, "You can go now."

As Jim pulled back on the road, he said, "What was that all about, Carol?"

"My dream. I had this horrible dream. I was driving behind a log truck, and one of the logs came off and crashed through the windshield, and then everything went black, and I woke up. Promise me that you won't follow any log trucks. Please, promise me."

Jim checked himself from saying that she was being ludicrous because he could see that she was terrified. There would be no reasoning with her. "OK, I promise. I won't drive behind any log trucks."

Carol put her feet back on the floor and let out a loud sigh. "Thank you."

The closer they got to Duluth, the thicker the fog became. It was as if they were driving through a cloud. When the wind picked up, the fog came at them like smoke from a campfire that turned on them.

"See if you can find a radio station, Carol. I want to hear the weather."

Carol played with the dial until they heard, "Areas of fog are affecting portions of the Twin Ports and the Iron Range. Some areas especially over the hill away from Lake Superior will see visibilities below one quarter of a mile. On Lake Superior, expect winds northeast twenty to twenty-five knots. Wind gusts up to thirty knots. Waves seven to nine feet."

"Oh no, no!" Carol grabbed the handle of the car door and turned to look at Jim.

"We're all right, Carol," Jim assured her.

Conditions worsened. Up in the hills, they could barely see the road, but coming down into Duluth, the road surface cleared, and only the scenery was obscured. Carol relaxed. She could make out ore docks off to the right and thought they looked eerie. They looked like docks in a watercolor painting that was beginning to run. It made a ghostly scene. Now the road was taking them up into the hills again.

"Oh no! The fog! I can't see. Can you see, Rod?" She had slipped back into using his real name. Terror gripped her. She thought the fog was a bad omen. First the log truck, now the fog. She was on an emotional roller coaster—fog and anxiety, clear road and relief. Was this how it was going to be? She could read the temperature on an illuminated sign. It was fifty-eight degrees. It just kept getting colder. Waves of fog were skimming the tops of the cars. When she looked out her window, she saw sheets of mist and fog passing and flags straight out in the wind. Her head began to ache, and she felt like her neck was going to snap. Her breathing quickened.

"Carol. *Carol!* We're here," Jim said as he pulled under the canopy of the hotel entrance.

Carol stared at him, not understanding. Finally, she said, "Oh, good."

CHAPTER | 10

SUNDAY, SEPTEMBER 17

Carol felt better in the morning. The hot bath and good night's sleep erased any feeling of unease. It was a new day, the beginning of a new beginning! The hotel breakfast was hearty and satisfying. While sitting in the breakfast room, Carol overheard a grandmother talking to her granddaughters. She was telling them that the freeway in Duluth, which they were going to take to Two Harbors, was closed due to a race. When Carol mentioned this to Jim, he said it couldn't be true. No one would close an interstate for a race.

When they left Hermantown at 9:45 a.m., it was sixty-two degrees. The rain and thunderstorms from earlier in the morning had gone. It was still misting and gray with low cloud cover, but the visibility had improved since last night. As they drove south on 53 down the hill to Duluth, the fog returned and did not dissipate until they reached the bottom. Traffic backed up, and they were stuck behind a delivery truck whose exhaust made Carol feel queasy. Then they were forced to take the signed detour to exit 256A Mesaba Avenue and into another snarl of traffic. Carol could sense Jim's rising tension.

"Look on the bright side, Jim," Carol said. "At least we're finally able to see freighters on Lake Superior. And the water is looking bluer."

"Yeah," Jim conceded. Later, as they drove through residential neighborhoods for thirty minutes, he said, "Well, we are getting the Cook's Tour of Duluth. I hope we didn't miss any detour signs. Put Two Harbors in the Garmin and see if it can get us out of this mess."

As they neared the turn for 61N and stopped the car to get their bearings, a peace officer at the intersection approached them. "Don't worry. I got this," Jim said with a forced smile.

Carol looked out her window to the right at the patrol cars with flashing lights near the wooden barricades. She placed her hands outstretched on her lap, smiled, and took slow, deep breaths.

"Good morning, Officer," Jim said. "We got a bit lost with the detour. Can we turn left? I mean, where does that race go? Are we OK?"

"Where are you heading?" the officer asked, bending at the waist to smile at Carol.

"Two Harbors," Jim told him.

"Yep. Turn left here."

"What kind of race is it?"

"Oh, it's the North Shore Inline Marathon. Starts just south of Two Harbors, goes along Scenic 61, rolls through the I-35 tunnels, and finishes at the Duluth Convention Center."

"Thanks, Officer."

"No problem. You have a good day now," the peace officer said, waving them on.

They took the turn, and Carol exhaled. She hadn't realized that she was holding her breath. "That was scary," she said.

"It's OK. We're OK," Jim said, looking in his rearview mirror. There was a line of cars but no patrols. He relaxed his grip on the wheel. "We're on our way!"

Two Harbors looked so inviting that Carol wished they were tourists. Quaint shops—Blueberry House, Vanilla Bean, Sweet Pea Gifts—all beckoned, but Carol knew she couldn't even suggest stopping. A banner advertising "Rock Show Today" hung across what looked like the entrance to a small park. Mothers pushed strollers. Boys about Will's age ran around playing tag. Teenage girls stood in a group giggling. "Maybe we can come back here someday," she said to Jim. He smiled but did not answer her unspoken question.

They passed through a tunnel at Silver Creek Cliff and then through another tunnel that was unnamed. Carol spotted Split Rock Lighthouse standing sentry on a cliff overlooking Lake Superior. When they passed the Minnesota Historical Society's sign for the lighthouse, Carol said, "You know, Elizabeth's husband worked for the Historical Society. I feel bad about sticking her the way I did."

"Don't worry about it. Don't even think back on it. She'll get over it," Jim told her.

They drove with the windows open. The air was crisp, and the sun shone through a cloudy, blue-gray sky. Rock outcroppings and pine trees proliferated the landscape. The whoosh of southbound cars passing them increased. Carol saw a sign, "Canadian Border 92."

She began to silently second-guess herself. *Should I leave the country—and with a fake ID? What if we get caught? What if I never see Will and Emma again? What if I never see my parents or sister or Jack's family—or even Jack?* She looked at the dead birch trees standing like whitewashed corpses among the pines.

Another log truck came into focus in front of them. Jim looked at her and pulled over. "Hey, don't worry about it. This is logging country."

"Do you think it's a bad omen?" Carol's voice was strained.

"Oh, for Pete's sake, *no*. I remember you telling me about your mother never putting new shoes on the table because she thought something awful would happen. She'd be upset if you forgot and would then worry about you. That's crazy, Carol. You grew up with superstitions brought over from the old country. Trust me. Nothing bad is going to happen." After several cars passed, Jim pulled back onto the road. When they saw the sign for "Temperance Liquors," Jim laughed. "Check that out! Not sure what is temperate about booze!"

"Why would they name it that?" asked Carol.

"Temperance River is here."

Small streams of water, like mini waterfalls, seeped down rock ledges. The beauty of the Superior National Forest wrapped them in a blanket of peace. Traffic became sparse. Carol read the sign, "Thunder Bay 98 miles." "What? I thought it was right across the border." She looked at Jim, her forehead wrinkled.

"No, it's about forty miles beyond the border." The vista was stunning coming down to Cutface Creek Wayside Rest. "Can you imagine what this would look like in a week or two? The colors?" Jim asked. "Too bad, but we couldn't have waited. Jack left, and Elizabeth came, and that was our out. We'll eat in Grand Marais."

They stopped at the Angry Trout Restaurant and were seated at a table in the corner of what looked like a three-season porch. The lake was visible from both sides of the table. The sky was still cloudy, but the lake was calm, with sailboats lazily bobbing on the water, sails gathered tightly to their masts. The grilled whitefish sandwiches, coleslaw, and chips were presented on pottery plates. Both Carol and Jim wrapped their fingers around their mugs, feeling the warmth of the coffee and savoring its rich aroma. Sydney had already been fed and was looking around, contentment evident in her visage.

"This place is like something out of a movie," Carol said. "Look at the chairs." The ladder backs were shaped as fish, with one fish facing right, the next facing left, each with a cutout circle depicting an eye. "Even the people look like a cast set in a northern fishing village." They wore jeans, sweatshirts, and baseball caps in the deep, rich hues of fall—green, gray, maroon, and gold.

Leaving Grand Marais, they saw the South of the Border Café. It was closed. Jim chuckled. "I bet they didn't serve tacos!" Carol didn't laugh. "Jim, I'm wondering if we should do this. Cross the border, I mean. Why do we have to leave the country? I think we should go back and work something out. It won't be easy, but it would be better than going to Canada. I don't want to lose my children."

Jim squared his shoulders and tightened his jaw. "Look, Carol, this is a hell of a time to start wondering. You weren't wondering when we were planning this. You weren't wondering when you were having an affair. You weren't wondering when you dumped the kids with Elizabeth. As I remember it, you went along with all the plans. You were excited about leaving. Were you leading me on, Carol? Were you? Come on. Think of all I've done for you. I've cashed out all my stocks, left my clients, my livelihood, my condo. I've broken the law for you in obtaining those IDs. I've given up everything for you. If this is the way you want to treat me, then fine, let's go back. But if we go back, you are on your own. On your own, Carol. Maybe Jack will take you back. I don't know. I doubt you'll get your kids after you abandoned them, and I'll want custody of Sydney."

Carol stared at him, mouth gaping, tears welling up.

"What?" Jim continued. "He is *my* son. Do you think I'd walk away from him? Do you think I wouldn't want to spend as much time as I could with *my* child? I wouldn't leave *my* kid."

Carol covered her face with her hands, crumpled forward, and sobbed.

After several minutes, Jim reached over and rubbed her back. "Hey, you're just tired and scared. You know I love you more than Jack ever did. He wasn't around. Yeah, he was working, but so was I, and I made time for you and for Sydney. You *know* we are good together. You don't want to go back and face the gossip, the judgment. Do you think your family is going to understand, to rally around you? Think again. This is your chance, baby. *Our* chance to lead a new life. But hey, I can turn the car around. Just say the word, and we'll go back and try to work something out. You know I love you. You know I love Sydney. You know that, don't you?"

Carol stopped crying, wiped her eyes, and nodded her head. "I know."

"OK then. Wipe your face and put on some lipstick. We don't want the border patrol to think I'm dragging you into Canada. I'm not dragging you. If you don't want to go, tell me now."

"I'll go," Carol moaned.

"Good. Good girl! Don't worry so much, Carol. This will be a piece of cake. It's nothing like an Arizona border crossing. And hey, keep this in perspective. It's Canada. It's not like we are falling off the face of the earth."

Soon they were driving up Mount Josephine in the Sawtooth Mountains. Fog was dense in the treetops. As they descended, they saw a state highway patrol car nestled among trees in a small roadway pull-off. Jim looked at Carol. She showed no reaction; she looked beyond caring. When they arrived at the entrance to Grand Portage State Park and saw the sign, "Customs & Border Protection ½ mile / last turnaround before border," Jim said, "Let's stop at the park and use the restroom. I don't know when the next one is going to be." He didn't need to stop, but he wanted to see what Carol would do. He was thinking that if she was going to bolt, better here than in front of border patrol.

Back in the car, they began crossing the Pigeon River, the boundary between the US and Canada. A big blue sign greeted them, "Welcome to Ontario." Then they were stopped in the middle of the bridge behind a "Vegas RV" from Illinois. Carol looked at her watch; it was 3:19 p.m. Traffic was at a standstill.

After a while, Jim asked, "You OK?"

"Yeah. I don't mind waiting. I just want to get off this bridge. Wasn't there a bridge that fell in Minnesota?"

"Change the phone settings to Global Roaming and Accept Data for all trips," Jim said as he handed Carol his phone. She did, and the time jumped ahead to 4:25 p.m.

They were moving again. There were more signs, this time in English and French: "You are entering the Eastern Time Zone," "Don't move firewood. Hitchhiking insects like the Emerald Ash Borer can kill forests," "Everyone must report to Border Inspection," "Declare all weapons to a Canada Border Services Agency Officer," and finally, "Please have your photo identification ready for inspection."

"Here we go. Look happy. They are going to take our pictures," Jim just finished saying before they drove through a line of flashing cameras. Jim handed their IDs to the agent who sat inside a booth. He took the documents and looked first at Jim, then Carol, then back at the baby mirror, which showed a sleeping Sydney. He handed them back to Jim and started the questioning: "Where do you live?" "Where are you going?" "How long are you staying?" "Do you have firearms?" "Do you have alcohol?" "Do you have tobacco?" "Do you have mace?" "Do you have a handgun?" "Do you have a stun gun?" "Anything that you plan to sell or leave behind or give away?"

Jim answered: "Minneapolis, Minnesota; Thunder Bay; two weeks; no, no, no, no, no, no, no."

"OK. Have a nice trip," the agent said, and Jim pulled ahead.

"That was unbelievable," Carol whispered. "No armed guards, no patrol dogs."

"What did I tell ya?" Jim said, smiling. "We can relax now. It's all going to be OK."

"Oh, this is too much," Carol said as she pointed to a flock of Canadian geese gathered at the welcome station.

"Yep. They pulled out all the stops to welcome us. Feeling better? I am!" he said and thought, *I should! I did it! A wife, a son, lots of money, and freedom!*

Carol felt in a suspended state. "I still can't believe it. I really can't."

Still telescoped in on his own euphoria, Jim said, laughing, "This is what illegals must feel like once they get on the other side of the Rio Grande, and we didn't even have to get wet crossing the Pigeon River!"

"Oh, stop it!" Carol said as she playfully punched Jim in the arm.

They passed a sign, "Thunder Bay 62." "What? Sixty-two miles? I thought it was closer," an alarmed Jim exclaimed.

"Everything is in kilometers here," Carol said.

"How are we going to know how fast to go? I don't want to get pulled over for speeding."

"It's easy. Just multiply everything by point six to get the equivalent in miles."

"Are you kidding me? How do you remember this stuff?" Jim was feeling disoriented.

"I had to learn the metric system in college. You'll get used to it. We can download a conversion chart once we get to a computer."

"OK. So if the maximum speed here is ninety kilometers, it's about fifty-four miles per hour. And Thunder Bay would be about thirty-six miles."

"That's right. You get an A."

"Oh, I'm going to get more than an A, teacher ma'am," Jim said, sliding his hand up Carol's thigh. This time, she didn't bat his hand away.

"I guess you are." Carol laughed. "And I'm going to give you a gold star."

Thunder Bay welcomed them with a sign stating the census statistic "Population 108,000." There were also piles of wood pulp and smoke belching out of stacks at a forest-products plant. "Not very scenic," Carol commented.

"It gets better," Jim assured her. And it did. Driving on the Thunder Bay Expressway on the route to their extended-stay hotel, Carol saw nice, suburban-looking houses, newer construction, a shopping mall with a Walmart and Safeway. But she also saw more logging trucks than she had ever seen before. She couldn't help but wonder if they were trying to tell her something.

"Look at all the Minnesota license plates," Jim said, tilting his chin up to indicate the cars in front of them. Most of the license plates were from Ontario or other provinces, but it seemed that almost all the American plates were from Minnesota. "I knew I chose the right state! Just remember to say, 'ya sure' and 'you betcha.' Gas is cheaper here too."

"The price is in liters, Jim."

"Oh," he groaned. And he groaned again when the thermostat in their rental was set to twenty-three degrees.

Carol was pleased with their accommodations. Two bedrooms, one and a half baths, nine hundred square feet. "How long do we have this place?"

"I rented it for two weeks. That should give me enough time to make the necessary arrangements for Toronto. You can rest up. Maybe we'll do a little sightseeing." Then he lifted Sydney into the air and said, "Just two more weeks, and you can ditch the pink outfits!"

CHAPTER | **11**

MONDAY, SEPTEMBER 18

When Carol awoke to Sydney's cries, she felt both apprehensive and sluggish. She looked down at him in his polka-dot sleeper decorated with dancing unicorns and shook her head. The sheet below him was wet, his face red and angry, his flailing hands balled into fists. "Jim? Jim?" Carol called out. There was no answer.

She soothed Sydney, changed him, and sank into the couch to nurse him. She heard keys in the door, then saw Jim walk in with a bag and a cardboard carrier holding two coffees. There was a newspaper tucked under his arm.

"Good morning, sunshine! There's a coffee shop just down the road. Got two of the cheese everything bagels," Jim said as he set the food on the table and tossed the newspaper on the couch. "How's our Sydney?"

Carol yawned. "OK. I think we are both just tired."

"Well, it will take a little bit to come to. We've literally been running." Jim came over and kissed the top of her head.

Carol flipped open the front page of the *Chronicle Journal*. Two headlines on the bottom caught her eye. She smiled at "Face fears, take plunge"—that was certainly what she just did. But the "From

104

tragic past to bringing cheer to present," with the accompanying picture of jubilant children singing and skipping down the aisle of a church, gave her an overwhelming sense of sadness. She read the caption and learned that they were members of the African Children's Choir. Children from Uganda, many of them had lost one parent or were orphans. She felt as though she would vomit. "So what's on the docket for today?"

"Well, we'll have to go to the grocery store and stock up. Then I thought while you are doing the laundry, I'd go buy a laptop. I need that conversion chart. I looked at the weather for today: sunny with a high of seventeen and low of eleven. I need something to help me figure it out quicker. It's driving me nuts!"

Later, at the grocery store, as they walked up and down the aisles, choosing milk, eggs, butter, and bread, Carol thought she was having a déjà vu experience. Except this time Will was not riding on the end of the cart while Emma tickled the feet of Martin, who rode in the front in his infant carrier. She looked at Jim, who was studying jars of spaghetti sauce.

"I thought we'd have spaghetti for supper," Jim said. "What do you want to make for lunch?"

Carol thought, *Me make lunch?* but only said, "Sandwiches?" She found it harder to make lunch than to make supper. She hated making lunch.

"Sounds good to me," a chipper Jim replied.

After lunch, as Carol put Sydney down for a nap, Jim readied himself to go shopping for a laptop. "Will you be back before Sydney gets up?" Carol asked.

"I don't know."

"Well, then, could I have some money in case I want to take her for a walk if you are not back?"

"Why do you need money to do that, Carol? It's free to walk."

"Jim, haven't you ever heard that you are not supposed to go out without some money? I feel funny not having any. I don't have credit cards anymore. What if I need to pay for something?"

"Like what?"

"I don't know. What if I pass an ice-cream shop or trip and have to go to an emergency room?"

"You'd better just stay home. We don't have health insurance here yet. We need Canadian IDs for that. Won't have those until we get to Toronto. Don't go out without me. Don't talk to people around here either. Keep to yourself."

Carol put her hands on her hips. "You mean to tell me that we are going to get another set of IDs? We are not going to be Carol and Jim and Sydney?"

Jim stared at her. "No. I figured out that we can't be Carol and Jim and Sydney. We are going to get lost in Toronto, get new papers, and be Canadians. That's the only way we will be able to get health insurance and jobs at some point. I'm working on it. That's the other reason I need the laptop. I need to make connections."

Carol was silent.

"I'll make it up to you tonight, babe," Jim said with a broad smile.

"No, you won't. Not tonight," Carol shot back with a scowl.

"What? Are you on the rag? Is that what this is all about?"

Carol bristled. Jack would never talk to her like that. He would never be so callous and disrespectful. "No. I just don't like the way this is all playing out, Jim. I don't like the running. I don't like the lies. I don't like feeling that I don't have any power, that I don't have any say in our decisions. I didn't think this is how it was going to be."

Jim laughed at her. "What did you expect, Carol? How *did* you think it was going to be?" He opened the door, walked through it, quietly shut it, and locked the deadbolt.

Carol dropped back down on the couch, crossed her arms, holding her elbows, and slumped forward. Her stomach hurt. Her breathing was labored. She thought, *What did I expect? I didn't expect anything. I just went along.* She felt herself spiraling downward, shame and regret beginning to smother her. Then she bolted upright. "I'll call Jack." She went to get her purse, but the phone wasn't in it. She checked her jacket, the luggage, and all around the rental. When it didn't turn up under the couch cushions, she realized that Jim had taken it with him. Then the truth slapped her into a new awareness—she was trapped.

When Jim returned from the computer store, he was still in a sour mood, roughly putting down items on the counter and glaring at her. She stayed out of his way and kept Sydney to herself.

Tuesday, September 19

When they awoke on Tuesday, it was as if nothing had happened between them the day before. They were back to being a happy threesome family. "Carol, my little chickadee," Jim said, his eyes twinkling, eyebrows arching up and down, and sporting a Cheshire cat smile. "How about we do a bit of sightseeing? Would you like that?"

Carol masked her budding anxiety, put on a happy face, and said, "Absolutely! I would love it! Where should we go?"

"I was thinking about Kakabeka Falls," said Jim. "It's about twenty-five minutes west. It's supposed to be the highest waterfall around here."

Although the weather was forecast to be sunny and sixty-eight degrees, the morning air was cool and brisk. Carol was glad that she had bundled up Sydney, who looked like a fleece ball nestled in the baby carrier on Jim's chest. They took the half-mile boardwalk walking trail crossing the bridge over the Kaministiquia River, so they could see the falls from both its east and west sides. Water thundered over the shale escarpment, rushing through the gorge on its way to Lake Superior. Carol and Jim stood silently, mesmerized by the cascading water and admiring the surrounding trees still sporting their lush green summer wardrobes. Carol found herself smiling at the clumps of daisies that waved to her from the tall grass. A feeling of contentment welled up inside her.

On their way back to the parking lot, they were stopped by a young couple who wanted to engage them in conversation. Jim gripped Carol's hand firmly and replied to them, "We'd love to stay and talk, but the baby just filled her pants. Eww! We've got to change her quick—only brought so many clothes."

Carol shrugged her shoulders and gave them her best sorry-got-to-run face. Jim didn't let go of her hand until they were at the car.

Once there, he said, "I think we have time to see the Terry Fox monument before we have lunch."

Carol said, "I read the article about the Terry Fox Run in Monday's paper, but it didn't explain who he was other than he had cancer and raised money for cancer research."

Jim explained, "When I was looking up places to visit, I found out that there was a monument to him, then did some research online. His is a compelling story. Basically, he was diagnosed with cancer when he was eighteen and had his right leg amputated above the knee. He trained for a couple of years. Then, three years after his diagnosis, he began to run across Canada. He ran twenty-six miles per day. After a hundred and forty-three days, he stopped running outside of Thunder Bay; the cancer had spread to his lungs. Before he died, at almost twenty-three years old, he raised twenty-four million dollars—one dollar for every Canadian. He's a national hero."

In the monument parking lot, Carol got out and reached inside the car to take Sydney out of the car seat. Jim pushed her hand away. "I've got her. I'll just carry her. We won't be here very long."

Carol maneuvered herself backward out of the car and stood up. "OK."

The monument, a bronze statue of a curly-haired young man being stilled in his stride, one leg strong and muscular, the other not more than a stick and a shoe, made Carol feel ashamed. Here was a young man who did something extraordinary to help others, and she had hurt everyone she loved. She knew that she was still a good person. She had made a string of terrible mistakes, but she could come back. She could make amends, somehow. She didn't know how, but she was going to try.

Jim was looking at the statue with satisfaction. He pointed up to it. "See, Carol, if this guy could grab success with one leg, think of what I can do with two! Yep, he didn't give up, and neither will I. No, not me. I'll win again. You'll see! Let's go to lunch." He took her hand and led her to the car.

They stopped at a Polish café in Thunder Bay. Carol again went to get Sydney out of the car seat, but Jim took the baby out first. "I can take her, Jim," Carol said. Her voice was clipped.

"No, when we go out, I'll take her. You have her at home. This is my chance."

"OK. But you can't nurse her," Carol said.

"Don't get cheeky, Carol. I mean you do understand, don't you?" Jim's eyes were steel.

"Of course I do." And she did. She understood now that Sydney was Jim's insurance—insurance that Carol would not cross him.

The food at the café was authentic and delicious. The pierogi and kielbasa reminded Carol of her mother's cooking, and that remembrance started to bring tears to her eyes. Her mother—what was she doing now? What would her mother think when she found out that Gloriann had left her family? More tears welled up, and she rubbed them away. "Jim, I think I'm going to have to take a nap after this. All the fresh air and now the food."

"That's OK. While you sleep, I'm going to do some computer work. I'm glad you enjoyed today. It's just the beginning of more to come," he said and laid his hand on top of hers.

She thought, *More to come?*

CHAPTER | 12

WEDNESDAY, SEPTEMBER 20

Billy White was driving. He didn't know where he would find a place where he could do what he needed to do. He couldn't go to the office. He called Destiny and told her he had a migraine and would not be in. He couldn't stay home. His parents were persistent in their questioning about his friend Rod: "Did you know Rodney was running away with this woman, Gloriann, and a baby?" "You don't think he kidnapped them, do you?" "Why would he do that?" "Did you know Gloriann?"

He had assured them that he knew about as much as they did. He didn't tell them that news of Rod's Ponzi scheme was all over the internet. He could imagine their questions then. Currently, he was driving around like a man without a country, trying to find a place where he could examine Rod's laptop. Rod had given it to him just before he quit coming to work at Pronghorn.

Rod had said, "Put this in a safe place in your house, Billy. I need to take a trip and will get it when I come back. You are the only one I can trust. Can't leave it at the office. Can't leave it at my place. You know someone was in my apartment. Don't know if it is that new manager or what, but anyway, don't leave anything there.

As a matter of fact, until I figure it out, don't even stop by the place. Maybe later we can put up security cams or something."

And Billy, empowered by Rod's trust, obediently hid the laptop in his bedroom closet. Now Billy needed to know what was on the laptop. He was nervous that Rod had files that would implicate him. That was probably why he gave Billy the laptop in the first place—to keep it away from the feds. Did Rod know he was taking off with the wife and kid of an FBI agent? Did he know that the Ponzi scheme was collapsing? And what about the bank accounts? What about the money he promised Billy?

He drove by a Starbucks but dismissed it as too public, and it had cameras. He thought about parking on a side street but knew that was an even worse solution. Finally, he decided to seek out Sean, one of his friends from high school. Sean had a townhome on Pueblo Ave off Forty-fifth and Broadway. He and Sean ran with the same group of guys. He figured Sean would be home since he was an HVAC technician who worked the later shift. Billy didn't bother calling but just showed up at Sean's door.

"Hey, Billy. What brings you around?" Sean asked as he opened the door to let Billy in.

"Sean, I've got to do some computer work in private, and I was wondering if I can do it here."

"Can't you do it at your office?"

"No," Billy said.

Sean could see that Billy was uneasy. He asked, "Billy, is everything all right?"

"No. Not really. You remember me telling you about my mentor, Rod Wilter? Well, he's missing with somebody else's wife and kid, *and* he's being accused of a Ponzi scheme. Can you believe that? I need to do some research, and I need to check some accounts. Can't do it at work with everyone looking sideways at me. Can't do it at home with the folks on my back about it. I thought that maybe I could do it here."

Sean was silent. He looked at Billy, and for the first time, he noticed that Billy was carrying not one but two laptops. He sighed and nodded. "You can stay and do whatever. But, hey, I don't want to know about it. In fact, I'm going to get ready and take off. I've got some places to go. Lock up when you leave."

"Thanks, Sean," Billy said with a weak smile. "I don't know what else to say."

Sean responded, "No need to say anything. Better that way. You can eat whatever you find. Take care, man."

As soon as Sean was out the door, Billy put Rod's laptop on the table and booted it up, wondering all the time what password he should try. He didn't have to wonder for long because the password prompt never appeared. Billy was looking at the Microsoft welcome screen. "What the heck," Billy said out loud as he went through the initial steps of choosing a language and time zone. When he was asked to set up a Microsoft Account to use the One Drive, he slapped his hand on the table. "Damn!" He checked the document folder on the computer. No surprise there; it was empty. No email account had been set up. He knew that Rod had reformatted the hard drive and wiped out whatever was on it.

"Wait a minute," Billy said out loud as he remembered that reformatting might still leave residual information. "I'm going to find out what you had on this puppy, Rod, old friend." He put his own laptop on the table and clicked "OK" to access Sean's internet. His computer had remembered the internet password from the last time the fight-night crew got together at Sean's to play *League of Legends*.

Billy researched data recovery programs and decided to try one of the free downloads. He carefully followed all the steps but was not successful. After more research, he discovered that Rod must have done a full format rather than a quick one. His only other option was to take the laptop to a data recovery specialist, an option that he could not pursue. "Why did you leave this with me, Rod?" Billy asked to an empty room. Trepidation gripped him. "Was it to stick me with the evidence? Huh, Mr. Rodney Wilter? Was it?"

Billy went from frustration at wasting hours on the laptop to raging anger at Rod for setting him up. He was going to make sure that no one was going to find anything on that laptop. He was going to make sure that there were no leads linking him to Rod Wilter.

He searched the townhome until he found Sean's tool chest. He held the laptop, flipped it so the back of the laptop was showing, and slammed it onto a wood cutting board that he had put on the counter. After he took out the battery, he used the smallest screwdriver available to remove the screws holding the plastic cover over the hard drive. Once he pulled out the drive, he held the approximately three-inch by four-inch rectangle in his hand and sneered at it, "You POS, no one is going to get anything from you!" He pried open its casing to expose the circuit board and platter, then scratched and hammered them beyond recognition. Finally, Billy stopped and took a breath. He looked around and decided he had better clean up after himself and leave.

He drove home and pressed the button on the garage door remote. As the door rose, he was relieved to see that both his parents' cars were gone. He drove in and lowered the garage door. Retrieving cardboard from the recycling bin, he piled it on the garage floor, placed the remains of the laptop on top, and proceeded to hit them with a sledgehammer. When he collected the remnants, he placed them into two plastic bags and threw them on the floor of the front seat of the car. Then he cleaned up the garage, got in his car, and left.

For the second time that day, Billy was driving around looking for the right place. He ended up steering first into one, and then into another empty neighborhood park having a trash dumpster. On his way back home, he felt secure.

Then his cell phone rang. He picked it up without looking at the screen. "Is this Billy White?"

"Who wants to know?"

"My name isn't important. Let's just say I loaned your friend Rod some money for his little start-up. Saw his name in the paper. Looks like he did a runner. So I'm asking you, where is he?"

"How should I know?"

"Aw, come on, Billy boy. Rod told me all about you. So where is he?"

Billy was scared. "I don't know. He told me he was going on a trip. He didn't tell me where. He told me he'd be back. I was stunned when I saw his picture in the paper. I had no idea. The chick's husband came to me, trying to find out where Rod was. I told him the same thing I'm telling you. *I don't know.*"

After what seemed like five minutes of interrogation, the caller said, "Well, he told me you weren't the brightest bulb in the bunch, even for being wet behind the ears. I guess he got that right." Then the man laughed. "Ah well, I didn't give him that much—nickel, dime. I'll save you the trouble, kid. There's no money at his apartment." Then he hung up.

Billy was shaking when he went through his recent call list to find out who had just called him. It turned out that it was Billy's name but not his number that displayed as the most recent call. What? Billy was afraid to hit the callback button. Did Rod really say those things about him? He decided to put the number into Google to see if he could get any information. There were hundreds of queries asking about the same number. Telemarketers had used the number to sell Florida vacations and cruises and time-shares. Billy realized the caller used a fake-call app, and he would probably never know who the man was. At least he hoped he never would.

By the time he got home, his cell phone rang again. This time he looked at the caller ID—it was a woman. He answered. An elderly woman in Minnesota told him that Rod had convinced her to give him $3,000, and now she was worried that she wouldn't see her money again. "Three thousand might not seem like a lot to you, but I'm on a fixed income, and I need that money for future expenses," she told Billy.

"Ma'am, I don't know how I can help you," Billy said.

"But Rod told me you were his right-hand man and that if I couldn't reach him, to call you. He gave me this number. I would like to get my money back."

Billy's stomach tightened, and his throat went dry, so dry in fact he didn't know if he could talk. After a moment, he said, "Okay, let me get a piece of paper to write down your information. I will make sure you get your three thousand back. It may take me a bit, but I'll do it. Is that all right with you?" Billy was stunned with the woman's understanding reply—yes, she would wait to hear from him.

He then called Destiny, asking her if she had heard anything new about Rod and explaining that he had no knowledge of the Ponzi scheme. He was as fooled as everyone else.

"I believe you, Billy, but I don't know if anyone else will. I've had a few calls here asking for you. Told them you'd be in tomorrow. Do you want to know what I heard about Rod?" And before he could answer, she continued, "My friend has a friend who lives in Rod's apartment building—same floor! She was walking by when an FBI agent was walking out the door, and she could see in the apartment, and it looked tossed. 'Trashed,' she said. Can you believe it? Good thing you weren't involved with him, because according to her, it looked like he must have made some enemies."

"Listen, Destiny, I was all set to take a two-week vacation, and I'm not going to cancel it. I'll see you when I get back."

"Billy, that's not a smart idea. It's not going to look good."

"Well, it can't be helped. I already had it planned. Just tell anyone who asks that I'll be back in two weeks. They can wait until then. Thanks, Destiny." Billy clicked the phone off.

Billy had some time before his parents came back from work; he knew he had to act fast. He packed his clothes and passport, then called his parents' landline and left a message telling them that he was leaving for a week or two, not to worry, and he would be back soon. When he finished the call, he took the SIM card out of his cell phone, put it in his wallet, walked out to the attached garage, picked up his dad's sledgehammer again, and smashed the phone. He wrapped what was left of the phone in newspaper and put it on the front seat of his car. Then he went back into the house, picked up his suitcases, laptop, and handgun. He packed the car and left.

First stop was another lonely dumpster where he could dispose of the phone. Then he drove to the bank and withdrew $9,000 in cash; he wanted to withdraw $12,000 to close the account but was afraid he'd trigger the $10,000 IRS limit, and he didn't want to fill out any paperwork. He wondered how much money Rod had withdrawn before he went missing and how he would have done it. Maybe there wasn't any money. Maybe Rod spent it or hid it or never even had it. Billy's head hurt. He felt as if cogs in his brain were grinding and smoking.

He thought back on Rod's scheme. Rod told him that he knew how to run a Ponzi scheme and how to get out of it safely in the end. He would entice initial investors by promising them a 20 percent return on their investment. Then he would get the next investors, promising them a 15 percent return but asking them for a larger initial investment, adjusting the amounts of percentage and return and investment as needed. He planned to invest a portion of the money and skim off what he considered windfall profits in addition to his broker's fee. He said he would do it slowly, carefully, and finish it with investments that provided high-yield profits to guarantee everyone got paid. The market was on an upswing. He said it was a win-win situation.

Rod had given him extra cash almost every week and said he would reward Billy generously for helping him get clients and handle paperwork once the scheme ended. The extra cash kept Billy engaged and excited about the final payout. It never occurred to him that Rod's scheme would not work. He knew what they were doing was illegal, but he rationalized away any concern because no one was going to lose money; no one would ever know.

Now, reality sucked Billy into a whirlwind of emotion, rotating him through self-flagellation, fear, hurt, betrayal, and anger, finally spitting him out into the land of resolve. Rather than trying to run and hide for the rest of his life, he would go hunting for Rod. He drove east out of Phoenix, checked into an economy motel, booted up his laptop, logged on to his virtual private network, and began his search.

CHAPTER | 13

Jack arrived in Tucson just as Helen and Stan were sitting down for their midmorning coffee. They were seated at the kitchen table eating jelly-filled doughnuts. They were both relieved and anxious to see him. Stan held up his doughnut and asked Jack, "Do you want a paczki? They are fresh."

"No," Jack replied, but on seeing Stan's face fall, he added, "Maybe just a half."

"I know we shouldn't be eating these, but I needed comfort food," Helen said.

"I know, Helen," Jack said.

When he finished explaining everything that he had learned about Gloriann's and Martin's disappearance, Stan stood up. "What the heck, Jack? I don't understand. What was she doing? What was she thinking?"

Helen started talking, more to herself than to Jack or Stan, "Where did I go wrong? I thought I raised her right. How could she leave those kids? Maybe she's had a mental breakdown. Or she got herself into a mess and didn't know how to get out of it. That no-good Rodney Wilter! What was he doing in St. Louis?"

Jack stopped her monologue. "Helen, I know the FBI talked with you two and asked general questions. They've probably already interviewed some of Gloriann's friends—I gave them a list of people. But you and Stan can help me. Now that we know more of what happened with Gloriann, I'd like you to talk with anyone you think might be able to tell us something new. They will probably be more relaxed with you. Don't tell them everything I told you. Just try to find out if they know anything we don't, especially about Wilter. Can you do that this morning? Oh, and remember, even if what they talk about seems inconsequential, it might be important, so write it down."

Stan said, "We got it, Jack. And don't worry. We are not going to tell anyone that our daughter left you and the kids and ran away with a scumbag."

Jack sighed. "Good. I'm going to go into the office and see what I can find out," Jack said, washing his hands in the kitchen sink to get the stickiness off his fingers. "I'll be back for supper. I'll pick up something, so don't cook."

"How about a pizza?" Stan offered. Looking at Helen, he added, "And a salad?"

"Sounds good to me. See you later," Jack said and headed for the door.

When he walked through the office of the Tucson FBI, people greeted him with a quiet, "Hey, Jack," knowing head nod, concerned eyes and forced smile, slight hand wave, or a combination of the four. It was as if Gloriann and Martin had died, and this was his first day back after the funeral. It made Jack uneasy, but he told himself that these were his colleagues, his friends who weren't quite sure how to respond to him. That's all it was—awkwardness birthed from heartbreaking circumstances.

He checked in at his former supervisor's office. Now that Jack was a private citizen on temporary leave from the Bureau, he knew he would not enjoy the access to information that he once did. But he also knew that agents would tell him what they could within certain parameters. He was not disappointed.

Jack learned that the Bureau had received hundreds of leads regarding the disappearance of his wife, as well as inquiries from anxious investors who had worked with Rodney Wilter. Gloriann and Rodney had been spotted in Florida, New York, Arizona, New Mexico, Texas, Missouri, Illinois, and Minnesota. Worried investors had called from all those states except Florida and New York.

The broad geographic scope of leads was daunting. There were people who honestly believed they had seen the missing persons, others who just wanted to be part of an investigation, some were members of crime-solving clubs, and still others were mentally unbalanced. But then there would be that person who really saw Gloriann—the person who would give the FBI the lead that they needed. Jack thought about the states listed. His mind went to the *Sesame Street* song, "One of these things is not like the other ..." He immediately dismissed Florida and New York.

The southern border states concerned him. Rodney and Gloriann were both fluent in Spanish. Would they slip into Mexico? And if so, what were Rodney's intentions? Jack's thoughts circled back to human trafficking. No, he would not think that way, not until he had more evidence. Jack gave no credence to Missouri or Illinois because he felt that those states would pose too great a risk of discovery for Gloriann and Rodney if they stayed there. That left Minnesota, another border state, another trafficking worry.

Minnesota also troubled Jack because that's where Elizabeth lived. Although the investigation cleared Elizabeth and he, himself, thought she was sincere in her declarations of innocence, he found it odd that Minnesota was listed as a possible sighting. It all seemed too convenient: Elizabeth's arrival and Gloriann's disappearance. And now he had Elizabeth and her husband driving to Green Bay to meet his parents and deliver the children's bags! Was that a mistake? Was Elizabeth a bit too eager to help? Were the children in danger?

While he was preparing to leave, Ken, one of the agents working the tip line, came up to him and asked, "How about going out for a late lunch? I'd sort of like to get out of here and grab something to eat. Thought we might catch up."

"Yeah, that would be great. Where do you want to go?" Jack asked, hiding his surprise.

"Meet me at the usual place, the sandwich shop on Congress."

As Jack drove the few blocks, he wondered about the lunch with Ken. They didn't know each other well enough to have a need to catch up. When Jack arrived, he saw Ken sitting in the last booth, his back against the wall. A red number fourteen was propped up on the side of the table. Jack walked to the counter and ordered a BLT and a Coke. The gal who took his order handed him a red number fifteen. He carried it to the last booth and sat down. Ken was silent for a moment, as if he was still deciding. Then he said, "So you are doing your own legwork?"

"Yeah, I have some contacts. Some PI friends if I need them. Right now, I'm just trying to get my head around all of this. Obviously, I want to find Gloriann, find Martin."

"I don't blame you; I'd do the same thing. I feel for you. So listen, I can't be a contact for you, but I'll help you this once on the QT. I think the best lead we got so far was the one from Minnesota. It was from a woman who belongs to an online crime-solving club. Said it helps her feel like she belongs to something bigger than herself, bigger than her small town in northern Minnesota. She's been checking the FBI Missing Person website for years. Never recognized anyone until she clicked on the photo of Gloriann and Martin. She's a waitress in a sports bar in Sturgeon Lake. Said she saw a man, woman, and baby come in late for supper on Saturday. She said that the baby was a girl though, not a boy."

"Did she say why she noticed them?" asked Jack.

"Yeah, she did. At first, she thought they were from Minnesota because she saw them get out of their car, saw the Minnesota plates. The restaurant has big windows facing the parking lot. But then the guy ordered a Hermann the German sandwich, and later she heard the woman ask the guy, 'Who's Hermann the German?'" Jack looked doubtful, agitation starting to take over his persona. Ken quickly said, "No hear me out. It makes sense." Their sandwiches arrived, and Jack was glad to have the distraction of eating.

In between bites, Ken explained, "The waitress didn't hear the guy's response, but she thought she could lipread him saying something like he wasn't going to ask because Minnesotans know who he is. She thought that was odd. He didn't say, 'We should know who he is,' but 'Minnesotans know.' Not only that, but people ask her all the time who Hermann the German is. She said this guy wanted to keep their not knowing a secret. It didn't make sense to her. Either they should have known or should have asked or not even have mentioned it. At least not be sneaky about it. It was as if they were pretending to be from Minnesota."

"Is there a Hermann the German that Minnesotans know about?" queried Jack.

"Yeah, there is. According to *Wikipedia*, a Hermann the German statue is in New Ulm, Minnesota, and is the third largest copper statue in the United States. The statue has Hermann raising his sword in victory over the Romans. 'In 2000, Congress designated the monument to be the official symbol of all citizens of Germanic Heritage.' So, it is important. I guess there are more Germans in Minnesota than there are Scandinavians. I'm assuming most Minnesotans would know about the statue, even if they didn't know the history behind it. Another thing, the waitress wanted to be helpful but didn't want to lead us on a wild goose chase. She emphasized that the baby was dressed as a girl, and Gloriann had red hair cut in a bob."

"You talked to this waitress?"

Ken nodded. "Yeah, I talked to her. I found her credible."

"So what did you do?"

"I contacted the field office in Duluth. They are going to look at tapes. The waitress told me there is a camera at the entrance door, the one by the parking lot. She doesn't want us to identify her, especially to her employer. I told her we wouldn't. If we need her down the line, then we'd contact her."

"How soon will you know?" Jack's knuckles were white.

"I'd say before the end of day tomorrow unless there are problems. Can't tell you anything more, Jack. That's all I got. One and done here."

"I understand. This was helpful. Thanks." Jack stood up, bussed his tray, and left.

Jack mulled over what he had learned as he drove back to his in-laws' house. In his mind, it was still a tossup between the southern and northern borders. Both held reasonable assumptions. He was hoping that Helen and Stan were able to gather information that would help him decide.

Helen could hardly wait for Jack to get through the door before she started talking. "Give him a chance to catch his breath," Stan warned as he took the pizza box and bag from Jack's hands. When they were finally settled at the table, Helen talked while Stan ate, and Jack picked at his salad. She had called friends, and friends of friends, and was able to patch together a quilt of Rodney's family life.

Rodney's mother, Francesca, married when she was nineteen and had her first son, Miquel, when she was twenty. Rodney was born four years later. Just a year after Rodney's birth, her husband was killed in an industrial accident. Francesca then took a job as a waitress, and a cousin watched the boys while she was at work.

"One of the gals knows her pretty well. She said that Francesca was a wonderful mother. She still writes to her. Francesca now lives in San Miguel, Mexico, as an expat. She has family there—two sisters and some other relatives. Went there about seven years ago after her son, Miquel, took up residence at the Monastery of Our Lady of Solitude. He became a Benedictine monk. This gal didn't know if she should tell Francesca about Rodney. Rodney has always been her worry—gave her nothing but trouble. So much trouble!"

"So, Helen, did this gal think that Rodney would go to Mexico?" Jack interrupted.

"No, she didn't! She said Rodney didn't do much with his mother or brother. He was embarrassed by them or something. Always thought other people were better. Preferred everyone else to his own family, and after his mother did so much for him! No, I don't think he would either. From what I've learned about Francesca, she'd turn him in for taking Martin. Not that she wouldn't love a grandchild, but not a kidnapped one. She'd do what's right." Helen finished her summation.

Jack hung his head. Helen and Stan were silent. Finally, Jack said, "I'm going to go to Green Bay. Make sure the kids are settled in. Check out some things in Minnesota. Gloriann and Rodney were spotted there. May be nothing, but I'm going to follow through. Do you think Elizabeth could be involved in any way?"

"Oh, good Lord, no! Give it up, Jack! I feel awful for my cousin, the way she was used," Helen said. She was defiant.

"The only reason they would be in Minnesota is if they are planning to leave the country through Canada. I can't believe this!" Stan said, standing up and pacing the room. "What the heck? I could kill Rodney!"

"Stan, don't say that. I know you don't mean it. *Do not say it.* Someone might believe you, and we've got enough trouble already," Jack cautioned. He studied them and felt as much pity for them as he did for Emma and Will. "Why don't you go to Green Bay with me? I'll have to leave from there to continue the investigation, but you could stay for a couple of weeks. Help get the kids acclimated. I'm sure my folks wouldn't mind putting you up. They'd probably like the support now too. We should all stick together through this. Mel is busy with work. I know if you went to Green Bay, it would ease her mind. How about it?"

Stan and Helen looked stunned, like deer in the headlights. Then their faces relaxed into thoughtfulness. Finally, they turned to each other and nodded. Stan said, "You know, that might work. I think it is a good idea. We can start out at your folks', and if we plan to stay for a while, we'll get a short-term rental. We'd love to see the kids and get away from all of this. Family should stick together."

"I'm going to fly out as soon as I can get a flight. I'll call the folks to give them a heads-up, and then why don't you call them and work it all out?" Jack prompted.

"Okay. We'll call them. It'll take us a few days to close up here. But goodness, I'm glad we are going to get out of here and actually do something," Stan said.

CHAPTER | 14

THURSDAY, SEPTEMBER 21

Carol was slowly learning the delicate dance of appeasement. She had to follow Jim's lead, anticipate his movements, match his rhythm, compensate for any missteps. If she didn't dance to his music, he became agitated, demeaning, even threatening. It was as if she was walking a tightrope trying to maintain balance while carrying Jim on her shoulders. She had never known life like this.

She thought back on meeting Rod for the first time. She was walking to a table in the food court of the mall, juggling packages, a plate of stir-fry, and a Coke. He accidentally bumped into her, causing the packages to jostle the plate and tip its contents onto the floor. He was mortified, so apologetic. He had wanted to make things right—wipe up the floor himself; order her a new stir-fry; bring it to her table. When he sat down, he was like a repentant child eager to please. She assured him that he was forgiven, and before she could put her guard up, they fell into easy conversation. She found him charming, delightful, and attentive. It was as if she had always known him. She forgot herself with him. Forgot her loneliness, her responsibilities, her husband, her children. They talked for an hour, and when she told him she had to leave, he asked her if she came to the mall often. She lied. "Yes, I like to mall walk here when the kids are in school."

"Maybe we'll run into each other another time then. Well, not *actually* run into each other," he said, laughing. Then he quieted, looked into her eyes, smiled, lightly touched her arm, turned, and waved goodbye.

On her drive home, she felt happier, lighter than she had felt the past several months. It was a good feeling, an exciting feeling—a handsome man noticed her and spent time with her! Even though it was out of her way, she started to walk the Chesterfield Mall several times a week. The next time she saw Rod, he said, "I don't want you to think that I'm being forward, because I'm not. I was just wondering if you wouldn't mind having lunch with me. I had a rough sales meeting, and I'd like to talk it out. If you wouldn't mind, would you?" Rod's face was pleading, expectant.

Of course, she didn't mind. She was willing to be a good listener. This time, they skipped the food court and went to a restaurant. They had met for lunch two more times when Rod suggested that if they wanted to talk in the future, they should talk in his hotel suite, where people wouldn't notice them. At first, Gloriann resisted, but Rod assured her that she was safe with him and that he was only concerned about her reputation. He didn't want anyone to get the wrong impression. He said, "I mean, Gloriann, think about it. What if one of your friends saw us and told Jack? He wouldn't understand that all we are doing is talking. There is nothing wrong with talking, is there? You trust me, don't you?"

Gloriann was put on the spot. There was no reason not to trust him, and she didn't want to upset him. "Of course, I trust you, and there's nothing wrong with talking," Gloriann remembered answering.

"We are adults, Gloriann. Aren't we? We are not doing anything wrong. Good Lord, are you one of those Catholic-guilt people?" Now he was teasing her.

"No. I don't have Catholic guilt! I can make my own decisions. I'll meet you at your hotel, just to talk though, Rod. I don't want you to have other expectations."

"No nefarious expectations, Gloriann. We'll talk—that's it. It'll just be easier, more relaxed. You'll see."

And it was easier. Rod was a good listener, and Gloriann could tell him about how hard it was for her since she moved to St. Louis. He was so kind and understanding. If she began to cry, he would hold and comfort her. He didn't say, "Don't cry." He never judged her. He offered such relief that she began to visit him several times a week. Before long, their talks became more intimate, and by the next month, she was pregnant. In horror, she realized what she had done! She checked her calendar, hoping that the baby was Jack's, but she knew it was Rod's. When she told Jack that she was pregnant, he was ecstatic. "What a surprise! What a wonderful, blessed surprise! I love you, Gloriann," he said as he lifted her off the floor and hugged her.

Guilt overshadowed her conscience. She couldn't tell Jack that she had been unfaithful. She couldn't tell him that the baby was not his. She looked to Rod to help her figure out what to do. She soon learned that Rod wanted the baby as much as Jack did. Rod told her that finally he would have the family for which he had always longed. "The gods smiled on me the day I met you," he said.

That's when her life spun out of control. Life at home kept to its routine schedule. Emma and Will were excited at the prospect of a baby in the house, arguing over who would win—Emma wanting a sister and Will sure he would have a little brother. Jack still worked long hours but tried to help more with household chores and whisked the kids away on weekend outings so Gloriann could rest.

Rod was over the moon. He became even more solicitous, fussing over Gloriann, making sure she did not exert herself in anyway. Once, when she protested as he knelt to take off her shoes, he said, "Doesn't Jack do this for you?" Rod was disappointed that he couldn't be present at the birth, but he said his time would come. He began to hatch a plan where he, Gloriann, and the baby would leave together, just for a while, until everything settled down and arrangements could be made. He said it would all work out in the end, that it would be better than a confrontation with Jack and her family—even her friends, whom he said would judge her harshly and blame her. She came to believe him.

Back then she compared Jack to Rod and found him wanting. Jack was predictable, involved with his job, familiar, and boring. Rod was new, exciting, focused on her. She had gotten sucked into the whirlwind of romance. Now she was slowly awakening from a dreamlike fantasy.

"How could I be so stupid?" Carol began to belittle herself. Finally, she held onto the realization that she wasn't the only one who ever made a bad choice. She thought about her friend Allison who was in an emotionally abusive marriage. Hadn't Carol pointed out to Allison that her husband was systematically isolating her from her family and friends? That Allison's husband ran hot and cold, blaming Allison for everything that went wrong but rewarding her for everything she did according to his wishes? It was all about him, about keeping the peace by keeping him happy. And that was exactly what was now happening to Carol. She accepted her complicity in this James-Russell-Johnson nightmare of hers and was determined not to remain a victim like Allison. She was not going to wear the blinders of gaslighting.

On Monday, she had wanted to call Jack. Why had that been her knee-jerk reaction to being upset with Jim? Thinking it over, she remembered what she had forgotten: Jack was a decent man. He loved her, and he would help her. And somehow she was going to contact him before she and Sydney were lost in Toronto. Yes, he'd be angry. Yes, her family would be upset. She'd have a lot of explaining and apologizing to do. But she would be back with her children, her family, her history. She had to get out of this darkness before no light was left in her. One step at a time, one foot in front of the other—that was her new plan.

CHAPTER | 15

It was almost 1:00 a.m. when Billy made up his mind. He had been on the internet constantly since he checked in yesterday afternoon, stopping only to buy candy bars and cans of Coke from the vending machine and to use the bathroom. He visited numerous sites and finally found two web pages—one on Facebook, the other an independent site. The Facebook "Help Find Rodney 'Rod' Wilter" page had been started yesterday and already had more than one hundred followers. Most of the comments were from women who had dated Rod. Some women were still pining for him, some wished him castrated, and others were neutral but curious. Billy read all the comments and realized that Rod had interacted with women in at least six states: the southern border states as well as Missouri and Minnesota. Billy was astonished, impressed, and disgusted all at the same time.

The other website was that of an amateur crime-solving club. In the upper right-hand corner of the home page was a login for members. The body of the page consisted of a mission statement, requirements for membership, contact information, and a box for public input that would be reviewed by the club before posting. The left-hand column was a box that had a list divided by the headlines: "Recently Missing" and "Unsolved Murders." He found the names of Rodney, Gloriann, and Martin directly below "Recently Missing." He clicked on Rodney's name, and a new window opened to a page with all three photos, basic facts of the case, law enforcement and newspaper links, bullet-pointed comments from the public, and a summary of the club's sleuthing. Gloriann's and Martin's names were linked to the same page as Rodney's.

The club's summary noted that a credible lead put Rodney, Gloriann, and Martin in Sturgeon Lake, Minnesota, on Saturday, September 16. Billy perused the public comments but saw no mention of Minnesota. The tip must have come from someone in the club. There was also information about Rod and the Ponzi scheme. Billy was relieved that his name was not mentioned on the site. He quickly checked Google search to see if his name was coupled with Rod's anywhere on the web. It wasn't. His relief was palpable.

He began to order his thoughts in a logical sequence. Law enforcement had not put travel restrictions on him; they didn't even name him as a person of interest yet. The *yet* was what made him want to hit the road and find Rod. Maybe Rod would still help him. Maybe Rod had a plan that he didn't know about. Maybe he could stay with Rod and his newfound family. True, it looked like Rod had thrown him under the bus, but maybe he hadn't.

He thought it plausible that Rod could be in Minnesota since that old lady called from there, and that was the only client call he received. Of course, he had destroyed his phone, so there could be more. Yet what if Rod wouldn't help him when he found him? *Oh, he's going to help me. He owes me*, Billy thought. "And if he won't?" the little voice in his head asked. "He's got to. He just does," Billy answered himself.

Billy decided to make a visit to the old lady to find out what she knew about Rod. He'd give her the $3,000 and explain how Rod duped him and that he, Billy, wanted to make things right. He hoped to have one investor who would bear witness to his innocence if he was brought to trial. He felt it was a good plan, but then again, it probably wouldn't get him any closer to finding Rod.

He finally concluded that the only way he would find Rod was to follow Jack Jurlik and let him take the lead. The heaviness of defeat pressed down on his back and shoulders. How could he follow Jack when he didn't even know where Jack was? Besides, he never followed anyone in his life! He pushed his laptop forward and rested his head on the desk. He was tired, but sleep did not overtake him; caffeine jitters kept him awake.

He sat up and typed Jack's name into Google and immediately brightened. Although the link for Jack only led to the staff listing of the FBI Tucson Field Office, Billy found several Jurliks who all resided in Green Bay, Wisconsin: Peter, a history professor at the University of Wisconsin, Green Bay; Joseph, a police detective; and a Ted who taught history and coached tennis at Green Bay Central Catholic. Following those leads, he was able to identify the men as Jack's father and brothers. Using "People Search," Billy found where Peter lived and was able to get the phone number of his landline.

"I'll head north, and hopefully something will come to me." Using Google Maps, he learned that he could either drive to Sturgeon Lake in twenty-six hours or fly to Duluth in a bit under five hours; it was a twenty-eight-hour drive to Green Bay or a flight slightly over three hours. He knew he couldn't fly commercial. He didn't want to have a trackable record, and the gun would be a problem. He didn't know anyone with a private plane. He'd have to drive, but he knew if he drove solo, it would take him at least two full days. He got up and paced the room. "Think, Billy, think!"

He remembered that Austin, another of his *League of Legends* friends, was upset that he lost his trucking job because his employer went bankrupt. Austin used to do long-haul trucking but then moved to a new start-up company that provided transportation locally. The company did well at first but never gained traction.

Austin was in the process of looking for a new job. He didn't want to do long-haul trucking again but said he would if he couldn't find something soon. Billy decided to forget the old lady and offer Austin the $3,000 if he would drive with him to Minneapolis. He knew that Austin was a night owl and would still be awake.

When Austin answered his phone, Billy explained his plan. They would drive nonstop to Minneapolis, alternating turns driving and sleeping. Once in Minneapolis, Billy would buy a used car, and Austin would drive Billy's back to Arizona. Billy would then begin to track a friend of Rod's whom he was sure knew where Rod was hiding. At first, Austin was surprised and concerned that Billy might be planning something illegal or getting in over his head.

"I don't want to be aiding and abetting something," Austin told Billy.

"No, no, you wouldn't be. I just really need to find Rod to figure out what is going on and what I should do," Billy assured him.

"I don't understand why you need to buy a used car, Billy. That's sort of crazy," Austin said. He was still not convinced.

"I know it sounds nuts, but I can't drive around in my car with the Arizona plates! Rod's friend would notice. No, I've got to blend in with the locals, have Minnesota plates. I need to be in Minneapolis by 7:00 a.m. Friday. Can you help me?"

Austin decided to change tactics. "Billy, you know I can really use the money right now, but I hate to take it in case your plan doesn't work. I don't want to lose your friendship—or worse, I don't want anything bad to happen to you."

"Don't think like that. If I can't find Rod, I'll just come back home. No worries. I am not going to hold it against you. I mean, you're helping me out, man."

Austin was still hesitant. After a few minutes of silence, he said, "All right, I'll do it. If you pick me up within an hour, we could possibly be in Minneapolis by 7:00 a.m. Listen, maybe I can help you out with the tracking thing too. I've got a real-time tracking GPS. I never told anyone this, but remember when I found out that Brittany was cheating on me? Well, that's how I knew. I put a tracker on her car. I took it off after we broke up. You can have it, but you'll have to pay the monthly service fee for it to work."

"Thanks, Austin. I appreciate it, man. Will you be ready to go in forty-five minutes?"

"Yeah, I'll just throw some stuff in a duffel. Say, why are you calling from a motel?"

"Oh, I was so upset when I learned about Rod's Ponzi scheme that I threw my cell phone against the wall and broke it. Then Mom got on my case, and I left to get some space. I'll pick up a new phone along the way and call home to smooth things over. It's all cool."

"Okay. I still think this is all crazy, but I'll do it," Austin said as he hung up the phone.

PART III

CHAPTER | 16

Jack landed in Green Bay at 2:30 p.m. and was surprised to see his brother Joe waiting for him at the luggage carousel. After they embraced, Jack said, "I thought you'd be at work. Mom was going to pick me up."

"I took time off. I want to hear what's happening before we get to the house. Are you carrying?" Joe asked.

Jack looked at him. "What, you think I went rogue? No, I'm not carrying. My Sig is in the checked luggage. I brought a few bags with more of the kids' stuff."

Joe exhaled. "Okay, good. I knew you took a leave of absence. I just wanted to make sure—"

"That I'm not screwing up my life any more than it is already screwed?" Jack asked.

"Well, yeah," Joe admitted.

Jack laughed. He was glad to see Joe. They were close growing up, only three years apart, and even though they lived in different states, the camaraderie had continued. Jack had tried to convince Joe to move to Arizona, but Joe said he was a Green Bay boy through and through. He could never leave the folks, his friends, the lake, or the Packers. On the car ride home, after Jack told Joe all that was happening with his investigation, Joe said, "Jack, you are holding

back on me, brother. I can tell. There is something you are not telling me."

Jack sighed. "I've never lied to you, Joe, so I'll just say maybe there is something. You'll just have to wait and see."

Joe was silent, then asked, "What are you going to do about Gloriann when you find her?"

"I don't know that either. I just need to find her and Martin. I still can't get my head around it."

"Well, Jack, I can't get my head around it either. I've always liked Gloriann, and this just doesn't fit my picture of her. Not to say good people can't get themselves in trouble. Heck, I see it all the time. I know you do. What was it Mom used to tell us? The devil never tempts with only bad things; it's always a mixed bag. He shows you the good and hides the evil until he has you hooked. I believe that's what happened to her. She never thought she'd do anything like this, but she let her guard down and got scammed by the devil."

"Yeah, but now we're the ones living in hell, and she put us there."

"Jack."

"Don't worry, Joe. I'm dealing with this," Jack said before he put his head in his hands, leaned forward, and sobbed. Knowing they would be home soon, Joe drove to a secluded area by the lake and parked the car. He waited until Jack's sobs turned to deep breaths and then to normal breathing. He put his hand on Jack's back but said nothing. When Jack sat up, Joe slipped his hand off Jack and back onto the steering wheel.

"I'm sorry," Jack said, wiping his eyes and rubbing his face. "I don't know what came over me. It's like if something is bothering me, the emotions always seem to well up either when I'm in church or when I come back home to Green Bay. I don't know why."

"You want a drink or something? A little liquid courage before you face the family?"

"No. No. I'm OK now. I guess it's just been building up."

"Well, it's a good thing you let it out now, Jack, because I don't know what the kids are going to do when they see you: rejoice, break down, or give you the cold shoulder."

"Oh, Lord. OK, give me the lowdown on the home front, Joe." Jack sat up straight and looked at his brother.

Joe began, "It's been a madhouse, really. Before Will and Emma came, each of the boys had their own rooms upstairs. We cleared out Andy's room for Emma, and we put Andy in with Charlie. Will's in with Ben. Ben is all excited to be bunking with Will, but Andy is not happy to be saddled with his three-year-old brother and is rather verbal about it. We are working on him. Will does well unless he gets upset with something; then he runs to Emma. She mothers him. She keeps up a strong front, but then we hear her crying at night, and she doesn't want our comfort."

"I don't know what to say. I didn't know what to do with the kids. Do you think it would have been better if they stayed with the folks?"

"No, I don't think the folks could manage it long-term. It would be too much for them. Plus, I can protect the kids better if they are with us. It's early days, Jack. Things will settle down. Just be aware you might get hit with all of this when you walk through the door. Tessa registered your kids for school today. Once they start on Monday, that's one more unknown off their plates. Plus, then we'll get into a better routine. I want us to be honest with each other. I'll tell you what's happening here. I won't sugarcoat it, and I expect you'll do the same. That's the only way we are going to survive this."

"You're right, Joe. That is the only way we are going to get through this. Thank you. I can't tell you how much I appreciate—"

"OK, shut up, Jack. It's all going to work out. Emma and Will are staying over at the folks' tonight. We thought it would be easier, just you and the kids and the folks. My kids still have school tomorrow. We'll all get together tomorrow night and take it from there."

"Good deal," Jack said as Joe started up the car.

They drove along Lake Michigan on Nicolet Drive, past the Communiversity Park Beach and the Shorewood Golf Course. "We had some fun times here, eh, Jack?" Joe said, smiling, pointing first to his left then to his right.

"Yep."

"You taught me how to improve my golf game," Joe continued.

"Yep."

Joe glanced over at his brother and saw the tightness in Jack's jaw, the rigidness of his spine, Jack's fingers gouging his thighs. He hated seeing him like this. He knew he could not imagine Jack's pain.

"Almost there," Joe said, breaking the silence. This time, Jack did not reply.

They took a right on Peterson, then a left on Kathy. As they neared his parents' street, Jack saw himself as a young boy, riding his bike, enjoying the warm summer sun. He had an idyllic childhood. A childhood that he had wanted for his own kids. A childhood they had until they moved to St. Louis. He should have insisted that Gloriann stay with the kids in Tucson. If he had, none of this would have happened.

Joe pulled into the driveway and stopped the car. Jack took in the familiar scene. A hanging basket bursting with pink petunias was anchored to the limb of the old maple tree. A colorful mix of impatiens encircled its trunk. Jack remembered when that tree was a lot smaller, and he and Joe used to climb it. Now its crown shaded most of the front lawn. The grass was as green and lush as ever. The American flag still flew from the post on the west side of the porch, and two wooden rocking chairs were still huddled together as if in conversation. As he got out of the car, he was relieved that no one was waiting by the front door or looking out the picture window. Of course, it was horribly hot and humid for mid-September; the house was closed tight, the air-conditioning on. Neither the folks nor the kids must have heard the slam of the car door.

When Jack rang the doorbell, he could hear the running of feet and Will yelling, "They're here! They're here!"

Will threw open the door and started jumping up and down. Jack bent down, picked him up, and tossed him into the air. "Good to see you, buddy!" When Will's feet again touched the floor, Emma grabbed Jack around the waist and clung to him as if he were the last fallen tree that could save her from being drowned in a rushing river. Jack put his arms around her shoulders and kissed the top of her head. From the corner of his eye, he saw a silent Will unsure of what to do next.

Just then, Jack's father, Pete, came into the foyer and said, "Hey, Will, let's finish that game of Candy Land. I bet Grandpa Pete is going to beat you!"

"No, you won't. I only have a few more squares to go," said Will, turning from his father to look at his grandfather.

"I don't think you're going to make it." Grandpa Pete laughed.

"You are not going to win, Grandpa."

"Come on. Bet you a quarter I will."

Will hesitated, then whizzed past his grandpa, singing, "I'm going to get a quarter. I'm going to get a quarter."

Jack put his hands behind his back and took hold of Emma's two arms. Disengaging her, he said, "Emma, let's go sit in the living room a minute, just the two of us. Tell me what's going on."

They sat on the couch and arranged themselves so that each could see the other's face. Jack waited, but Emma did not speak. Finally, Jack said, "Emma, talk to me. Tell me how you feel, what you like, what you don't like."

"I don't like anything!" Emma crossed her arms across her chest and glared at Jack.

Jack knew he had to turn the conversation around. "Did Aunt Tessa take you and Will to school today?"

Emma kept staring at him, then relented. "Yeah, we saw our classrooms. I'm in Mrs. Bader's fifth-grade class. Will and Ben are in kindergarten together. They have Ms. Audrey. We only saw those classrooms, the school office, cafeteria, and gym. We didn't see Andy's classroom because he's in fourth."

"Well, what did you think?" Jack prompted.

"Does it matter?" Her voice was snotty. "I have to go on Monday whether I want to or not. I want to go back to St. Louis, where I have friends—no, wait. I want to go back to Tucson, where I have even more friends. At least Will has Ben in class with him. I don't know anybody here! I don't have anybody to play with. No one will eat lunch with me. It's not fair."

"Wait a minute. You haven't even started school here yet. You made friends in St. Louis, didn't you? I don't remember you eating lunch by yourself there. What makes you think you won't make friends here?" Jack said, trying to get Emma to look on the brighter side.

"Mom's not here. *You* won't be here. I'm not living in my own house. These kids don't know me. But they are going to know that mom ran away with another man, and they won't like me because of it. My life is ruined!"

Jack was stunned. For a moment, he wondered if Emma had memorized a mental list and was now reciting it. He anticipated the anxiety about the lack of friends, but he hadn't thought about the repercussions of gossip or publicity surrounding Gloriann's disappearance. At that moment, he hated Gloriann and the situation she put them in.

"Would you feel better if I told you that by the time you are in middle school—you know that starts in sixth grade—that we'll be in our own house?" Jack asked.

"In Tucson? Or are you going to make us go somewhere else?" Emma asked.

"I don't know where that is going to be, Emma. But wherever it is, we'll have our own house."

"Will I have to keep changing schools?"

"Emma, I promise that I'll do everything in my power to keep you in the same school system from middle school through high school," Jack said. He surprised even himself with this assertion.

Emma thought for a moment. "What if the kids ask me about Mom?"

"Well, tell them the truth. Say, 'I don't really know what happened. I'm still waiting to find out.'"

"What if they say they know she left with another man and kidnapped Martin?"

"Emma, even I don't know what really happened. I'm trying to figure it out. You know that. Tell them that yes, your mother left with Martin, but you don't know why or what's happening. If you don't get defensive or angry, they'll leave you alone. Kids can be like that. Either they are simply curious, or they are just mean and want to upset you. They don't need to know diddly-squat. Don't let them get under your skin."

Emma pondered Jack's words, then asked, "But what if we never see Mom and Martin again?"

"Emma, I don't think that is going to happen. I believe we are going to find them. Yeah, there's a slim chance we might not, but listen—don't think about that. Consider all the good things that could happen and try not to dwell on the scary stuff. Remember, you are not alone. We are all in this together, and we will each do what we can do to make it easier. It is not always going to be easy, Emma. We are going to have good days and bad days. But you know what? Even Grandpa Stan and Grandma Helen are coming to Green Bay to help out!"

Emma's face lit up, and her body relaxed. She gave Jack a hug, then said, "Grandma Sophie and I made three-cheese manicotti for supper and chocolate chip cookies for dessert. You are going to love it! Don't tell her I told you though. It's supposed to be a surprise!"

After supper, they all watched a movie, and Jack was grateful for the low-key evening without any questions or expectations. He carried the sleeping Will up to the kids' room and got him ready for bed. When Emma got into the other twin bed, he tucked her in, then went down to face his parents. He met them coming up the stairs.

"Do you mind if we call it a night?" his mother asked him. "It's been a long day, and we are both bushed."

"Tomorrow's another day. We can talk then," added his father.

Jack nodded and headed for the guest room. Just as he was about to fall asleep, his cell phone rang. He looked at the caller ID; it was his St. Louis supervisor, Dave Harlan. Dave told him that the FBI had new information about Gloriann and Martin. They were last seen in Sturgeon Lake, Minnesota, with Rodney.

"We got them on a security video at a restaurant. They changed their appearance; the baby was dressed as a girl. We are assuming that they are headed for Canada, and I've alerted the Canadian Border Patrol and the Royal Canadian Mounted Police (RCMP). They will be looking at border tapes, but it might take longer than we'd like," Special Agent Harlan said.

"But if you got them on video, you got the car make and plates, right?" Jack was hopeful.

"No. That's the thing. The security camera was positioned in such a way that we can see them coming into the restaurant and the cars directly behind them. They parked farther away from the door, so we don't have a visual. All we know is that their car has Minnesota plates."

"Did anybody remember them?"

"We have one witness. She didn't get the plate number and wasn't sure of the make of the car. We know it was a grayish-silver sedan. Jack, you know we'll find them on the border tapes. If we don't, then they didn't go into Canada. Where are you anyway?"

"I'm in Green Bay with my folks. Trying to get the kids settled."

"Good. I'll keep you posted with whatever we find out. Take care, Jack." Special Agent Harlan clicked off.

The call confirmed what Jack had surmised from the previous report from Ken. Gloriann and Rodney were in Minnesota, presumably headed to Canada. He knew he would have to keep moving if he was going to find them. He was so tired; he could not analyze the situation anymore. "Dear God, give me direction. I need your help. Keep me on the right path," were the last words he remembered praying before nodding off.

CHAPTER | 17

FRIDAY, SEPTEMBER 22

Billy and Austin drove I-40 east through New Mexico, skimmed the panhandle of Texas, picked up I-35 in Oklahoma City, and shot north past Kansas City and Des Moines. The night sky awoke from its slumber. Clouds, once obscured by darkness, dressed in the reflection of the rising sun. At first, only a thin line of red was seen on the eastern horizon—a single note heralding the beginning of a new day. Then arose the chorus of orange, yellow, magenta, and blue-gray filling the sky with a triumphant finale.

It was a little after 6:30 a.m. Austin was tired and sweaty. Neither he nor Billy had taken the time to shave or change clothes yesterday. They were now just south of Lakeville, only forty minutes from Minneapolis. "Billy, get up," Austin said as he shook Billy's shoulder.

"Are we here already?" a groggy Billy asked.

"No, but we will be soon. Why don't you look up 'used cars near me' so I don't have to drive into the city during rush hour."

"Can I use your phone? Remember, I don't have one," Billy said as he stretched out his hand.

"It's in the cup holder."

"Hey, we're in luck. There's an Economy Used Cars just about five minutes from here." Billy was fully awake now. "Let's check that out."

Economy Used Cars was visible from the road. A huge gorilla statue was perched on the flat roof of a small brick building. "Economical Reliable Cars" was sprayed on the front window with yellow paint. Plastic red, white, and blue pennants flapped lazily in the breeze. There was a man in black slacks and a turquoise, short-sleeved shirt washing off the parking lot with a hose.

"Do you think he's open?" Billy asked.

"Look, even if he's not, he'll sell you a car. This place doesn't look like it gets a lot of business."

Austin was right. Even though the sign hanging on the door still said, "Closed," the salesman was cordial and eager to make a sale. Billy bought a 2001 silver Honda Civic with 190,000 miles for $1,500.

The salesman was a bit surprised when Billy laid out the $1,500 in cash, but he took the money and completed the paperwork without comment. When he asked Austin about the Arizona plates on what he assumed was Austin's car, Austin said, "Well, I'm from Arizona. Just a friend of Billy's. He needed a ride, so I helped him out."

When they left the car lot, Billy followed Austin to the Kwik Trip they had passed on the way to Economy Cars. "Hey, do you want to go get breakfast?" Billy asked as they both got out of their cars.

"No, Billy, thanks. I just want to settle up. I'll stop at that small café down the road. I know you want to keep heading north. Best we split now."

"Are you going to try to drive back nonstop?"

"No, I'm going to take my time. Drive until about one o'clock and see if I can get into a hotel room early. I just want to take a shower, get some sleep, watch a movie. When you get your new phone, call me and let me know. I'll keep you posted on when I get back to your house," Austin said.

"Oh, Austin, I think it's best if you just left my car at your place. No need to take it to my folks." Billy was nervous.

Austin looked at him for a long while. "That's not going to happen, Billy. I'm not going to be the one to leave your parents hanging in the wind. I'll drop the car off and tell them I drove you to Minnesota, where you bought a used car for your vacation. I'm not lying for you, Billy. That's not me. I helped you out getting here, but that's as far as it goes."

Billy knew he could not sway him without arousing more suspicions than Austin already had. "I understand," Billy said. "Let me get my luggage out of the car and give you the three thousand dollars. Don't worry. I'll call the folks, Austin. When do you think you'll be getting back?"

"Well, I'm going to take my time. Probably Sunday night or Monday morning."

Billy was tentative. "OK. Thanks for everything, Austin. Drive safe."

And then Austin was off, waving his hand out of the driver's side window.

Billy topped off the tank of his new wheels, headed into the Kwik Trip to pay, picked up a coffee and hot dog, and got directions to the nearest Walmart. He pulled the car around to the back of the Kwik Trip and parked under the shade of an oak tree. While he ate, he thought about his next moves. Should he buy a cheap burner phone or a regular phone? What should he tell his folks so they wouldn't worry and end up calling the cops?

The first stop was at Walmart, where Billy decided on two cell phones: one burner and one regular. He needed the options on the full-service cell as well as the anonymity of the burner. He had the SIM card from his old cell and put it into the new one. He decided to call his parents. He wasn't concerned about the time; he knew they would be awake and getting ready for work. As expected, they were happy to hear from him and eager to know about his vacation. He told them that he had a new cell phone number because his old phone got fried when he accidentally dropped it in water. He said he got the new number because he was getting too many crank calls on his old one. That made sense to them.

Then he told them that he was in Kansas City seeing the National World War I Museum and the Steamboat Arabia Museum. Said he would keep them posted as he could. Asked them not to give out his cell phone number, as he decided to keep this one more private. Also wondered if anyone had called for him in his absence. He discovered that no one had. He told them he loved them, ended the call, and let out a sigh of relief. He knew they believed him. That was the beauty of cell phones—it was so easy to lie about one's whereabouts.

Now, Billy used the burner phone to call the house of Jack's parents.

"Hello," Jack's mother, Sophie, answered the phone.

"Is Jack there?" Billy asked.

"Jack?"

"Yes, I'm an old friend of his, and I heard he's in town. Maybe I got the date wrong." Billy held his breath.

"Oh, yes, he's here, but he's still sleeping. I hate to wake him. I could have him call you. Your name is—" Sophie waited for a response.

"John. I'll tell you what. Don't let Jack know that I called. I'll call back later and surprise him. When do you think might be a good time?"

Sophie was silent for a few seconds, then offered, "Why don't you call around noon? He should be here for lunch."

"Thank you, Mrs. Jurlik. I'll do that." Billy was grinning as he hung up. Bingo! He figured that Jack was either in Sturgeon Lake or Green Bay. He had wanted Green Bay because it would be easier to find Jack, and now he knew for sure that Jack was staying with his parents.

He used his regular phone to get the driving directions. "Good thing Austin didn't want to go into the city," he said out loud to himself. "I can avoid Minneapolis and be in Green Bay by suppertime! Oh, man, this is working out better than I had hoped!"

CHAPTER | 18

Carol was lying awake in bed, waiting to hear Sydney's cries. The light in the room was becoming brighter, but Carol was too tired to put her feet on the floor to start the day. Sydney had woken more than usual during the night, and Carol slept fitfully after feeding the baby. She tried to remember what day it was, finally deciding on Friday.

She thought to herself how cruel it was to ask nursing home residents the day of the week upon awakening. How could they possibly remember? One day was just like another—same surroundings, same routine, same people. That was how she felt now, like she had been institutionalized. It was always only her, Jim, and Sydney. She could not leave the house alone; she could not sit outside; she could not even use the phone. Jim rolled over in bed and nudged her. "Wow! Sydney must have slept through the night. Did not hear her at all. Isn't it great to be able to sleep in? Gonna be a good day, girl!" He got up, stretched, and headed for the bathroom.

Their morning was typical. Carol fed the baby while Jim made breakfast. After showering, Jim went out for the paper while Carol picked up or did the laundry. When Sydney was awake, they played with her. Then Carol read, and Jim worked on the computer until lunch.

It was after lunch, when Jim went back to the computer, that their slow, rhythmic existence changed. "Son of a bitch!" Carol heard Jim exclaim. He jumped up from the desk and strode quickly toward her. He was wearing his mask of anger. She took a few steps back, bracing herself.

"Do you know what I just found?" He raised his voice. "Do you?" She was so startled that she was frozen in silence.

"I'm asking you a question. Do *you know* what I just found?" She managed a "no."

"Well, I'll tell you. *We*, dear girl, are on the internet. *All* of us: *you, me, and the baby.* And do you know *why* we are on the internet?" Carol shook her head.

"Because of *you*, Carol! Because you just had to stop at a restaurant." Jim put his hand below his neck and, mimicking Carol's voice, began to whine, "I can't take it anymore. I feel sick." He dropped his hand to his side, and Carol saw the flex of his bicep, the balled fist. His voice, quieter now, was hard and clipped. "Oh, and then you started to cry. Big crocodile tears. I gave in because I felt sorry for you, because—hell, *I'm a nice guy.* I told you we were taking a chance, but did you listen? No, because you were thinking only of yourself. I should have stuck to my plan. You pushed me, Carol. *This is your fault.*"

"Jim, what are you talking about?" Carol dared to ask.

"Remember that place in Sturgeon Lake? Where you had the chicken soup? Well, somebody spotted us, and a lead about us is now on the net." Jim was talking through clenched teeth.

"But how could they?"

"Some frickin' crime club. Do-gooders."

"Maybe this is their first posting," Carol offered.

"*No.* This is not the first post." Jim's face looked like it would explode.

"Well, it must be. You would have seen it earlier," Carol said, trying to smooth things over.

"What? So now it's *my* fault? No, I did not see it earlier. I've been trying to get us new IDs, make plans for Toronto. I was looking forward—not backward. Gosh, you can be stupid. I only looked because one of my contacts told me." Jim was now standing toe to toe with her.

"It doesn't matter now; we're in Canada."

Jim took a step back and began mocking her again. "It doesn't matter now; we're in Canada!" He raised his hand, and she instinctively cowered. He stopped, arm in midair. "Can't you hear the baby crying? Go deal with her before the neighbors wonder what's going on."

She hurried to retrieve Sydney and put the baby to her breast. She was so upset that her milk would not let down.

Jim came into the room. "What are you doing? Why is Sydney still screaming?"

"I need a drink, Jim. I need something to calm my nerves."

"Calm your nerves? Are you kidding me? What the hell is wrong with you that you can't even nurse the baby!"

"Please, Jim."

He could see that the baby was not going to settle if he did not help Carol. He left the room, then came back with a tumbler half-filled with bourbon. As Carol downed the liquor and could feel the heat of it going down her throat, her milk let down, and the baby quieted. Jim looked down at her in disgust, made a *th* noise with his tongue, turned on his heel, and left.

CHAPTER | 19

"Daddy, get up!" Will was jumping up and down on the bed. "Grandma said you slept enough." He dropped to his knees, then tackled Jack.

"What time is it?" Jack moaned.

"Time to get up!"

Jack stretched out an arm to turn the alarm clock toward him, while Will still hung on to his back. "Ten o'clock? I can't believe it." But he could believe it; he could have slept forever. He never got up once during the night; he doubted he even moved. "Hey, buddy, Daddy's got to take a shower and get dressed. How about you ask Grandma to put the coffee on? I'll be down real soon. Promise."

"Okey dokey!" Will said as he bounced off the bed. Jack watched him run out of the room, envious of his unbounding energy.

Jack stood in the shower letting the hot water loosen his neck and shoulder muscles. The bathroom fan was running, but the room was still a fog of steam. He wondered how long he'd been in the shower and chuckled at the memory of his dad pounding on the door, saying, "Hey! We only have one hot water tank! The rest of us have to use it. Come on, Jack. Get out already!" Jack knew no one would tell him to get out today. He knew they felt sorry for him, and although he appreciated their consideration, he did not want their pity. He laughed out loud at the irony. "Heck, I pity myself." Then he shut off the water, got dressed, and went downstairs.

"Well, you look one hundred percent better," said his mother. She was pleased.

Jack sat at the kitchen table drinking his coffee, while Emma, Will, and his parents all kept him company. He was glad for it. He relished the normalcy of the moment, its ease, its warmth. They talked about what the day would bring. Emma wanted Jack to take her and Will to shop for school uniforms. Will thought shopping was a horrible idea and wanted to play instead. Sophie and Pete were getting ready for that night's big family dinner and were hoping Jack would take the kids. It was finally decided that Jack and Emma would go shopping and out to lunch; Will would go back to Aunt Tessa's house to play with Charlie; Sophie and Pete would have the day to themselves.

Then Emma asked Jack what he was going to do to find Gloriann. Pete told her, "Emma, we don't need to talk about that now."

"Dad, it's OK. The kids need to know; you need to know," Jack said. "Last night, right before I went to bed, I got a call from St. Louis. There is a lead the FBI is following. Gloriann and Martin were seen in a restaurant in Sturgeon Lake, Minnesota."

"What about the man? Was he there?" Emma demanded to know.

"What man? What man, Emma?" Will was confused.

Jack winced and shot a "don't say another word" look at Emma. She got the message and pursed her lips.

"What man, Daddy?" Will persisted.

Jack glanced over at his parents. They were as immovable as stone. "Will, Mommy and Martin are traveling with a man. We don't know much about him. But we are going to find the three of them, and then we'll know."

"Is he a bad man?" Will asked. He was worried.

"We don't think he's a bad man, Will. Like I said, there is a lot we just don't know. That's why I'm going to find them and get all our answers. Think of it as a puzzle—every time we find out more, it's like another piece of the puzzle. We keep finding more pieces until the puzzle is done."

"I don't like this puzzle!"

Silent tears were wetting the tops of Sophie's cheeks just below her glasses. Pete was biting his lip. Emma looked guiltily at Jack and tried not to breathe. Jack again felt their pain, and the rage rising inside him was hard to contain.

"I know, Will. None of us like this puzzle. But today is going to be a good day! Grandpa is making his famous barbeque ribs; Grandma has the potato salad in the fridge; Aunt Tessa is bringing ..." Jack looked at his mother.

"Fruit salad, and Uncle Ted is going to make us all ice-cream sundaes!" Sophie acted excited.

Emma took the cue and said, "Dad, I'll be ready to go in ten minutes. Grandma said she'll give you directions to the uniform store. Will, get your stuff. Charlie can't wait to see you!"

"Oh, Jack, I almost forgot. One of your friends called this morning and said he'd call back around noon, but now you won't be home. He didn't want me to tell you. He wanted to surprise you. Said he heard you were in town," Sophie said.

"Who was it?" Jack asked.

"He said his name was John. Didn't give me a last name."

"I know a lot of guys named John," Jack said as he walked to the phone to look at the caller ID. The "private" message unnerved him. Who would know that he was home? Maybe he should not leave the folks and go shopping. Was he being paranoid? No, the call was too much of a coincidence. It hit him—it could be Rodney! Gloriann certainly knew the phone number. Were they tracking his movements? Did they know the kids were in Green Bay? Sturgeon Lake was less than six hours away. Had they decided to get the kids? *Damn it*, Jack thought. He could not leave the house now. He would have to come up with a new plan and pitch it to the kids. He knew that he would have to convince Tessa to drop Charlie off at the house and go shop for the uniforms by herself. Then he heard Emma in the foyer calling for him. He sighed as he walked toward her. "Emma, change of plans."

A little after two o'clock, the phone rang, but before Jack could get his hands out of the dishwater, Emma picked up the receiver. He was poised to take it from her in case it was the elusive John, but then he heard the excitement in Emma's voice as she said, "How are you?"

Jack stood in front of Emma and silently mouthed, "Who is it?"

Emma, covering the mouthpiece, said, "Elizabeth."

Jack was perplexed. Why was Elizabeth calling his parents' house? He continued standing in front of Emma until she glared at him. Then he returned to washing the dishes, making sure he did not make noise so he could hear Emma's conversation. It amazed him that Emma talked for almost five minutes before yelling, "Grandma, telephone. It's Elizabeth."

When the call was finished, Sophie said, "Well, we are going to have two more guests tomorrow evening. That was Elizabeth. She and Carl planned to come up this weekend but did not realize there is a Packers home game on Sunday. They cannot find a hotel room for miles around. I told them they could stay here."

"Why are they coming here? How do you know them?" Jack was astonished.

"Dad! They are bringing our stuff! Remember? They were driving up our stuff from St. Louis!" Emma said. She looked at Jack as if he had lost his mind.

The flush of red started at Jack's collar, moved up his neck, and lit up his cheeks. He did forget. At that moment, he realized that he was not thinking clearly; he was losing his edge, and it scared him. He had managed to get Tessa to purchase the uniforms, which she took home to wash. He kept the kids out of his parents' hair so they could get ready for tonight. He was spending quality family time, even keeping the kitchen tidy, but what he was not doing was figuring out why Gloriann was in Sturgeon Lake and where she was now. He had lost his focus.

"Jack are you all right?" his mother asked.

He assured her that he was. Then he excused himself and went upstairs to call Lou. He explained to her that Special Agent Harlan had called last night to inform him that Gloriann was seen in Sturgeon Lake. "What else can you tell me, Lou?"

"We theorized that they are headed to Canada, but we don't know if they crossed the border yet. The Canadians have been helpful in sharing information according to our mutual Beyond the Border Action Plan. We've obtained the entry information from the Grand Portage/Pigeon River Port, but there is no mention of Gloriann, Rodney, or Martin. If they are already in Canada, they had to use false IDs. We know they have changed their appearance and are driving a car with Minnesota plates. They must be traveling with cash and burners—no credit card or phone trail. Jack, they thought this out. They knew how to stay off the grid."

"Judas priest!" Jack said as he dug his fingers into his scalp and ran them through his hair.

"Listen, we are going to look through the tapes. If they crossed, we would find them; just might take us longer," Lou said. "Plus, we are checking the cameras at Grand Portage State Park. See if they stopped to use the restrooms. A lot of people do that before hitting the border. If we spot them there, we can get a time frame."

"Do you think it feasible that they took a side trip to Green Bay? Do you think they are coming for the kids?" Jack asked.

"I thought of that, but looking at it logically, no, I don't think so. First, they have been extremely careful to avoid detection. I doubt they would chance it. Second, how would they even know the kids were in Green Bay? And here is the bottom line: if they wanted to take the kids, they would have done it at the beginning. They would not have had to wait for Elizabeth's visit. You were out of town when they disappeared. They could have left, and you never would have known until you got home."

"Yeah, you're right. Of course, they would have taken the kids in the beginning. I kept thinking that Gloriann would come back for them. I just could not accept the fact that she left them. Me? Well, yeah, maybe, but leaving the kids? Never thought that would ever happen." Jack paused, then continued, "My mother got an odd call from someone asking for me this morning. The guy called himself John, said he knew me; said he'd call back, but he never did. No number on the caller ID. I'll admit that I thought of Rodney and panicked a bit. Who would know that I'm home? Or who would be trying to figure out if I were?"

Lou responded, "Think reporter casting a net. Someone will probably waylay you for an exclusive."

Jack laughed. "Well, that's not going to happen! Thanks for the update, Lou. I am going to go to Canada, see if I can find anything. Keep me posted. I'll let you know if I get any leads."

"You'd better, Jack. Do not get yourself in trouble. I am telling you, we got this. We'll find them," Lou said, finishing the conversation.

CHAPTER | 20

Billy was making good time speeding along Wisconsin 29 in light traffic. He was halfway between Chippewa Falls and Wausau when he heard sirens approaching from behind. Checking his rearview mirror, he saw the squad in his lane and slowed down so it could pass. The squad's sirens changed from a constant wail to short bursts of *whoop, whoop*. He looked in the mirror again. "Shit."

Billy pulled onto the shoulder and turned off the car, leaving his window partway open. He put both hands on the steering wheel and waited. Had they already linked him to Rod? For a moment, he thought of driving off. Why not? He imagined himself, as if in a movie, leading the cops on a car chase. Was there a mall he could drive through just like in the *Blues Brothers*? Too bad there weren't construction cones that he could pop like Bill Murray with his mini. He could be *The Man Who Knew Too Little*. He chuckled but got serious as soon as the officer approached his window.

"Do you know how fast you were going?"

Billy looked at the officer with skepticism. "What? No. I think I was going the speed limit."

"Well, son, you were doing fifteen over."

"Oh, Officer, I'm sorry. I didn't check the speedometer. I just bought this car this morning, and I guess I'm not used to it. It didn't seem like I was going too fast." Billy was sincerely apologetic.

"Let me see your license and registration."

Billy handed them through the window. The officer stood looking at them and then headed back to the squad. Billy watched him in the driver's side mirror. He knew the officer was going to run his information through the computer. Would he find a warrant there?

He remembered the little wallet card that the American Civil Liberties Union had distributed on his college campus. It was an outline of what to do if stopped by the police. He had read it and threw it out; never thought he would need it. Now he was trying to recall its information. So far, he felt he had done everything right. He knew that if he was arrested, he did not have to answer questions, but he should be polite just the same. It was never good to antagonize the cops; they usually had the power in a situation.

The officer came back to Billy's window and returned his license and papers. "How is it that you have an Arizona address, bought a car in Minnesota, and are driving east through Wisconsin?" the officer wanted to know.

Billy was fairly sure that he didn't have to answer; he wondered if the cop could even ask the question. He looked at the officer and decided to be friendly. "Officer, it's a long story, but basically, I just moved to Minnesota. Flew in yesterday. Bought a cheap car until I get settled. And today, well, I am driving to Green Bay to meet some college friends. Packers play on Sunday."

The officer gave Billy a huge smile and relaxed his stance. "So, you're a Packers fan. Do you have tickets to the game?"

Billy knew the answer. "No, no, Officer. We would have loved to get tickets, but it's a sellout. We're going to a bar to watch the game."

After exchanging more sports banter, the officer said, "OK, listen. I'll let you off with a warning. You'd better learn how to keep checking that speedometer until you are used to this car. If you get pulled over again, you're not going to be as lucky."

Billy thanked him, and when he saw that the officer was safely inside the squad, he pulled out onto the freeway. He was relieved that he got off with only a warning and ecstatic that he was not a wanted man. He wondered if he could possibly be in the clear; maybe they could not link him with the Ponzi scheme. If that were the case, he would not have to pursue Rod. He decided to call Destiny when he stopped to eat.

Billy sat at the McDonald's in Abbotsford, eating a Big Mac combo meal and washing it down with thirty-two ounces of Coke. He knew the Coke would run through him and add more stops to his trip, but he needed the caffeine and sugar to stay awake. He threw away his trash but kept the ice in the cup to chew on the way. Once settled back in the driver's seat, he started the car, opened all the windows, shut the car back off, pulled out his burner phone, and dialed his office number.

"Pronghorn Financial Services. Destiny speaking. How may I help you?"

"Destiny, it's Billy. How are you? I'm just calling to check in. Any important calls for me?"

"Billy, where are you?" Destiny asked.

"I'm in Kansas City, seeing the sites. I'll be back next week. Anything I need to know? Any news on Rod?"

"Haven't heard anything new about Rod. Lots of buzz here, but same old same old. The FBI assigned an agent to me. I'm supposed to keep track of all the calls for Rod that come to my desk and give out the agent's phone number if the person says they've been scammed. She calls me every other day for updates."

"Any calls for me?" Billy was fishing.

"That's the thing, Billy. Some of the scammed investors *are* calling for you—said Rod gave them your number, but you aren't answering your phone."

"Destiny, Rod may have given them my number, but I swear I didn't know about his scam."

"Well, Billy, then you have nothing to worry about. Nothing to worry about as long as there is nothing connecting you with Rod." Destiny sounded distant.

"No, there isn't. I'll be back next week and help clear this all up." Billy was matter-of-fact. But when he hung up the phone with Destiny, he remembered the old lady from Minnesota. He regretted telling her that he would get her $3,000 back. He should have acted surprised, told her to call the police, been insistent that he could not help her. Even after he unthinkingly took her information, he should have called the FBI. How could he distance himself from that mistake?

He now understood that his goal of walking away from involvement in the Ponzi scheme would not be attainable. He would have to salvage what he could to avoid going to prison for a long time. "I'll turn state's evidence! That's what I'll do," Billy said to himself. But then he thought, *What if they have enough evidence to convict Rod without my help? What if they have enough evidence to convict me? How could I possibly get a lenient plea deal?*

He threw his head back, put the cup to his mouth, closed his eyes, and chewed the ice while hatching the designs of a new plan. He would locate Rod, find out where he hid the money, then call the FBI to turn him in. No! Better yet, he would bring Rod in; make a citizen's arrest. He had the handgun; he could do it! There was only one problem, the same problem that he had been denying all along: if he followed Jack to Rod, Jack would get to Rod first. Billy would have to make sure that did not happen; he was more determined than ever.

He finished chewing the ice, drank the remaining amber-colored water, crushed the cup in his hand, and threw it on the passenger-side floor. He twisted his body to duck under the steering wheel and feel along the floorboard beneath his seat for the handgun. It was still there.

He made it to Green Bay in two hours and decided to first drive around, looking for a place where he could spend the night in his car undetected. He would not use his credit card at a motel. He found a neighborhood on the east side of Green Bay just west of Main Street that was heavily populated with older, worn-looking apartments, not far from East Town Mall. The neighborhood by the apartments looked a bit rough, but that was perfect for his purposes. No one would bother him, and if they did, he had the gun. There was a Walmart Super Store and numerous fast-food restaurants. He was satisfied with the setup.

Using Google Maps, he entered Pete's address. It was fifteen minutes northeast of Billy's location. As he drove by the southeast tip of the Bay Beach Wildlife Sanctuary, he took in the beauty of the landscape. This was a whole different world, only fourteen miles from the one he just left.

He drove by the house and could hear children in the backyard. Someone was grilling; it smelled like barbequed ribs. No one was in the front of the house. Neighbors were nowhere to be seen. The day was still unseasonably hot, and people were staying inside. There were three vehicles in Pete's driveway, all with Wisconsin plates: a minivan with a sticker that said, "My child is an honor student," a SUV with a kayak strapped to its roof, and a Toyota Avalon. Billy looked at the three and then wondered how he would get the tracker on the Avalon with no one noticing.

He knew he had to take the chance. He parked opposite the driveway, opened his door, left it open, walked to the back of the Avalon, and placed the tracker on a flat, magnetic surface under the car. It took him ten seconds—had anyone seen him? He walked back to his car, closed his door so quietly that the open-door light on the dash lit up, and drove away.

CHAPTER | 21

Carol and Sydney were both asleep when Jim came in to wake her. "You really knocked out, Carol. Come on. I made supper." Jim bent over and kissed her lightly on the forehead, then walked back to the kitchen.

Carol sat in the recliner a moment longer, trying to get her bearings. She looked over at Sydney sleeping in the portable crib. Her thinking was foggy. She remembered parts of the argument with Jim and drinking the bourbon. He was so gentle now. He had made supper. Carol was off balance; she did not know what was happening; she did not know what to expect.

"Hey, sleepyhead! Are you coming?" Jim called from the kitchen. His voice was teasing and light.

"Yeah, I'm coming. Just a minute," Carol said quietly as she slowly lifted herself out of the chair and headed for the kitchen. A steaming bowl of spaghetti was on the table, along with garlic bread, tossed salad, and a bottle of red wine. Carol smiled at Jim, who was beaming.

"I've figured it out, Carol. My contacts in Toronto are willing to hide us for as long as it takes until they can get all our papers together." He guided her to the table and pulled out her chair. Before he went to sit down, she felt his warm lips start to kiss her tenderly on the neck. She tilted her head, putting her ear to her shoulder, and giggled.

Carol's mind was moving in slow motion, while Jim was on fast-forward talking to her. She was not processing. "What do you mean hide us?" she asked as she reached for the garlic bread.

"Carol, we need to *go to ground* as they say. We don't want to be found, and the feds may be on our tail. If we are hidden for a while, then we will probably become a cold case, and finding us will no longer be a priority." Jim realized that Carol still had not comprehended what he had just told her. "Think of it this way. It's like the government witness-protection program. We will live in a safe house. Only, we will not be protected by the government; my contacts will protect us, and we will pay them for the service."

"I thought you said we'd just get lost in Toronto. I don't know why we need your contacts to hide us. Can't we just hide out ourselves? We've done it so far," Carol said, still looking perplexed.

"Well, that all changed when we were spotted at the restaurant in Sturgeon Lake. The FBI has the means to track us now that we have shown our hand. We need to make sure we don't get caught before we can get settled and get on with our lives." Jim was patient.

"*If* we were caught, what could they do to us? I mean, really, all they would do is send us back to the States. Isn't that what the United States does with illegals crossing the Mexican border? I can't imagine that Canada would do anything different. We are Americans for goodness sake." Carol was confident. The food was helping disperse the clouds in her head.

"Carol, that's right … sometimes. It all depends. If the illegals have committed a crime, even American illegals, then they are jailed, and a judge decides what to do with them. That's what would happen to us."

"But we are not criminals, Jim. You know that." Carol was insistent.

"Carol, we are criminals. You took the baby without Jack's permission, crossed state lines, and even fled the country."

"But he's not Jack's baby. You're his father." Carol looked confused.

"Biologically yes, but legally no. The legal father is the one on the birth certificate if the mother and father are married at the time. Then there is the business of the fake IDs and lying to border patrol. It starts adding up, Carol." Jim remained calm.

Carol was silent, thinking. Odd that she never gave much thought to the legality of her escapade with Jim. She thought about the backlash from her family and friends if they found out about her affair with Jim and the truth about the baby. Looking back, she realized that all she wanted to do was to get away and deal with it all later. Even when she thought about calling Jack, it was because she was upset with Jim, upset that her freedom was taken away, upset that she left Jack for a man who was so volatile. That was why she wanted to call Jack. She wanted to get her life back; she was not worried about being arrested.

She was beginning to unearth a new vein in the mine of her ignorance, and the discovery awed her. She had abandoned her children, detonated her marriage, kidnapped her own baby, and was now a bona fide criminal. Jim must have known that what they were doing was criminal, and yet he did not explain the seriousness of his plan to her ahead of time. He did not warn her. Is that why he'd been isolating her and keeping the baby in public? He was worried she'd go to the police? Carol thought it was because he did not want her to leave him—that he needed her. No longer a fugitive from reality, she said, "But these Toronto contacts, what if they turn us in? You said you have to pay them. What if they take the money and kill us?"

"Carol, don't worry about that. They run a successful business. They wouldn't last long if they killed their customers. They help us, and we never ever mention them to anyone, ever."

"What if we did? Like accidentally."

"Well, then they *would* kill us, Carol. We'd just disappear, all of us. They might sell the baby, but we'd be dead," explained Jim.

"They wouldn't though. Someone would know. They'd be caught," Carol reasoned.

"Carol, once they help us and we get our papers, we are fiction. We can never tell people who we really are. We have no extended family, no history, no hometown, no nothing. We are just their creation. In a way, even though we are alive, we don't actually exist in the eyes of the law. We'll still have good lives. It will just be a different life. That's all," Jim assured her.

Carol hesitated, then said, "Jim, maybe we should take our chances and go to the police ourselves. Forget Toronto and the contacts. I bet Jack will not press charges if I explain what I was going through. Then that leaves the fake IDs and the border patrol, but even that, Jim, would probably be … what? Probation? We are first-time offenders. We could go back to the States, start a new life there, and we would still have our history, our families."

Jim poured Carol another glass of wine, pulled out her chair, and led her to the couch. "I have something to tell you." As she sipped the wine, he began to talk. He told her about the Ponzi scheme, how it started out innocently enough, how he genuinely believed it would work and no one would lose their money, and finally, how it all got away from him and imploded. Like Carol, he just wanted to get away from his situation, but he couldn't leave her; he couldn't leave his son. He loved them so much that it hurt. That's when he devised the plan to go to Canada and start a new life. He was sorry that they were seen in Sturgeon Lake. He should have been the man, taken charge, not let Carol diverge from the path. But he felt sorry for her, and his heart overshadowed his thinking.

"Can you forgive me, Carol, for loving you and Sydney so much?" Jim's eyes were pleading. "I am very sorry. You have been so good to me, helping every step of the way—changing your name, your appearance, even passing off Sydney as a girl. And now we are both in the lineup if you know what I mean. Do you, Carol, know what I mean?"

She did. She was silent, unscrambling her thoughts. She put down her wine glass and took his hand. "Jim, I do know what you mean, and now that we are in this together with eyes wide open, I have a favor to ask." He nodded, and she continued, "I want to be treated as an equal. I know that I don't always do things the right way or think things out, so if I could just ease into being an equal partner, that would be all right with me." She was searching his face for an answer, and he was squinting his eyes, trying to read her mind. Finally, he agreed to give her a bit more freedom, just a bit, until he was sure she was ready.

Satisfied, she asked, "So when do we leave for Toronto?"

Jim laughed. "Now you're talking turkey!" He explained that they needed to go to Walmart as soon as Sydney was finished eating to get supplies for their trip. "Can you make up a quick shopping list?"

"Wait, are we leaving tomorrow? I'll never be ready." Carol was alarmed.

Jim assured her that was not the case. He wanted to leave for Toronto on Sunday morning. He planned to spend Saturday tying up loose ends with his contacts and hoped Carol could spend the day doing the laundry and packing. He also planned to pay for the room through Tuesday, even though they would be leaving early on Sunday, because he thought it would throw people off.

"Do you think we can make it to Toronto without being caught?" Carol was desperate to know.

"Absolutely. The feds may have that Sturgeon Lake lead, but it will take them time to gather information, look at film. No. We're ahead of them now. There is no way they will catch us. We can take turns driving to Toronto. I'll drive most of the way. You will just have to spot me from time to time so I can rest. It will be a long day, but we can do it. Once we are there, we're home free!" Jim was confident.

"Good!" Carol smiled and acted relieved while swallowing the acid that had made its way up her throat. "You get Sydney, and I'll make the list." As they drove to the store, Carol was multitasking: listening to Jim's chatter, responding when he asked a question, yet still rehearsing her plan in her mind. When he parked the car, she was patient as Jim got Sydney out and placed the baby carrier in a shopping cart that had been left in the lot. She did not try to remove the invisible rope that bound them together in public: Sydney to Jim and Carol to Sydney.

She purposely stuck close to Jim when they entered the store. Looking at her shopping list, Carol suggested they buy her items first. She needed to get more nursing pads, tampons, panty liners, lipstick, and hair dye. He rolled his eyes and stared at her.

"I can't help it, honey. I need..."

Jim sighed. "It's OK. Take a basket and go get what you need. I'll take Sydney and get the diapers and other stuff. I'll meet you by the baby clothes. Don't take long."

Carol was hoping Jim would want to avoid the tampon aisle; most guys did. She left Jim and headed to find the lipstick. "Oh, God, help me!" she pleaded. She did not know how to get herself and the baby away safely. "Please, God." When she rounded the corner of the makeup aisle, she saw two teenage girls discussing eye shadow. One was wearing an Iowa Hawkeyes T-shirt; the other sported a Nebraska Cornhuskers muscle shirt layered over another T-shirt. They looked like sisters—blonde hair, blue eyes, same build. She saw the bulge of a cell phone in the older girl's back jean's pocket. Carol looked up at the ceiling. "Thank you, God," she whispered.

She glanced around and did not see Jim, did not see any mirrors that would reflect what she was going to do. She took a deep breath, curved her lips into a smile, and approached the girls, "Hi! How are you doing? Hey, I was hoping you could help me out. My husband accidentally took my phone, and I need to call him. Could I use yours? You know, I've never been to Canada before, first time out of the States. Can't believe he took my phone."

Both girls were taller and heftier than Carol. They sized her up, looked at each other, then came to a decision. "Sure. Keep it short though," the girl said as she handed the cell to Carol.

Carol took it and nodded. She dialed Jack's number. "Answer it, Jack. Answer it," Carol said, willing him to pick up. She heard the ringing stop. "Hi! I'm ready for you to get me. Yeah, you took my phone when you dropped me off in Thunder Bay. Look, I can't talk now. Just come as soon as you can. No. You just come. You can leave the kids for a few minutes. Love you too. Bye." Carol ended the conversation without ever hearing Jack's voice. She handed the phone back to the girl, shrugged her shoulders, and said, "Thanks. You're a lifesaver. He forgot where he dropped me off. Can you believe it? Honestly, sometimes guys are clueless."

Both girls giggled, but as soon as Carol was out of earshot, the older sister said, "Boy, he must be a tool."

To which the younger replied, "Yeah, you'd better curve him. Mom can be so extra about the phone."

Carol did it! She called Jack! She wanted to jump up and down, scream even. Her heart was pounding; her hands were sweating; suddenly she could not breathe. Her excitement evolved into panic. What if Jim saw her? What if the girls came to talk to her while she was with Jim? No, she would not think like that. She made the call; no one saw her; she would avoid the girls. Jack would come help her. True, he never had the chance to speak, but she believed he would come. She just had to calm down.

Inhaling deeply through her nose and exhaling slowly through her mouth helped her get control of her breath and slow her heart rate. She wiped her hands on her slacks. "I can do this," she told herself. She finished her shopping and arrived at the baby clothes before Jim. When she saw him approaching, she picked up her blue shopping basket from the floor and held it high for him to see. Her stance was one of triumph.

"Wow! You were fast. Did you find everything?" a pleased Jim asked.

"Yep! Guess I was just lucky; found everything I needed. How about you? Do you want to buy anything else?"

"No, I'm just bummed. They ran out of ice," Jim said, then paused. "Oh, heck, we can pick up a bag as we leave town on Sunday."

"That will work." Carol looked first at Jim, then at Sydney, then at the checkouts. The two sisters were nowhere in sight. "If we hurry and check out now, maybe we can catch the beginning of that comedy you wanted to watch."

Jim perked up and started to push the cart toward the registers. He moved so fast that Carol had to power walk to catch up with him. He found a cashier that had no customers waiting, and they were out of the store within minutes, much to Carol's delight. In the car, on the way home, Jim asked her, "Are you OK with what I told you earlier? You seemed preoccupied on the way here."

"Oh, sorry. Yeah, I was preoccupied. I was thinking of all the things I need to do to get ready for Sunday. What the weather is going to be like, what I should pack, how much food to take—those sorts of things," Carol explained.

"But are you OK with what I told you?" Jim queried.

"I am. Jim, I'm sort of relieved. I can't explain why. I just am. I'll admit that at first I was alarmed, but the more I thought about it as I was making the shopping list, the freer and more empowered I felt. It's like when we first met, and we could tell each other everything. We leaned on each other. I found strength in that connection, and I found that same strength in you telling me the truth."

Jim wanted to believe her answer. He had noticed a change in her but was unsure what that change meant. He took a chance and probed deeper. "Tell me the truth, Carol. What about Emma and Will? How do you feel about them?"

Carol looked sad. "I miss them. I always thought that once we were settled, we'd work something out. I never considered that I might not see them again. But you know what? There are statutes of limitations for a lot of crimes. We haven't done anything that awful. As long as we are not caught, we could find out the statute of limitations for what we've done, and when we pass that time, we can go back to the States. That's my hope. So I am going to work very hard to not get caught."

Jim was astonished at her investment. She would go along with his plan, expecting to wait it out until she could see her kids. Even he had not thought of that angle. What a stroke of good luck! He looked over at her. "I love you so much, Carol."

She smiled back at him. "And I love you, Jim."

22

"William, stop!" Jack reprimanded. The little boy stopped so quickly that his cousin Ben ran into his back. Will fell on the floor, and Ben fell on top of him. They both looked up at Jack, then jumped to attention when Jack said, "Get up." Jack rarely used that tone of voice or called Will by his full name. The boys had been chasing each other around the house while an exasperated Tessa pleaded for them to get in the van. She finally gave up and headed out the front door.

Jack did not soften his demeanor. "Look, when Aunt Tessa," he said this to Will, then looking at Ben, added, "your mother asks you to do something, you do it. When she gives you the fifteen-minute warning, you know you will be leaving. And when she tells you to get in the van, you get in the van. Do you understand me?"

"Yes, Daddy."

"Yes, Uncle Jack."

They looked thoroughly chastised. He appraised the two of them: sweaty hair, dirty knees, barbeque sauce on their faces and shirts. He bent over and gave them both a hug, "OK then. You are going to apologize to Aunt Tessa," Jack said.

The three of them walked out to the driveway where everyone was saying their goodbyes. Tessa was already buckling Charlie into his car seat. Andy was talking to Uncle Ted, one hand and foot in the van, the other foot still on the cement. When he saw Will and Ben approach, he heaved himself into the van and sat down to wait. "Emma? Are you coming?" Andy yelled, leaning over his youngest brother.

Emma stood torn between two worlds. She looked at the van, then at her father, then at the van again. Tessa, who was now making sure Ben and Will were secured in their seats, glanced over her shoulder and saw Emma's indecision. "Emma, if you want to stay here another night, that's OK. I can get you tomorrow."

"Thanks, Aunt Tessa. I'll stay and help Grandma," a relieved Emma said. She was not ready to go back to the frenzy that the four boys would inevitably create when they got home. She was glad to stay with her father and moved closer to him.

Joe walked over to the driver's window and kissed Tessa. "I'll be back shortly to help you."

"Joe, take your time. It's not often you three brothers get together. Andy can fend for himself, and I'll give the little ones a bath and get them to bed. They are all tired. Then I am putting my feet up and watching my show. So do *not* hurry," Tessa said, eager for solitude.

"OK, I hear you. And, Tessa, thanks," Joe said as he kissed her again, then slapped the roof of the van twice to indicate it could hit the road.

As they were walking back to the house, Jack's cell phone rang. He looked at the name, Katelyn, and the number but did not recognize either. He hesitated, then answered. Before he could say hello, a woman began to talk. He stopped and listened as the rest of the family followed one another into the house. Jack stood on the driveway immobilized, holding his phone at arm's length, staring at it. Then he began researching his account to see where the call originated. Finally, he slipped it into his back pocket and walked slowly to the house.

"Man, you look like you just saw a ghost!" Ted said when Jack entered the kitchen. Jack's face was devoid of emotion as he turned to consider his brother. Immediately, Ted regretted saying anything. He did not know Jack well. There was a fourteen-year age difference between them. Jack had gone off to college when Ted was only four and stayed in Arizona after graduating. Joe, eleven years Ted's senior, was the brother he knew. Joe never moved from Green Bay.

Pete strode up to Jack and put a hand on his shoulder, saying, "Let's go into the living room." Ted hesitated to look at his mother before Joe grabbed him by the elbow and tugged him along behind Jack. Emma began to follow until Sophie said, "Emma, stay here. You can join them in a bit. Let's finish these dishes. You know how I hate to see a dirty sink in the morning."

Jack took his cell phone from his back pocket and sat down on the couch. "Gloriann just called me."

His father and brothers looked astonished. Joe got up and extended his hand for the cell phone. Jack gave it to him. "Jack, the last call was from a Katelyn. Are you sure it was Gloriann? What did she say?" Joe asked.

"She didn't give her name or use mine, but it was definitely her voice. She said, 'I'm ready for you to get me. Yeah, you took my phone when you dropped me off in Thunder Bay.' Said she couldn't talk, that I should come get her, come soon, don't bring the kids, come alone, that the kids would be OK for a few minutes. That was it. Eighteen seconds."

"That's odd," Ted said quietly to himself but loud enough that Jack heard him.

"I don't think she could speak plainly. Someone was listening. The way she spoke, the inflections in her voice and the quick pauses would have made the listener believe I was responding to her, that she was answering my questions," Jack explained.

Ted jumped in again. "Did you call her back?"

"No," Jack said. "She was trying to be elusive. I didn't want to blow her cover and put her in danger."

"If she is to be believed," Joe used a respectful tone, "then she is in Thunder Bay."

"Hey, you can check that out. Just access your phone bill and see where the call came from," Ted said, eager to help.

"I did that. But it didn't list the city. Those call records are used by phone carriers for billing purposes—billing you and settling accounts with other carriers. Sometimes you will get the information you want, sometimes you won't. I'll call Lou, my colleague in the St. Louis office, and give her the details. She'll figure it out. But I do believe Gloriann. I was already planning to go to Thunder Bay. I'll just leave earlier."

"When were you planning to go?" Pete asked.

"I wasn't sure, but now I want to leave as early as possible—tomorrow. Do you think I can take Mom's car? I can rent one, but I couldn't get it until nine o'clock in the morning. They are already closed tonight."

"No, you don't need Mom's car! I'm going with you; we'll take mine," Joe said.

Jack looked at him and shook his head, while Pete and Ted turned theirs to stare at Joe. "No, you are not coming with me, Joe." Jack was back to his authoritative dad voice. "And leave Tessa with all the kids? What about work? No, absolutely not!"

Emma came rushing into the room from the doorway, where she had been listening unnoticed. Holding a dishtowel in one hand and balling her other hand into a fist, she dug her heels into the carpet and stiffened her legs. "You can't go alone. Uncle Joe has to go with you. I'll help Aunt Tessa. You just *can't*!" Tears started to stream down her face as she stared at her father.

Joe broke the silence. "Jack, I figured you would go to Canada, and I decided to go with you. Tessa and I already talked about it. I cleared it with the chief. It's OK. There are officers willing to cover for me as long as it takes."

"Unpaid leave, Joe? With three kids? I can't ask you—"

Jack was cut off by his father, who said, "If Joe needs money, your mother and I will help him."

Joe shook his head and started to respond to his father, but Ted cut him off. "Yeah, and I'll help Tessa. I can go over there every day after school and stay until the kids are in bed."

Pete added, "I can drive the kids to swimming and practice. And your mother will help. You know that."

Jack was blindsided by their response. He hesitated, then reconsidered. Throwing up his hands, he capitulated and said, "OK. You win. Joe will go with me, and the rest of you will take care of everything on the home front. I'm grateful. Truly I am. Thank you."

When arrangements had been finalized, goodbyes had been said, and Emma was asleep in bed, Jack called Lou. He told her about the phone call from Gloriann and gave her the number and name on the caller ID. She said she would go into the office early on Saturday and find out who owned the phone and from what tower the call originated. Jack knew that a single cell tower would at least place the call in a geographic area. To get more specificity, Lou would use cell tower triangulation—the distance from three different towers used to advance the call. That would result in being able to home in on the location within a one-mile area. She could call the phone's owner but would have to vet them first to be sure not to endanger Gloriann.

"I'll call you as soon as I know something. When were you planning to go to Canada?" Lou asked.

"Joe and I are leaving for Thunder Bay tomorrow morning."

"Jack, I hope you and Joe are not taking your guns with you." When Jack did not respond, Lou cautioned, "You can't. You know that. There is no Non-Resident Firearms Declaration form for the guns you are carrying. They are not just restricted; they are totally prohibited. Zero tolerance, Jack. You do remember that, don't you?"

"Yes." Jack's voice was clipped. But again, he capitulated. "I hate to go unarmed, not knowing what I'm walking into and exposing Joe too. But, no, I'm not going to make things worse by violating Canadian law."

"Good!" Lou was relieved. "Jack, we're making progress. We'll find Gloriann and Martin. Just please don't do anything stupid."

"*Please* quit telling me that! Can't you say anything else?" Jack asked, frustration emanating from his voice.

Lou did not respond directly but said, "Yeah, good luck. I'm pulling for you, Jack."

CHAPTER | **23**

Billy had just dozed off in the back seat of his car when an alert sounded on his cell phone. Jack's car had started moving. "Shit!" Billy said as he sat up. He opened the tracking app and watched as the car drove a few miles from Pete's house then stopped. Zooming in on his Google map, he could see that the location was another house on a residential street. He was tired and wanted to sleep—needed to sleep. He decided that Jack must be visiting someone, as Rod was certainly not staying at a house in Green Bay.

SATURDAY, SEPTEMBER 23

Billy slept fitfully. Temperatures stayed in the high sixties, with the humidity at almost 90 percent. The car was like an oven. He had cooled it off with the air-conditioning and closed the windows, thinking that might help. It didn't. Every time he awoke, he would turn the car back on and open the windows a bit more, finally stopping at halfway, not caring if someone could put an arm through. He got up with a splitting headache at 4:00 a.m. His back hurt, and his clothes were wet with sweat. He needed relief. He pressed the microphone icon on his cell phone, and when he saw the word, "Listening," he said, "Beaches near me." Bay Beach, near Jack's house, was the only option. Billy sighed. Both the Fox River and the East River were closer, but they didn't have beaches. There was no way he was going to jump into an unfamiliar river; it would have to be Bay Beach.

He was glad it was still dark when he stripped down to his shorts, grabbed a bar of soap, and headed for the water. Not one to put his toe in to approach the coldness with caution, he ran in, stopping only when he was submerged up to his armpits. After bathing and shampooing his hair, he let the bar of soap drop and swam parallel to the shore for a few minutes. Back at the car, he dried himself off and put on clean clothes. He brushed his teeth, used bottled water to rinse his mouth, then spit it out on the blacktop. Then he took two Excedrin and headed off to get breakfast.

He arrived at the restaurant early enough to order their all-you-can-eat pancakes, but he didn't want pancakes. He wanted bacon and eggs and toast and black coffee, lots of black coffee. He had eaten half of his breakfast when the tracking app sounded another alert. Jack was on the move, driving back to Pete's house. *Early start*, Billy thought. He had finished off the bacon and eggs when the tracking app alerted again. Jack's car was leaving Pete's house. Billy kept eating his toast and drinking coffee as he waited for the car to stop. It didn't; it was moving in a northwesterly direction.

Billy drained the rest of the coffee, left a tip on the table, walked to the counter to pay his bill, and headed for his car. He did not have to hurry. The app would show him Jack's movements in real time, anywhere in the US, Canada, or Mexico. He didn't have to worry about the transmitter's battery; it should last at least a month even with heavy driving. Before he started his car, he looked at the app again to see Jack's location. Then he used Google directions to find the fastest route to Jack. Billy was pleased that the app was so easy to use. It alerted again, indicating that Jack had stopped. Billy did not want to overtake him, yet he wanted to see Jack.

When he found him, he was surprised that Jack was not alone. There was another man with him. The other man was pumping gas, while Jack went into the store, coming out later with two coffees. It was light outside now, even though the sun had not yet risen. Billy realized that if he could see Jack, Jack could see him if he only looked. There was not much traffic this early on a Saturday, so Billy thought it prudent to let Jack's car get ahead of him by ten minutes.

CHAPTER 24

Jack put the coffees in the car's two cup holders and opened the bag that his mother handed him as he left the house. "Mom made us ham and cheese sandwiches. There are two apples and lots of chocolate chip cookies," Jack said.

"Good! We won't have to stop to get breakfast. Unwrap the sandwich. I'll eat it while I drive."

"Officer Jurlik, I'm not sure that's allowed under Wisconsin Statute—"

"Shut up, Jack. Just give me the sandwich," Joe said as he backhanded Jack's shoulder.

Jack handed him the sandwich and laughed. "Looks like it will take us about nine hours if we take Twenty-nine over to Chippewa Falls, then pick up Fifty-three and head north. It'll be too soon to eat before we get to Superior."

Joe said, "Well, it will be busy, but there's a lot of restaurants. Unless something turns up, let's stop there for lunch."

"Sounds good to me."

Joe continued, "OK, Jack, you told me everything you know about the case. What didn't you tell me?" Jack looked over and gave Joe a "Who me?" face. "I need to know, Jack. I don't want to be blindsided by some after-the-fact revelation that could jeopardize my career."

"What you don't know, you don't know. Didn't Mother Teresa say, 'You can't give what you don't have?'" Jack told him.

"She's right, but I don't think I could use that as a defense. No proof—just my word and yours. I'm not going to bale unless it is something horrific, Jack," Joe said, looking over at him.

Jack was silent. Telling Joe was a gamble, but not telling him was also. If only Jack had not been pressured to accept the family's help. But he had to admit he was glad to have Joe alongside him. "OK, but no one else knows this, and I mean no one. If you want to bale after I tell you, no problem; just take me to a car rental. Do you still want to know?" Jack looked over at Joe, who was nodding his head.

Jack continued, "Things just weren't the same between Gloriann and me after we moved to St. Louis. At first, it was fine. She and the kids were excited about the adventure, but that eventually wore off, and I knew she regretted moving, though we never discussed it. When we got pregnant with Martin, the kids and I were ecstatic, but Gloriann was on edge. I chalked it up to the pregnancy. Then when Martin was born, he had brown eyes." Jack stopped and turned his head to Joe.

Joe's face was expressionless except for his raised eyebrow. He remained silent, kept his eyes on the road. "Go on."

"Remember simple genetics from biology class? Two blue-eyed parents can't have a brown-eyed child? I thought Martin's eye color would change, and when it didn't, I started to do some research. Found out it can happen, but it is rare. That got me to thinking, wondering if I was Martin's father. I had to know, Joe. He didn't look like me; he didn't look like anyone in our family. I did DNA swabs on me and the baby and sent them to an accredited DNA lab. You know, you can send them in as long as it is not for a legal paternity test, so I didn't have to go to a lab and have it done by trained lab techs. I didn't have to worry about the integrity of the chain of possession. They sent the results to my PO box."

"You have a PO box?" Joe was surprised.

Jack answered, "I got one just so I would have anonymity with the test. I didn't want Gloriann to know I doubted her fidelity. What if I was wrong? The results indicated what I had already guessed. I'm not Martin's father. I paid a hundred and seventy-nine dollars to have my world shattered."

"Ah, geez. Then what did you do?" asked Joe.

"Nothing. But it ate at me. That's why I went back to Tucson for a bit. I had to get away. I had to think about what to do, how to handle it. Then I got the call that Gloriann and Martin were missing. I didn't tell anyone that Gloriann had an affair. So, yes, I withheld information. I didn't want to become a murder suspect with a motive. I didn't want them to figure she just up and left me; that would destroy any urgency in finding her. And I certainly didn't want our personal scandal splashed all over the papers and internet."

"Oh, Gee, Jack. Is that all of it?" Joe asked.

"No. I found her diary after the cops' first cursory search of the house. There was nothing in it as to whom her lover might be. She journaled everyday stuff as well as some feelings of despondency. Nothing about running away, nothing that would help find her. In my professional opinion, they didn't need to see it, so I did not give it to them. I don't think any of this will come back to bite me, Joe, as long as we don't talk to anyone about it."

"What a frickin' mess! So even after we find them, after it's over, it's not over at all. I don't know how you're surviving this. Good Lord, I don't know if I could. In a way, I wish I didn't know; knowing is a burden. But, Jack, I'm glad you told me. I'm here for you. And don't worry. I won't say anything, and I would deny that I ever knew if asked. Oh no, I'm ... what a frickin' mess."

Jack sighed. "Thanks. It feels good to finally get it off my chest, to share it with you. I can tell you, Joe, I don't know what I'm going to do when this is all over."

"Yeah, not just you, but the kids and Martin. Poor Martin."

"That is one thing I decided when I was in Tucson. Martin is my son. I was there for his birth. I walked the floors with him, and I listened to his breathing on the baby monitor to make sure he was OK. My name is on his birth certificate. I'll fight for him. He's not getting stuck with Rodney Wilter for a father."

"And Gloriann?" Joe dared ask.

"I don't know. Right now, I feel like I got hit in a head-on crash and wasn't wearing a seat belt. I don't know if I'll ever heal from this—the betrayal and hurt are pretty deep. I still love her, Joe, but I just don't know what is going to happen."

CHAPTER | 25

By the time Billy hit Highway 29, traffic increased but was scattered with wide spaces between vehicles. He saw cars with kayaks on their roofs; trucks pulling fishing boats; SUVs with trailers hauling all-terrain vehicles. He heard the music and felt its heart-thumping base before the convertible with four young men whizzed past him. He envied all these people. He liked to fish, go boating, and hang out with his friends. But now he was playing bounty hunter.

Billy snickered to himself, "That's not a half-bad idea. I could be a bounty hunter." He thought about how he successfully investigated Rod's whereabouts and how he was now tracking Jack. It only took him two days to get this far, so how hard could it be? Billy thought, *I could be a bounty hunter, get out of the office, make my own hours. True, I'd probably have to get a criminal justice degree and take some self-defense classes, but I already know how to handle a gun. I could do this!*

Billy sat up straighter in the car. He smiled as another camper pulled up to his left. He was not being passed by; no, he was being invited to join a future party. All he had to do was bring Rod in, testify against him, and help give the fraud victims their money back.

When Jack's car headed north on Highway 53, Billy knew that Jack was probably going to Canada. He thought about the border crossing. He would have to hide the gun in his luggage and hope his car wasn't searched. He had Minnesota plates, which would be a help. He was Caucasian, which he thought would help, but he was a young man traveling alone, and that might arouse suspicion. He decided he would wear his glasses even though he didn't need them, put a pen in his shirt pocket, and throw a map on the front seat. He put his hand to his face and felt the stubble. He hadn't shaved in two days and figured he looked a bit too ragged. He pressed the microphone icon on his phone and said, "Rest stops near me."

Within forty-five minutes, Billy pulled into the parking lot of Chetek Rest Area 34. It was a low-slung building set amid fields and sporting a brown roof and windows along the front. No one was parked next to him. He reached under the front seat for his gun and slipped it into his pants' front pocket. Then he hung his arm down his side to cover the gun's handle. When he opened the trunk, he put the gun on the trunk's floor. He unlatched his suitcase to get out his shaving kit and hid the gun in a folded sweatshirt, then placed the suitcase to the rear of the trunk.

On his way into the building, he stopped to read the Wisconsin official marker. It was titled *Pine Was King*. He learned that government-owned acres of virgin white pine were sold to the Knapp, Stout and Company for $1.25 an acre. The company began its logging operation in 1847, and twenty-three years later, the Knapp, Stout and Company was lauded as the "greatest lumber corporation in the world." They continued their success until 1901, when there were no more trees to harvest. Billy looked around—the land was flat with fields of corn; only a few trees stood tall.

Billy went into the restroom and took a sink farthest from the door. He was glad that the facility was clean, and the men who came and went paid him no attention. Before he left, he looked at the tracking app again. Jack was still driving north. Not knowing when Jack and his friend would stop for lunch, Billy bought a candy bar and Coke from the vending machines. He picked up a map from the rack and headed to his car.

CHAPTER | # 26

Jack's cell phone rang. He answered, "What d'you got, Lou?" He listened briefly, then said, "I'm going to put you on speaker so Joe can hear this. He's driving. We'll make Thunder Bay by evening."

Lou agreed to be on speaker, then explained, "We traced the cell phone that Gloriann used to call you. The call originated from Thunder Bay. She must have had to borrow that phone to make the call, so we are guessing she was in a store or something, maybe the Walmart there. The number is part of a family cell phone plan. The account holder is a Kevin Taylor. He works for an insurance company in Des Moines. No criminal records for him or his family. We called his office, and his secretary told us he was on vacation. Checked the Facebook accounts for his teenage daughters and confirmed that they are vacationing in Northern Minnesota and Canada. Unless we need specific information from the daughter with the phone, we are not going to contact."

"Why not?" Joe asked.

"The girls post everything on Facebook. No secrets there. I doubt that even if they were given orders not to disclose the nature of our inquiry, they would be indiscreet. Can't take the chance of Rodney discovering Gloriann's call," Lou answered.

"What's the next step?" Jack asked.

"The RCMP have been updated. Still do not know what type of car they are driving, and they could have changed rides. But we are working on the tapes. We should know soon. Gloriann and Martin must be OK if she was out and about. What are you planning to do?"

"Get to Thunder Bay, drive around, see if Gloriann calls again, wait to hear from you," Jack said. Lou agreed and ended the call.

"So, tell me this, Jack. If we find—when we find—Gloriann and Martin, what are you going to do? Take Martin? Drag Gloriann home? What if she doesn't want to come? Just asking," Joe said.

"She wants me to come get her. That was evident from the call. And, yes, I'm going to take Martin. We are all going back to the States together. And Rodney? He's wanted for fraud. He'll be extradited back to face charges in the Ponzi scheme."

Joe's mind was thinking of the legalities involved, but he did not share his thoughts. As they passed over the Nemadji River, he said, "Jack, do you want to check restaurants near us?"

"Hey, Joe, let's go to Grandma's. I haven't been there in years."

"That's going to put us back. They'll be busy now."

"That's OK. I'll buy you lunch, and afterward, I'll drive. We are not going to be able to do much in Thunder Bay tonight anyway. Might as well enjoy the journey," Jack said.

They began crossing the John A. Blatnik Bridge connecting the Twin Ports of Duluth and Superior, informally referred to as the High Bridge. From about 120 feet up, they looked to their right and saw the vastness of Lake Superior, the largest freshwater lake in the world, then to their left at the St. Louis River, the largest freshwater estuary in North America. "I love living near water," Joe said. "I don't know how you can live in the desert southwest."

"It has its advantages, Joe. No humidity, nice winters, and when the desert blooms, it is indescribably beautiful. The summer is a challenge, but no more of a challenge than the winters here. I guess it's pick your poison."

"I'll stick with up north. Love the winters, love Green Bay, can't leave it." Joe nodded his head. "Watch for signs for Canal Park. I don't want to miss the exit."

Grandma's was busy, but they got lucky and did not have to wait long to get seated in the upstairs pub. They both ordered the same thing: iced tea and chicken salad sandwiches on cranberry-wild rice toast. "Geez, it's hot today. I thought Duluth was the air-conditioned city," complained Joe.

"You know, it usually is cooler. Today is an exception. There are people down in Arizona who are seriously thinking of buying property in Duluth, hedging their bets that it will be one of the most livable areas as climate change heats up the coasts. There's also the water, freshwater, and lots of it. They might be right."

"Well, big brother, come back to the north country. Let your kids get to know their cousins. The folks miss you guys. You can bring Gloriann's parents. Think about it." Joe gave Jack his puppy-eyed look.

"Ah, Joe, just one thing at a time."

As they left the restaurant, they spotted a freighter about a mile from the harbor; Duluth's aerial lift bridge was already making its ascent. When the ship entered the canal, its captain blew the horn in the friendly salute of a long-short-short sequence. Then the bridge operator signaled back in the same way. "Saltie or Laker?" Jack asked.

"She's too big for a Saltie. I bet she's a Laker bringing in limestone and picking up iron-ore pellets," Joe said, pointing at the 1,000-foot-cargo ship flying the American flag.

"Yeah, she'd never fit through the St. Lawrence Seaway," added Jack. "I'd love to stay here longer, but we better hit the road."

CHAPTER | 27

Carol awoke even before Sydney stirred. She did not feel the familiar weight of Jim next to her. She extended her arm and patted his side of the bed. It was empty. She got up and walked through the apartment but did not find him. She looked out the window. The car was gone. He left no note.

She immediately looked for her phone. Jim had taken it once again. "Not an equal partner yet, I guess," she said. Then she panicked, realizing that she hadn't heard Sydney. She ran to the crib, then let out a sigh of relief. The baby was still asleep. She hesitated. Maybe she should call the police. But what if Jim came back before they got there? What if she tried to leave, and he caught her? Before she could come to a decision, she heard his key in the door.

"Jim, you're up early. Where did you go?" Carol asked.

He walked in holding two bakery bags and a cardboard tray with two coffees, shut the door, and headed for the kitchen counter. "Thought I'd do a last coffee run. Tomorrow, we'll get out early and stop on the way." He put the bags on the counter, making a loud thud.

"Sounds like pretty heavy scones there, Jim."

"Did you just get up? Carol, why don't you grab a shower before you get Sydney? Then we'll have breakfast. I'll put the coffee in a thermos."

When Carol was ready and the baby fed, they sat down to eat. Jim had scrambled the last of the eggs and sliced two oranges. He put a scone on each plate and poured the coffee from the thermos. It was still steaming. When they finished their breakfast, Carol pointed at the remaining bag on the counter. "So is that a surprise?" Carol asked.

"Yes, as a matter of fact," Jim said as he got up to retrieve it. He put the bag gently on the table. No thud this time. He put his hand in the bag and pulled out a gun.

Carol gasped. "What is that? Is that a gun, Jim?"

"Yep, it's a Kriss Vector SDP .45 ACP Special Duty Pistol with a thirteen-round magazine," Jim said proudly.

Carol's heart was racing. She thought she would lose her breakfast. She realized she was cradling her face in both hands just like the painting, *The Scream*. Slowly, she lowered her hands, crossed them over her chest, and leaned back in her chair, "Ah, OK, Jim. Why does it look so funny?" she managed to ask.

"What do you mean?"

"Well, it looks like some kind of handsaw or something," Carol said.

Jim turned the gun over. "Yeah, I guess it does. Like a small reciprocating saw."

Carol shook her head. "Whatever. I didn't know guns came in tan."

Jim laughed. "It's not tan. It's called flat, dark earth."

"Dark earth? Where did you get it? I thought handguns were illegal in Canada."

"Well, I got the dark earth Vector on the dark web. There are illegal guns in Canada, and guess where they come from? Yes, the U-S-of-A. So while we have guns being smuggled in over the southern border, Canada has them smuggled in from us. This baby came from Detroit via Windsor all the way to Thunder Bay. Got her at regular price too, about fourteen hundred dollars." Jim was bragging.

Carol could not help herself; she was curious. "I've heard of the dark web, and all I know is that I shouldn't go there. It's supposed to be the underbelly of the web, and it is dangerous. How do you even get to it?"

"It's not hard to do. The surface web, the one you know, uses search engines like Google, Yahoo, or Bing. These search engines take all the available information on the web and index it, so when you type in a search word, they know where to take you. The next layer down is called the deep web."

"I've never heard of that," Carol said.

Jim continued, "Google can take you to the deep web's front door, but to get in, you have to fill out a form, or agree to certain rules, make a payment, that sort of thing. Now the dark web is the wild child of the internet. Its content cannot be indexed, and everything is encrypted so there are no virtual footprints. To get on, all you have to do is download a Tor browser. Then there are no longer dot coms or dot orgs. Everything is dot onion. It's slower but anonymous, and you can find almost anything you want," Jim said, relishing the teacher role.

"Is that how you found the guy to sell us the IDs in Minneapolis?"

"Yep. He was an odd fellow. Called himself Idman. Told me his name was a double entendre: Idman for a man who markets IDs and for a man who follows his id. Must have been some sort of psychology major."

"Was he a student, Jim?" Carol asked. She was concerned.

"Naw, he was an old guy. Probably an original hippie," Jim assured her. He noticed her looking at the gun with interest. "Do you want to hold it?"

"No. No, I don't like guns." Carol was firm.

"Well, you've been around them. I am sure Jack had guns. I think you should overcome your fear, Carol. Someday you may have to use this. You should know how." Jim was bouncing the gun in the palm of his hand.

"OK, someday I will. But for now, would you just put it away? Do you really think that you need to have a gun? That I might need a gun?" Carol asked.

"I'm not going to lie to you. Yes, we need a gun. I am ninety-five percent sure that we will be OK, but that leaves five percent that we might not. The gun gets rid of that five percent. We would be stupid not to prepare for our Toronto contacts. It's insurance, Carol. I'll do whatever I have to do to protect us." Jim then lapsed into silence. Finally, he pushed back his chair and stood up. "OK, that's enough school for today. Let's get packing."

"Looks like you are already packing," Carol quipped.

Jim looked at her and smiled. "You're OK, Carol. More than OK." He walked over, put his arms around her, and kissed her.

CHAPTER | 28

After driving for over two hours, Jack pulled into the parking lot of Naniboujou Lodge. Joe asked, "Do you want me to take over?"

"No, I just want to go in and get some postcards for the kids. I haven't been here in ages, and I want to see it again," Jack explained.

"What? Come on, Jack. We're not that far from the border. We can stop at the park and use the facilities. Let's just go," Joe said and threw up his hands.

Ignoring his brother, Jack got out of the car and started walking toward the lodge. He turned around and jingled the car keys so Joe could see them. Joe was sitting in the passenger seat, arms now crossed over his chest, glaring. Jack greeted the woman at the counter and started to look at the postcards when the door opened, and Joe walked in. Before leaving, both men stopped in the dining room and admired the Cree Native American designs on the walls and two-story-high ceiling. The designs were painted in bold colors: blue, red, golden yellow, lime green.

"See that fireplace?" Jack said to Joe. "I believe it is largest one in the state of Minnesota. "Have you ever seen anything like it?"

"No. The stonework is beautiful," Joe admitted. "There is a plaque by the door that said Naniboujou is on the National Register of Historic Places."

"Yeah, it opened in July of 1929. A private club for the rich and famous. Jack Dempsey and Babe Ruth were some of the first members. Then the stock market crashed later that year, and Naniboujou fell on tough times. Thank goodness people preserved it."

"How come you know so much about it?" Joe asked.

"First time I saw it, I couldn't believe there was something like this in northern Minnesota. It intrigued me, so I read about it." Jack smiled at his brother. "Naniboujou is said to be the great benefactor of the Cree Native Americans. He is revered for his wisdom and gentle spirit," Jack said as he left the lodge and walked back to the car.

Jack got behind the wheel, and Joe settled himself into the passenger seat. "Jack, I didn't mind stopping, but I don't understand. This is not like you. Usually, you are eager to get going, hot on the trail—let's find Gloriann. Seems to me that you are dragging your feet a bit. Is it just that you're tired?"

Jack did not respond.

Joe continued, "Look, we are partners on this. Same squad. I'm just asking you what I would ask any other guy I'm on a case with." Joe waited. When Jack still did not speak, he asked, "Are you afraid that you won't find Gloriann, or are you afraid that you will? I get it that you don't know how this is all going to play out, but what is still holding you back?"

Jack sighed. "Did you ever wonder why they don't let cops work on cases involving family or friends? I mean really wonder? I always thought it shortsighted. We are professionals. We have a vested interest, an interest that I thought of as an impetus, not a hindrance. Well, I was wrong. Maybe some guys can keep a clear head and detach, but I can't, no matter how hard I try. I want to have an answer before I proceed. I need clarity. What's the endgame?"

Joe thought about what Jack said before answering, "Yeah, I get that. But here is a reality check—you won't know what the endgame will be in this case until you find Gloriann. Period. You can take more time, but that is not going to change anything. You still will not know. So my best advice to you is do not overthink this. Just focus on finding Gloriann and Martin."

Jack nodded, but his physical assent did nothing to dissipate the tension in the car. Within forty-five minutes, they arrived at the border crossing, joining a long line of cars inching forward. Thankfully, the line kept moving, only stopping momentarily as each driver was interviewed at the booth after producing identification. No one was detained. Jack and Joe were eager to get back on the open road, but after their visit with border patrol, they were told to pull the car over to the side.

They did as they were told and waited, windows down, hands visible on the steering wheel and dash. An armed CBP agent stood in front of the car, and another came to the window. "Your last name has been flagged in our system. Do you know anything about that?"

"Yes, sir. My wife, Gloriann Jurlik, is the subject of a BOLO. My brother and I are driving to Thunder Bay on a hunch that she might be there." The agent looked doubtful. Jack continued, "I'm an FBI agent on leave. My brother is a police officer in Green Bay."

"Are you here in any law enforcement capacity? You didn't show creds."

"No. We are here as personal representatives of our family. No official capacity."

"May I see your creds?"

Joe said, "They are in our pockets. Should we get them, or do you want us to get out of the car?"

"Keep one hand visible and pull out your wallets," the agent instructed. Joe handed over his law enforcement ID, and Jack said, "I had to hand in mine when I took a leave of absence."

"OK, we are going to do a quick search of your car while we make the necessary calls. Due diligence, you understand." The agent took a relaxed stance.

"No problem," Jack said. They got out of the car and stood by the side of the road. People who had just left the border crossing were slowing to look at them as one of the agents searched the car and trunk. "Smile. We're on the perp parade," Jack whispered to Joe. Suddenly, within Joe arose the threat of a full-blown laughing fit. He clamped his lips shut and could feel the pressure building in his throat and cheeks. Jack looked over at Joe and was contaminated by the same hilarity.

"All ready to go. Thank you for your cooperation and patience. I hope you find your wife," the CBP agent said.

Jack's vocal cords were so taut from trying not to laugh they hurt when he responded, "Yes, thank you." As soon as Jack and Joe were out of sight of the border crossing, their laughter erupted. Tears were running down their faces, and Joe had doubled over, holding his stomach. Every time they tried to quiet themselves, they failed. Jack was the first one to catch his breath. "Oh, Lord, I haven't laughed like that since we were kids."

"And Mom found the fart jar," said Joe, starting to hoot all over again.

"Joe, stop. I can't take it. I'll be sick," pleaded Jack.

It took a minute for both men to breathe normally. They had been panting as if they had just finished a 220-yard dash. "Good thing we didn't bring the guns. Can you imagine?" Joe broke the silence.

"It would have been bad. That's for sure," Jack said. "Why don't you look for a hotel near the Walmart in Thunder Bay. We'll get settled, grab some food, make plans, hit the sack early. Tomorrow, we'll drive around the parking lots and look at license plates, inquire at hotels. Maybe Lou will call with a lead."

"Are we contacting the locals?"

"Right now, no. Let's get the lay of the land first. See if we find anything," Jack answered.

"Ah, Jack, there are three Walmarts in Thunder Bay. Which one do you want me to choose? Joe asked.

"Three! Damn. Three? Lou didn't tell me which one."

"Maybe there's a reason for that," Joe offered.

"No. I'm going to call her. I can't believe she would purposely not tell me," Jack said as he pulled the car over and connected to Lou's cell. After Lou told him the location of the Walmart, he asked, "Is there anything else I should know?"

"Not that I can speak of," she replied.

When the call ended, Joe said, "I heard her. Nothing she can speak of? Does that mean she knows, but she can't say, or she doesn't know anything new?"

"Yeah, I'm beginning to wonder how much they are not telling me." Jack sighed. "She said the Walmart was just off the Thunder Bay Expressway and Dawson Road 102. What hotels are near there?"

"Quite a few," Joe said as he began to list them for his brother.

"Where's the police station?"

Joe was working his phone. "Balmoral Street, not far from the Holiday Inn Express."

"Let's try that," Jack said.

Once in the room, they ordered in pizza and spent the rest of the evening doing research on extended-stay accommodations and pouring over the map of Thunder Bay. Joe had picked up *Thunder Bay Experience—The Event Issue* from the rack in the lobby. "You know, Jack," he said, "there's a ton of stuff to do here. Someday I'm going to bring the family."

CHAPTER | 29

Billy kept checking his tracker. When he saw that Jack's car was not moving, he realized that Jack must have stopped to eat lunch. The car was in Duluth, just across the bridge. Luckily, there was one more exit before he would commit himself to I-535 and the river crossing. He found a nearby bar and grill in Superior and ordered a hamburger and fries. He wanted a beer but thought better of it. While waiting for his order, he took out his phone and researched border-crossing tips.

He had already taken care of the first one: he was clean-shaven, dressed in a shirt with a collar, and looked unremarkable and risk-free. He would need to tidy up the car, making sure nothing was lying on the floor, and dispose of any opened bags of food. He knew to be polite to the border guards, to stay calm and answer plainly. Driving at the correct speed, not too slow or too fast, up to the checkpoint was one tip he had not considered. Another, "Don't bring oranges," made him laugh. *No, no oranges. Just the gun in the trunk,* he thought, grinning.

He looked around the bar, and sobering thoughts overshadowed him. He would have to show his passport. What if his name triggered an alert warning? What if the guards searched his car? No, there was nothing he could do now except play the game and hope for the best.

He would not come up with plan B; he would not send plan B out to the universe. "I can do this. I am doing this. I am being successful," became his mantra.

The burger was juicy, and the fries hot. He finished off another Coke. Jack's car was on the move again. Billy waited fifteen minutes, left a tip, paid the bill in cash, and walked out to the parking lot to clean up his car. Driving north on Hwy 61, he got the alert that Jack's car stopped again. "What's with this guy? Why doesn't he just drive?" Billy was irritated. His anxiety to get the border crossing behind him was hard to shake off. He looked again at the map on his phone. He had just passed Beaver Bay and was about thirty minutes behind Jack. He decided that if Jack did not move soon, he would stop in Schroeder and have a look around.

When Billy's phone alerted again that Jack had been stopped at the border, his stomach clenched, and he could not catch his breath. "I can do this. I am doing this. I am being successful," he said out loud. He repeated it several more times, but hearing his own voice did nothing to dispel the one in his head: *Who are you kidding? This isn't going to work. You messed up. You're a dead man.* He shook his head. "No. I can do this. I am doing this. I am being successful. I'm going to stop at the state park and wait. You don't know a damn thing. I can do this." He was passionate in his rebuttal, then felt sheepish for arguing with himself.

At Grand Portage State Park, he went to the restroom, washed his face, and brushed his teeth. When he was alone before the mirror, he practiced a relaxed, friendly look. That exercise gave him confidence. He stood up straight and visualized a successful crossing. As he walked back to his car, he intoned his mantra one more time. He was ready.

Billy lingered behind several cars until it was his turn to drive up to the booth. He read the signs, looked at the scenery, checked his rearview mirror—all to distract himself from what was coming. When the car in front of him left the check-in booth, he looked straight ahead, drove at the expected speed, and ignored the cameras along the way. The border agent proved matter-of-fact and professional, and Billy acquiesced to his authority. He was asked to produce the car's registration, then explain why he had just purchased it. He did not change his demeanor when asked about mace, a handgun, or a stun gun and casually answered no to each one. Finally, he was told to have a nice trip and to drive safely. He drove away controlling the impulse to punch the accelerator and beep the horn in triumph. Once he was safely out of view of the border, he took a quick peek at his tracker.

Jack's car was moving around Thunder Bay. Guessing that Jack was looking for a place to stay, Billy decided that he would also spend the night there. This time, however, he would relax at a hotel, confident that using his credit card would not put him in danger. He was not on anyone's radar yet since he had not been stopped at the border. Billy waited until he was on the outskirts of Thunder Bay to pull over and use his phone. He just had to talk to Austin.

"What's up?" Austin asked.

"Hey, where are you?" Billy answered.

"Wichita. Decided to take my time going back. Stop and see the sights that I never had time for when I was driving truck."

"Where are you going next?" Billy asked.

"Tomorrow night, I'll be in Tucumcari; Monday night in Flagstaff; home on Tuesday. I'll drop your car off Tuesday," Austin explained, "so you'd better call your parents before then."

"Definitely will. No worries there. I'm tracking Rod's friend, and I've got this feeling that I'll find Rod real soon. It is sort of fun, Austin. I'm even thinking that when this is over, I'm going to become a professional bounty hunter. No kidding. I'm giving it some serious thought."

"You are just going to talk to him when you find him, right?"

"Yeah, yeah, I guess so."

"You guess so?" Austin's voice rose with alarm. "Don't get ahead of yourself, Billy."

"Nah, you worry too much, Austin. All's good," Billy assured him. "Hey, I gotta run though. Got to get a room yet. Get some sleep." Billy looked at the tracker. Jack was still on the move in Thunder Bay. "Oh geez, when is this guy going to stop?" Billy asked out loud. Tired of waiting for Jack to decide, he researched hotels in Thunder Bay and chose an inn on Dawson Road because it was farther out than the others and close to a Walmart if he needed anything. He was confident that Jack would not notice him before he found Rod.

CHAPTER 30

SUNDAY, SEPTEMBER 24

It was still dark when Jack awoke. He turned over in bed to reach for his phone, thinking he could put it under the covers to see the screen, so as not to disturb Joe.

"Are you up, Jack?" a raspy-voiced Joe asked.

"Yeah. I can't sleep anymore."

"Me neither. What time is it?"

"Five ten. Do you want to get moving?"

Joe switched on the light next to his bed and sat up. "Just let me use the bathroom. Then you can take your shower first."

By 5:40 a.m., both men were showered, shaved, and packed. Jack collected Joe's room key, and Joe put a tip on the desk before they headed out the door. As Jack dropped the keys at the front desk, Joe said, "Let's get the coffee here and look for a doughnut somewhere else."

"OK. You got our itinerary for today?"

Joe held up his phone. "All ready to go."

Billy's phone alerted him awake. "Shit," he said as he realized that Jack was on the move. Luckily, he had showered and packed the night before. In a frenzy, he got himself dressed, hair combed, teeth brushed, and in his car within fifteen minutes. His heart was pounding so fast he thought he might faint. Jack had left the Holiday Inn Express and stopped at a bakery near the police station.

"Are you kidding me?" Billy asked the empty car. Wanting something to eat, he drove to Walmart, hoping they were open. If not, he'd have to be satisfied with the warm can of Coke and the bag of chips he left in the car. He pulled in and parked.

Jack was wiping the sugar off his face when his phone rang. He picked up the phone and looked at Joe. "It's Dad." Joe put down his coffee and turned to Jack, concern overshadowing his face. Jack put the phone on speaker and said, "Hey, Dad! Everything all right? Little early for you. Kids all right? Everybody OK?"

Pete responded quickly. "Yes. Everyone is fine. Look, I have something to tell you. Couldn't sleep and figured you are an hour ahead, so I'd give you a ring. It may be nothing. Probably is nothing ..."

"Dad, just tell us. We are both listening."

"OK. Elizabeth and Carl came in yesterday. Nice people. Kids were excited to see them. They brought the kids' stuff. We had a nice time."

"Dad, you didn't call us this early to tell us you had a nice time," Joe said.

"No. Later in the evening, when we were alone with Elizabeth and Carl, she said she had a newspaper clipping to show us. She had a short article from the Minneapolis paper about a dead body that was found in an old, abandoned silo near the University of Minnesota campus. The deceased was not identified, but the article said that police think it was a student whom they suspect was a purveyor of false IDs. Estimated day of death was when Gloriann was probably in the area. Elizabeth thought you should know. I would have called last night, but it was getting late and—"

Jack interrupted, "Dad, did Elizabeth say if she called the police?"

"She didn't call anyone. She thought she would give the article to you, and you could decide what to do with it. Do you think this has anything to do with Gloriann? I can't imagine, but it scares me."

"Dad, I got a text that I need to take. I'm sorry. Don't worry. I'll get back to you soon." Jack ended the call and read the text aloud, "Walmart."

"Should I call it in, Jack?" Joe asked.

"Not yet."

"Then when?" Joe asked. His anxiety was growing.

"I'll know when we get there," Jack said as he started up the car.

"What if it's not the same Walmart?" Joe asked.

"We'll know when we get there," Jack repeated as he picked up speed.

Billy's phone alerted. Jack was just turning north on Oliver Road. "Where's he going?" Billy asked himself. Several cars were now entering the Walmart parking lot. As he alternated between looking at Jack's movements and people getting out of their cars, he was jolted by what he saw—two people were exiting a car with Minnesota plates. The woman waited for the man, who was leaning into the back passenger seat. When the man emerged, he was holding a baby. It was Rod!

Billy looked down at the phone. "Shit! Damn it!" He dropped the phone, leaned over to grab his gun from under the front seat, opened the car door, tucked the gun into his waistband, and ran toward Rod and the woman. He was nearing them when they were halfway between the car and the store. "Rod! Rodney Wilter!" he yelled.

When Rod turned, he saw a red-haired man who looked like someone he knew, but he just couldn't place him. As Billy strode nearer, Rod made the connection. "Billy? What... what are you doing here?"

Billy was confident. "Hey, Rod, I've been looking for you. You're my ticket to freedom."

"What?" Rod's eyes narrowed as he stared at Billy. "What are you talking about?"

Billy laughed. "Ever hear of a bounty hunter, Rod? That's what I am now, I'm a bounty hunter, and I'm here to take you in."

"Billy, have you lost your frickin' mind? I'm not going to go anywhere with you, and if you're smart, you are going to come with us right now and get the hell out of here. Just come with us, and you'll be fine. We are going to get back in the car, and you are going to get into your car and follow us out of town," Rod said with calm determination.

"Not going to happen, Rod," Billy said, pulling the gun out of his waistband and pointing it at Rod.

"So what? Now you are going to shoot a baby?" Rod said, holding up Martin as a shield.

Gloriann's mouth dropped open. She wanted to scream, to reach for Martin, but she could not move; she was paralyzed.

"Rod don't screw with me. Jack's coming. I've got backup. It'll go better for you if you come with me." Billy's voice was loud and forceful, but his hand was beginning to shake.

PART IV

CHAPTER | 31

Jack pulled into the Walmart parking lot, mulling over what he would do if he encountered Gloriann. How would he approach her? Would Rodney put up a fight? Joe was methodically scanning the lot. Suddenly, he grabbed Jack's forearm with one hand and pointed out the window with the other, "Look! Isn't that Gloriann?"

Jack's eyes widened. He was horrified with the scene unfolding in front of him—Rodney holding Martin; Billy pointing a gun; Gloriann planted where she stood. He stopped the car far enough away to approach Billy from behind. He knew he couldn't wait for backup. Opening the car door, he started to say, "Call for backup," but didn't finish the sentence. Joe was already speaking into his phone.

Jack walked at an angle toward Billy, keeping his eye on the gun and assessing Rodney. He thought of the conversation that he just had with his father. While still twenty yards away, he heard Billy say to Rod that Jack was his backup, and he knew that if Rod was a murderer, Billy had just entered shark-infested waters.

"Jack!" Gloriann called out to him. She looked like she would break ranks and run to him, but the bond with Martin held her in terrorized indecision.

215

When Billy turned his head to glance in the direction of Gloriann's gaze, Rodney flung the baby at Gloriann. She tried to catch Martin, but he slipped from her arms. She caught him by the hand, jerking his body to a halt before he hit the blacktop. Martin began shrieking, not just baby cries of distress but piercing screams of pain.

Billy reeled to face Rod, but it was too late. Rod was upon him, trying to wrench the gun away from him. The two men were swearing as they jostled each other, each holding on to the gun. They fell to the ground entangled together like two wrestling bear cubs.

Jack ran toward Gloriann. He could hear the sirens of approaching police cars getting louder, Martin's unrelenting cries, Gloriann gulping for air, the gun going off once, then again. He reached Gloriann and stood between her and the heap of men on the ground. Rodney was on top, blood diffusing to cover the lower back of his shirt, Billy was pinned beneath him, blood coming from his thigh. Neither moved. Jack could not see the gun or their hands.

Jack looked back at Gloriann. Joe was already there, ushering her and the few onlookers away. Keeping his arm around Gloriann's shoulder, Joe herded everyone toward the store. He yelled to his brother, "Jack, you can't help those two anymore. Leave it to the locals."

But Jack couldn't leave it. He was drawn to Billy and Rodney as a moth to the fire. He didn't think they were alive, but if they were, they needed help. He walked to Rodney and, leaning over, put two fingers on Rodney's neck. There was no pulse. Then he startled when he heard a strained voice say, "Get him off me. I can't breathe." Jack's heart began to race. He had no bulletproof vest, no gun, no backup, no nothing.

"Where's the gun, Billy?"

"I can't. I can't breathe, Jack."

"Where's the frickin' gun, Billy?"

Billy's breathing was labored. "I, I don't know. It's between us, somewhere between us."

"Oh shit."

"Jack, please. I don't have the gun. Please."

"All right, Billy. If you find the gun, don't touch it. Slide both your arms out to the side where I can see them. I'll lift Rodney just a bit to help you. Make a wrong move, and I'll, I'll… just don't do anything stupid, Billy," Jack said as he straddled Rodney, grabbed him under the armpits, and strained to lift his dead weight. Billy managed to free his arms and put them out as if he were making a snow angel. Jack jerked Rodney up and dropped him facedown not far from Billy's right arm.

There was the gun, lying on Billy's abdomen just below his belt. "Don't move, Billy. Just breathe. Take slow, deep breaths." The wound in Billy's thigh was bleeding more heavily now that the weight of Rodney was not compressing it. "Billy, I have to put a tourniquet on your thigh, or you are going to bleed out." Billy's chest was heaving up and down, his breathing labored; he did not answer Jack or move. Jack took off his belt, knelt, and began to fasten the belt around Billy's upper thigh. He was tightening it when he saw the police cruisers speed into the parking lot.

He looked at the gun again but wasn't going to risk touching it; the scenarios of all that could go wrong flashed through his mind. "God, help me!" Jack said out loud and immediately realized what he needed to do. He knelt, straddling Billy's chest but not resting on it, the gun directly behind him. Facing the incoming squads, Jack said, "Billy, let me take your arms." Billy groaned as Jack took hold of Billy's two wrists and raised them in the air so the approaching squads could see all four hands clearly. Then he waited.

Two squads and an unmarked pulled up close to Jack, an ambulance not far behind. Two more squads raced to the front of the store. Four officers approached Jack with guns drawn. There was a momentary standoff. It was at times like these that Jack often had humorous thoughts come to him: *I bet they don't know what to do. They can't say, "Police! Put your hands up!"* He wanted to smile but didn't. Instead, he called out to them first. "I'm Jack Jurlik. Off-duty FBI. Rodney over there is dead. Billy here is critically wounded. Neither of us are armed."

They lowered their guns and started to approach. Two detectives got out of the unmarked and began walking toward them. Jack knew then that the FBI had been working with the Thunder Bay police. He let out a sigh of relief. He held his position, and when they were close enough to touch him, he said, "The murder weapon is right behind me on top of Billy. We didn't move it. I couldn't wait for you to get here. He was bleeding. I had to help."

"Don't you move until we bag it," an irritated officer said.

"I'm sorry I didn't tell you about the gun. I was afraid. I didn't know how you'd react," Jack said simply.

"You can stand up now." Two officers took Billy's arms and lowered them, while two others helped Jack to his feet. EMTs started working on Billy, while one of the detectives squatted to put evidence bags over Billy's hands and secure them with a flex cuff.

"Gunshot residue?" Jack asked, even though he knew the answer and knew he shouldn't ask. He couldn't help slipping back into his FBI role.

The detective didn't answer but the EMT did, "Yeah. We'll take samples in the ambulance. May not help, but just in case. If we don't bag 'em, they won't run the test."

"Makes sense," Jack said, although he wondered if it would make a difference. Both Billy and Rodney would have GSR on them because of where the gun was when it discharged not once but twice. He was guessing that the shooter might have more residue on his hands, but then again, maybe not. Testing was the prudent thing to do though—cross all the Ts.

Billy, now on the gurney, was loaded into the ambulance. An officer jumped in after Billy was secured, and the ambulance sped away, lights flashing, siren screaming. The detective stood up and turned to Jack. "Let me see your ID." After he looked at it and was satisfied, he gave it back to Jack. "OK. Follow me. We need to clear this area." Jack did as he was told. When they were well behind the squad cars, the man said, "Are you armed?"

"No!"

"OK. Up against the car. I want to make sure." When the man finished, he said, "I am Inspector Emile Tremblay. I have a few quick questions for you. How is it that you knew Gloriann was here?"

"My brother and I were eating doughnuts when my father called. During his call, I got a text, and all it said was 'Walmart.' I figured it had to be Gloriann because I'm sure it was her who called me on Friday night. I never got a chance to speak, but I recognized her voice, and the call was traced to an area near here."

"And when you got today's text, you did not call it in?"

"No. I thought it was this Walmart, but I wasn't sure. I wanted to be sure. As soon as we got here, we saw them, and Joe called it in. It was instantaneous. We could see that Billy was pointing a gun at Rodney, and Rodney was holding up the baby as a shield. I couldn't wait for you to arrive."

Inspector Tremblay nodded. "Did you know Billy was here?"

"I didn't. That was a complete surprise."

"All right," Tremblay said as he listened to something in his earpiece. "We'll need your witness statement. But first, your son needs your attention," explained Tremblay. "You are lucky that the FBI gave us advance warning about you and your personal involvement. They vouched for you to take custody of Martin, and the State Department has given the go-ahead. Martin appears to have suffered an injury to his arm but does not need an ambulance. You'll have to take him to the ER." He took a card out of his pocket and gave it to Jack. "Keep us posted on his progress and report in person to the station when he has been released."

"I don't have a card with me. I can give you my information," Jack offered.

"We already have it and your brother's. Joe has Martin. They are waiting for you in the store." Tremblay jerked his head toward the entrance. Jack waited. "You can go now, Jack. Keep me posted."

Jack began his sprint toward the store. He saw that the crime scene was already secured, Rodney's body hidden by a tent. When Jack entered Walmart, two officers were waiting for him. They escorted him past a gathering of onlookers to a more secluded area near the exit doors. Joe was sitting on a chair, cradling a sleeping Martin. Gloriann was not there.

Joe's eyes welled with tears at the sight of his brother. His relief was palpable. Then he scanned Jack's body, beginning with Jack's face, but he stopped when he got to Jack's waist and legs. His face registered alarm, and he gave Jack a questioning look.

Jack looked down at his clothes. His lower shirt was spattered with blood, and his slacks were heavy with blood from the knees down. The sight stunned him until he realized that his clothes were stained because he had moved Rodney's body and then knelt in blood while aiding Billy. "I'm OK, Joe. I'm OK," Jack reassured him. He started to walk toward Joe, but before he could, officers intercepted him and began to brief him on the situation.

They told him that Martin had been evaluated by the EMTs, who decided that he might have a fractured arm or dislocated elbow. They felt that Jack could safely transport him to the ER. "Did they give him something for pain? Why is he so quiet?" Jack asked.

"No. The baby is just exhausted. Infants will do that. They'll just fall asleep until they are moved and the pain returns," the officer explained. He told him where the hospital was located, and that Jack would just have to wait for service as in any emergency room in the US. "They triage patients as they come in. If you don't need immediate care, you'll have to wait until it is your turn. First come, first served, unless you have a life-threatening emergency; then you go to the front of the line." Jack nodded. He'd been in ERs before and knew the drill.

"The baby will need to eat. Where is Gloriann?" Jack asked, looking around.

"Gloriann is being transported to the station."

Jack knew she would be but hearing it in real time unnerved him. "For questioning?" Jack asked.

"Yes. You'll be given an update when you get to the station. You don't have to hurry; she'll be there whenever you arrive. Take care of your boy. But first, you'll have to change your clothes. You'll scare the heck out of people looking like that. Besides, we need to bag them. Crime scene evidence."

Jack nodded. "I'll have to get my clothes from the car," he said.

"No. There are clothes for you in the restroom, compliments of Walmart. Your brother told us your sizes. Come on. Let's go," the officer said, pointing in the direction of the men's room.

As Jack was changing clothes and cleaning up, he said to the officer, "You know Gloriann was nursing Martin. I don't even know if she'd have formula with her. Maybe she did. There must be a diaper bag. If he's hungry now, what am I going to do?"

The officer sighed. He felt for Jack; what a rotten situation! "Jack, Walmart also is donating a car seat, diapers, and ready-to-feed formula. If there is other feeding equipment you need, the hospital should be able to help with that until you figure it out."

"Thanks," Jack said.

"Some of the customers who saw Joe with Martin wanted to help. They bought a bunch of baby clothes. *Boy's* clothes. Baby detergent too. The ladies wanted me to tell you to make sure you wash the clothes before you use them." The officer smiled at Jack.

Jack found it hard to respond. He nodded his head, bent over the sink, and fought the tears. When he gained control of himself, he held on to the sides of the sink and raised his head to look into the mirror. He glanced at the officer, who was busying himself with the evidence bag, his back toward Jack to afford Jack privacy. "Thanks. Thank you so much," Jack said as the officer turned to face him. Jack continued, "The kindness of these strangers—it is just overwhelming. Hard to believe how they just stepped up and helped. I'll never forget their kindness. Good people. Thank God for good people!"

"Yes. Thank God for good people. Ready?" the officer asked.

"Yeah. Yeah, I am."

As they walked, the officer told Jack that one of the Walmart staff, a new dad himself, installed the car-seat base in Joe's car and put the other purchases in the trunk. "Stop by the crime scene and let them know you are on your way to the hospital. They can give you the diaper bag from Rodney's car. That's the store manager next to Joe."

Jack walked over to the store manager and extended his hand. "Thank you. I'm so grateful. Words can't express …"

"You are very welcome. It was the least we could do. We hope it all works out for your family and that the baby is OK," the manager said, looking down at Martin resting in the car seat next to Joe's feet.

Joe stood and hefted Martin's car seat up by the handle, being careful not to jostle it. Jack and Joe said their goodbyes, then smiled and waved at the onlookers and mouthed, "Thank you," before exiting the store.

"I'll drive. You can sit in the back with Martin," Joe said to his brother.

"Those people were so kind, Joe. They touched my heart. I wish Gloriann could have seen the support they offered."

"Well, she did see it until the cops cuffed her. Then their concern and pity turned to astonishment and anger. You could see it in their faces. She was aware of the transformation. Public opinion is not on her side," Joe said. "You can't blame them for their reaction though." Joe paused, then added, "Hey, let's not think about it, Jack. We've got to get Martin to the ER."

CHAPTER 32

When they entered the emergency room, Jack smiled at Joe. "I think we lucked out, brother."

"Unless all the beds in the back are full," Joe said, shrugging his shoulders.

"Listen, if you don't want to wait with me, you can go back to the hotel, and I'll call you when I'm done."

"No. I want to stay, Jack. I'm not complaining. I'm just stating the obvious. We still might have a wait ahead of us. Besides, we checked out of the hotel."

"Ugh! You're right. Damn. Hey, I'm glad you're staying though. I really didn't want to wait alone. I'll go register; you can have a seat." Jack walked to the registration window and explained his situation. The woman behind the desk was both professional and sympathetic. She assured him that a triage nurse would be with him shortly to assess Martin. She also inquired as to how he wanted to handle the bill, explaining that the cost would be at least $825 which included $650 for hospital costs and $175 for the physician's assessment. Any tests or equipment would be extra. Jack assured her that he could pay by credit card but needed a detailed bill for reimbursement from his American health insurance. He was also asked to sign a waiver, which stated that any malpractice suit that he might initiate would be filed in Canada rather than in the United States, as this helped doctors avoid costly legal action in the US. Jack finished the paperwork and went back to sit next to Joe. That's when the triage nurse greeted him and led him and Martin through the doors to the emergency treatment area.

They entered a small room with three chairs: two for patients and one for the nurse who was seated in front of a computer. As they discussed Martin's situation, he started to squirm. He was furiously sucking on his pacifier. Then, opening his eyes, he spit it out and began to scream. "What should I do? Should I pick him up? I don't want to hurt him. I know he's hungry." Jack's voice was pleading.

"Just leave him there for a minute. I need to check something," she said as she left the room.

Jack bent down and tried to soothe Martin. Talking softly and stroking Martin's legs, Jack was able to get the pacifier back into the baby's mouth. Martin began to suck, and Jack thought of how his father always called pacifiers "foolers." Jack knew that it would not fool Martin much longer.

The nurse came back and led him to another room, this one bigger with more medical equipment. Jack placed the car seat on the exam table. Cyril, the second triage nurse, was ready to help him. He told Jack that he had called pediatrics, and they were bringing down a bottle and diapers. Jack thought of the diaper bag that he had left in the car and wished he had remembered to bring it in. Cyril asked Jack to explain exactly what had happened to Martin. When he finished, Cyril said, "Let's have a look at this little guy."

Martin was screaming again. Still, Cyril took his temperature, listened to his heart, and pressed on his abdomen. He unbuckled the car seat and touched Martin's arm. The screams intensified. Jack's heart was racing, and sweat was breaking out on his face. Cyril looked at Jack and said, "I know it is hard to hear him scream like this, but he was quiet before, and that's a good sign. Once we get him fed, he should be better, and we can evaluate his arm. I'm going to wrap it next to his body to immobilize it. As soon as the bottle gets here, you can feed him."

"He's never had a bottle before. My wife was breastfeeding him," Jack said.

"He'll take the bottle. He's too hungry to refuse it," Cyril said. He took Martin out of the car seat and laid him on the exam table. Once he had secured Martin's arm, he handed him to Jack. A nursing assistant walked in with the bottle and burp cloth.

At first, Martin gripped the nipple in his mouth and shook it like a dog with a rag. He settled after that and sucked greedily. Jack held the bottle up at an angle so Martin would not gulp down air. As Martin continued to feed, Jack relaxed. He savored the warmth and softness of Martin's body, his infant hands, his big eyes, the little noises he made as he ate. When he had drained the bottle, Jack laid him against his shoulder and, rubbing Martin's back, coaxed out a burp.

"Whoa! Now that's a burp! Feeling better, Martin?" Jack cooed as he laid Martin down on the exam table. Martin grinned, and Jack smiled back. As Martin's grin grew, so did Jack's smile. Jack started to cluck his tongue, and Martin's face lit with delight. That's when Cyril reentered the room.

"I see he is doing much better. Let's get him changed, and then you can take him back to the waiting room. Someone from x-ray will come to get you."

"Cyril, I'm worried about feeding him. Walmart gave me formula, but I don't know what to do about bottles. It's been five years since the last baby, and Gloriann did not wean the kids until they were six months old. I've never fed a baby this young," Jack said.

"Jack, I know you are concerned, but don't worry. Someone from the nursery is coming down to talk with you. She'll meet you in the waiting room. You can have a seat back there. Why don't you put Martin back in the carrier and follow me?"

Joe looked up from his phone. "All done already?"

"No. Martin needs an x-ray, but he's fed and changed," Jack explained as he picked up Martin and held him on his lap.

"I could hear him screaming."

"Yeah, he was hungry. He's OK though. It's his arm. Hence the x-ray," explained Jack.

"You'll be happy to know I got us a room at the Hampton Inn. It's a suite: two queen beds, bar sink, microwave, and mini fridge. Should make things easier with Martin. They'll have a portable crib in the room for us, and I got an early check-in." Joe beamed.

"Thank you. Did you have a chance to call anyone?" Jack asked.

"Yeah, I called Tessa and told her just the basics—Gloriann and the baby are OK; Rodney was shot in an altercation with Billy; Gloriann is being held for questioning; and you have Martin. She'll let the folks know, and she'll call Mel."

"Good. Thanks, Joe."

"Jack Jurlik?" a young woman in scrubs inquired.

"Yes."

"I'm from pediatrics. Do you mind if I talk to you right here?" she asked, looking at Joe.

"No problem. This is my brother Joe. He can stay and listen."

She nodded and pulled up a seat across from the two men. "I brought you some samples that should hold you over until you can get to a store tonight or tomorrow. These are microwave sanitizing bags." Joe and Jack looked at each other and shrugged their shoulders. Then they looked back at her with keen interest.

She chuckled. "OK. This is simple. You can add tap water to the bag, put in the nipples, and microwave them. They'll be sanitized. The instructions are on the package. Here's a bag with two bottles, two nipples, and extra bottle liners. The bottles and nipples are already clean and ready to use. Do you have formula?"

"Yes," Jack replied. "Walmart gave us a case of ready-to-feed formula."

"Good. When you get back to the States, you may not find the exact same brand of formula. So just buy some and see if the baby likes it. If not, try another brand. Do you know how to warm the formula?"

"Yes," both men replied this time. Jack continued, "I just didn't know how much I had to sanitize things with a baby this young."

"You can use a dishwasher to sanitize the bottles and nipples. Or even wash them in hot, soapy water and let them air-dry. Unless you are worried about the water source, if it's other than city water, then you would have to keep sanitizing the equipment. You'll do fine. Contact your pediatrician when you get home." She stood up to leave. "Good luck. He sure is a cute little guy."

Jack waited another fifteen minutes before x-ray summoned them. Leaving the car seat behind, Jack carried Martin and followed the x-ray technologist. Martin didn't seem to mind the cold, hard x-ray table or the tech gently unwrapping his arm and positioning it. Jack was asked to put on a lead apron and instructed as to where to hold Martin to keep him from moving. Then the tech went behind a wall with a window and activated the x-ray machine. He came out and repositioned Martin and took another x-ray. He told Jack to keep holding Martin in that position until he could check the x-rays for clarity. When the tech was satisfied, he came out and wrapped Martin's arm so it wouldn't move and told Jack that he would take them back to the waiting room. A radiologist would read the x-ray and send the results to the ER doctor.

Within a half hour, Jack and Martin were again summoned, this time to see the doctor. "Good news," the doctor announced when they walked into the exam room. "Martin does not have a broken arm. No fractures. He has what is commonly called *nursemaid's elbow*."

"What is that? Can you fix it?" Jack asked.

"Oh, yes," the doctor said as he unwrapped Martin's arm, shushing Martin to calm his beginning cries. He gently felt Martin's arm and hand. "In babies and young children, the ligaments that hold joints together are looser and only tighten as the child ages. Nursemaid's elbow is when a ligament gets caught between the two elbow bones. Martin's arm and hand are warm, not cold. If I pinch them, he doesn't like it, so they are not numb. That tells me that his elbow has not trapped any blood vessels or nerves. The x-ray shows a simple dislocation. There's no avulsion fracture, which sometimes happens when a torn ligament pulls off a tiny bit of bone from where it was attached."

"Did this happen when he fell, and my wife caught him by the arm?" Jack asked.

"I would think so. It can be caused by jerking the arm or swinging a toddler by their hands."

Jack winced. He'd done that with his two older kids. Even he and Joe would swing their younger brother, Ted, as high as they could. "It doesn't always happen though," Jack said.

"No. All kids are different. It's not a good idea to swing kids by their hands. I know a lot of people do it. It can happen with something as simple as pulling an arm though a sleeve. The good news though is that we can fix it, although Martin is not going to like it. You have to help. Are you going to be OK if he screams?"

"What are you going to do to him?" Jack was alarmed.

"I'm just going to gently put his elbow back in place. The procedure is called a reduction. It only takes a few seconds. Then we'll give him some infant Tylenol and put an elbow immobilizing splint on his arm, so the ligament doesn't slip out again. He'll have to wear the splint for two weeks. You can remove it to dress or bathe him; it has Velcro strips. Just be careful to not twist or jerk his arm."

Jack nodded. The doctor instructed Jack to sit on a chair and hold Martin in his lap. He took Martin's arm, straightened it, and bent it upward. Martin did scream. Then the doctor brought Martin's arm back down and, keeping it straight, turned Martin's palm toward the floor. Martin screamed again, but soon his cries subsided to cries of protest, not pain.

"He did very well, and so did you," the doctor said. "I'll just get that splint on, and then the nurse will come in with the Tylenol for Martin and discharge papers for you. She will give you instructions and the number to call if you have any questions. Billing will help you settle your account. Then you can be on your way."

Soon Jack was back in the waiting room. "We're good to go, Joe," a relieved Jack told him.

"Cute splint. What's the story?" Joe started to put away his phone and pick up the car seat.

"I'll tell you in the car. Now that he's going to be OK, I need to go to the police station once we are settled," Jack informed him. Martin fell asleep in the car and did not awaken until the contents from the trunk were in the hotel room. Then he began to cry and would not take the "fooler" this time.

"You change him, Jack, and I'll get the bottle ready," Joe said as he began to rummage through the bags on the bed. When he had prepared the bottle, he said, "OK, now give him to me. You go to the station and let them finish their reports. I can hold the fort."

"Thanks, Joe," Jack said as he handed over the baby. Before he opened the door to leave, Jack looked back at his brother and Martin. A tinge of jealousy stung him—Joe was a natural at infant care, much better at it than he. Consoling himself, he reasoned that Joe must have had more experience, more time to practice the skill. Jack knew that his life would need to change. Fate had just signed him up for the short course on childcare, and he would need more than a pass/fail grade if his family were to thrive. Shaking off his burgeoning self-pity, Jack told himself to man up. He had been in complicated and dangerous situations in his job; he had a good relationship with Emma and Will; he could certainly take care of a baby! He was relieved to feel the familiar armor of determination bolster him.

When he arrived at the station, he gave his name and asked to see Inspector Tremblay. Soon, Tremblay appeared and led him to an interview room. "Would you like coffee or tea or anything?" Tremblay asked as he motioned for Jack to sit down.

"If the coffee is any good, I'd take a cup."

"OK. Give me a minute," Tremblay said and left the room. He returned with two cups and handed one to Jack. "How did everything work out with your boy?"

"Good. He had a dislocated elbow—nursemaid's elbow they call it. He'll be fine, just has to wear a splint for a couple of weeks." Jack looked at Tremblay. The man was genuinely interested in Martin's welfare.

"Well, that's a relief! The little guy has had quite an ordeal. OK, let's get started. Our interview will be recorded and may be used in court if Billy is brought to trial."

Jack nodded.

Tremblay turned on the video, then gave his name, rank, the date and time, and added that he was interviewing Jack Jurlik, a United States FBI agent currently on leave. "Jack, tell me what happened from the time you drove into the parking lot until the police arrived."

Jack did.

After having Jack clarify several points, Tremblay asked, "How was it that you were in the parking lot at the same time as Billy?"

Jack explained that he was searching for his wife, Gloriann, and their son Martin. He indicated that she had sent him a one-word text, "Walmart," and that he had a sense that she would be at that location. When he arrived, he encountered Billy, Rodney, Martin, and Gloriann.

"Did you know that Billy would be there?" Tremblay continued.

"No. I was stunned."

"You did know who Billy was though, right?"

Jack explained how he knew about Billy but was adamant that he had no idea that Billy was even in Canada. "Were you able to ask him why he was in Canada or how he knew that Rodney would be at the Walmart?" Jack asked, trying to read Tremblay's face.

Tremblay answered, "I'm the one conducting the interview, yes?"

Jack nodded. "I just can't understand it, that's all. I'd like to know Billy's side."

Tremblay's eyes widened; he looked exasperated. Jack looked back at him with a classic sorry-can't-help-it expression. It was Tremblay's turn to nod. "We can't ask him, Jack, because he is still receiving medical attention. Let me ask *you* this: could he have been tracking you?"

"Well, I don't ..." Jack stumbled on his words. "I don't know how he could have. How would he know where I was? How would he know to track me?"

"Do you regularly check your car for a tracking device?"

"I do because of my line of work, but I don't have my car here. We took my brother Joe's car. It never entered my mind that someone would put a tracker on it," Jack said, disbelieving.

"Mind if we check?" Tremblay asked.

"No. Go for it. I give you my permission to check the car for a tracker. I'll give you the keys." Jack started to reach into his pocket.

"Keep the keys. You can come with us while we look over the car."

Two officers accompanied Tremblay and Jack out to the parking lot. It wasn't long before one of the officers found the tracker below Joe's trunk. He showed it to the others, then put it in an evidence bag. "I'll be darned," Jack said. "I wonder how he knew where I was." Just then, the light bulb went on in his head. "I know how he did it!"

Before Jack could explain about the mysterious phone call to his mother, Tremblay said, "Don't tell me yet. Save it for back in the interview room so we can record your statement."

When the formal interview was over, Inspector Tremblay shut off the video recorder. Jack knew this was his chance to ask him questions off the record. "Can you tell me what is happening with Gloriann?"

"To a point. She signed a release of information to include you and her parents. We told her of her right to contact the US consulate office in Toronto, and she followed up. The consular officer will contact whatever family and friends she might have indicated. Also, the officer will provide a list of attorneys and arrange transfer of any money needed to pay legal costs, bail, or fines. We gave Gloriann the eight hundred number for the Canadian duty counsel, which will allow her to speak with an attorney who is contracted with legal aid."

"May I speak with her?" Jack asked, even though he knew that was doubtful.

"She hasn't seen a judge yet, and we don't usually allow visitors at this time," Tremblay said.

"I understand that, but this is a child welfare issue. Gloriann has been the main caregiver for Martin and has been nursing him exclusively. I've helped with bathing and dressing him, but I do have questions. Even as to if he is current on his immunizations and what pediatrician was seeing him in St. Louis. We have been living there temporarily due to my current job assignment. I need to know how to care for Martin. It is definitely a child welfare issue. There must be some leeway for special circumstances," Jack said and squared his shoulders.

Tremblay thought, then said, "I can give you thirty minutes. That should be enough time to get your questions answered."

"Thank you," Jack said and extended his hand.

CHAPTER | **33**

Jack sat at a small cubicle with a phone on one side and a glass partition in front of him. The room on the other side of the glass was empty. He thought about how odd it felt to be waiting for a telephone visit with his incarcerated wife. He was relieved that she was safe, pitied her, hoped she was coping, but beyond that, he felt nothing. He was numb, and he was tired.

Gloriann entered the room accompanied by a guard. She was dressed in the same clothes she had been wearing at Walmart. He could tell she had been crying. When she sat down and picked up the phone, he realized that her tears were not those of sorrow but of frustration and anger.

"Jack, they won't bring Martin to me! I told them I was nursing, and he had to be with me. But they said that they don't allow babies in jail. Can they do this? Can you talk to them? Do something?" Gloriann was frantic.

"Gloriann, listen to me. They can do this. You cannot have Martin in jail. It is just not done. He'll be OK. Joe and I have already fed him a couple of times, and he is taking the bottle just fine. Try not to worry about him." Jack was reassuring.

Gloriann's jaw dropped, and she stared at him. "I figured he'd take formula, but what am I going to do, Jack?" She held the phone

236 | *Kathryn Tokar Haidet*

with one hand and stretched her other hand over her breasts. "They feel like rocks! I just can't quit nursing! I'm hand expressing, but it isn't doing much to help. I guess I can hold out until tomorrow when I'm out of here. You know, I'm not going to wean Martin yet."

"How do you know you will be out tomorrow? Did they tell you that?" Jack asked.

"No, but I'm going to see a judge tomorrow. One of the gals back there"—Gloriann jerked her head toward the prisoner door—"said that if you enter Canada with a fake ID, they just deport you. No big deal."

Jack ignored her assertion. "Gloriann, we don't have much time to talk. I've got some questions about Martin. Then we can talk about your case until they come get you."

"What kind of questions?" Gloriann asked.

"I need you to tell me what pediatrician you were using in St. Louis. Doesn't Martin need shots at three months?"

"Why are you even asking about that? He's got all the shots he needs right now. I took him to the Children's Clinic in St. Louis. Is Martin hurt?"

"No. He has a dislocated elbow, but they fixed it, and he should be fine."

Gloriann said, "Then why are you asking me about Martin's doctors? I'll take him for his appointments. You don't have to."

Jack blew out air and looked up at the ceiling. "Gloriann, you may not be released as soon as you think. Even if you are not held on the illegal entry, there's still the matter of an international parental abduction."

"What? Are you kidding me? Are you pressing charges, Jack?"

"No, I'm not, but you don't understand. It is not up to me. You've broken the law. I can't stop the wheels set in motion. You denied my parental rights and took Martin across state lines. That's a crime, Gloriann. You even took him out of the country!"

"That's crazy, Jack. He's not even your son!" Gloriann blurted out. Then, looking horrified, she put her hand over her mouth.

Jack gripped the phone receiver so hard he thought the tendon in his thumb would snap. He hung his head.

"Oh, Jack, I'm sorry. I'm so sorry. I didn't want you to find out like this. I did not want to hurt you. I really didn't. I was so, so … I don't know. I just wasn't happy in St. Louis. I should have stayed in Tucson with the kids. You were right about that. Rod made me feel better. Then one thing led to another. I didn't know how to tell you. It was all such a mess. Jack, I didn't want you to find out like this, but it is true that you are not Martin's father. So we had every right to take him," Gloriann said.

Anger gripped Jack's heart, squeezing it so hard he became dizzy. Then his heart hurt as if someone had put a knife in it. Finally, his breath came back to him, and his head quit spinning.

"Gloriann," he said, lowering his voice and speaking through clenched teeth, "I may not be Martin's biological father, but I am his legal father. He was born while we were married, and my name is on his birth certificate. I am your husband, Gloriann. You had other choices. Whether you think it is fair or not, you are guilty of a federal crime. And, Gloriann? What about Emma and Will? You had no right to abandon them; you had no right to put our family's future in jeopardy; you had no right to hurt us all the way you did. At this point, it is probably best for you to ask for medical help to take care of your breasts because I am certain about this—you won't be feeding Martin anytime soon." Jack looked at his watch. There was still time.

Gloriann looked stunned. "Why? What happens now?"

"Now you face the consequences of your actions, Gloriann. Call the Canadian duty counsel. You have the number. See what the judge says tomorrow. The US consulate will keep me informed. If you are brought back to the US, I'll arrange for an attorney. I have one more suggestion for you. If Rodney's mother comes to get his body, make sure she knows about Martin, her only grandchild."

"Rod doesn't have any family. He told me they were all dead," Gloriann said and began to cry.

"He told you a lot of things, a lot of lies. He has a mother and a brother."

"What? Don't tell them! What if they take Martin?" Gloriann was alarmed.

"They can't. They have no legal standing."

"But I don't want anyone else to know who Martin's father is. Don't do this to me, Jack." Gloriann's tears had dried.

"I'm not doing anything to you, Gloriann, that you haven't already done to yourself. We can't pretend none of this happened. Eventually, it will all come out. The kids, the family—they need to know now. We have to save them from a whole lot of hurt down the road. I am not going to lie to them, Gloriann."

"Don't do this to me, Jack. I beg you," Gloriann said.

The guard came forward and said, "You have one minute."

Jack nodded to the guard. "Gloriann, I'm not doing anything to you. Listen, you have the right to request a clergy visit. I suggest you do that," Jack said and hung up the phone. He did not look at Gloriann. He stood up, turned, and left the room.

34

"How did it go?" Joe asked when Jack got back to the hotel.

"It went," Jack said, putting the car keys on the desk. He turned the chair around and sat down to look at Joe. "I don't want to talk about it right now."

Joe was sitting on the bed, back against the headboard, legs straight out and spread wide. Martin was lying on his back between Joe's legs, gurgling and cooing as Joe dangled a toy above him. Joe looked at his brother. "OK then. I'll tell you about my day first. I had a visitor."

Jack was surprised. "Who?"

"A nice detective from the Thunder Bay Police. He came right after you left. Questioned me about what I saw. We got along rather well. He did tell me a few things that you probably don't know."

"Such as?"

"The baby clothes." Joe did not look up; he kept entertaining Martin.

"Does this have something to do with the reason that Martin is dressed in that bright pink sleeper?" asked Jack.

Joe laughed. "Well, yes, big brother, it does. Seems like all the baby clothes in the car were girl's clothes. There were no boy clothes. And they are keeping those clothes for the feds. This fashion item was in the diaper bag. Wasn't it, Martin? And we had to clean you up, didn't we, buddy?" Joe teased as he started to play the this-hand-is-going-to-get-you game. Martin watched Joe's hand hover above him, and when it came down to tickle his tummy, Martin squealed with delight, his little legs softly thumping the bed. "I've taken all the tags off the new boy's clothes, but we need to wash them. I had to wait for you because there's no way I could carry Martin and the detergent and the clothes down the hall." Joe looked at Jack and smiled.

Jack remained silent. Finally, he said, "So, they must be keeping them for evidence that Gloriann helped plan the deception. I wonder what she did with all the clothes she took from the house?"

"My guess is that she didn't know Rodney would chuck them and pass Martin off as a girl. The fact that she took his clothes might help her defense."

"Oh, Cripe! What else did you find out?" Jack wanted to talk now.

"We may be here a few days. You need to get a birth certificate for Martin so we can get him back over the border. The only documents found in the car were fakes. Also, the feds want to talk to Gloriann about that murder Dad told us about this morning and possibly Rodney's Ponzi scheme."

Jack shook his head. "What!"

"So, Mrs. Lincoln, how was the play? What did Gloriann have to say?" Joe asked.

Jack sighed. "You know, Joe, she didn't even ask about Emma and Will. Didn't even ask! She didn't say, 'Thanks for saving me, Jack.' Nope, nothing like that. She was only worried about not being able to nurse Martin and what would happen to her. She was rather indignant about the whole thing. Didn't think she should be in jail, felt unjustly treated. Oh, she did tell me she was sorry that she didn't mean to hurt me."

"Well, that's something," Joe said.

"She told me that only after she told me that I was not Martin's father, that she and Rodney had every right to take him."

Joe winced. "She just came right out and said that? In a jail conversation? She told you that you are not Martin's father?"

Jack continued, "She told me after I told her that she would be held for international child abduction. She couldn't see how my rights were denied since Rodney is Martin's father. I explained to her that her knowledge of the law was woefully lacking. I also told her that I would not hide the truth of Martin's paternity."

"How'd she take that?" Joe was interested.

"Not well. She begged me to keep her secret. I told her I wouldn't. I told her she should ask for a priest, and then I left," Jack answered.

"And that's it. You're done with her or what?"

"No, I'm not done with her. I can't do anything right now anyway. When she gets back to the States, I'll get her a lawyer and do what I can to help her. But for right now, she is going to have to buck up and deal with the consequences of her actions. We'll see what happens. If she starts to flounder, they'll get in touch with me. She did list me as a contact with the consulate and signed an information waiver, so I'll know what's happening. Joe, right now I've got to deal with Martin and Will and Emma and the folks and Mel and my job."

"OK! Stop! I got it. I'll call our side of the family; you touch base with Gloriann's folks and sister; we'll split the Martin duties. I don't know how long it will take to get the birth certificate, but my guess is that we'll be home by Wednesday. That should give you time to get things squared away at work."

Jack moved over to the bed and squeezed his brother's calf. "Thanks, Joe. You know I couldn't have done this without you."

"Yeah, I know. Just shut up. Here, take Martin. I'll throw the laundry in, and then maybe I can get to the store to buy some beer before they close. Why don't you find a pizza place that delivers?"

After the beer and the pizza, with Martin now asleep in the small crib, the brothers made their calls. Joe called Tessa, explaining the day's happenings in more detail, and left it up to her to inform the folks and to filter the information for Emma and Will. He called his brother Ted, and when he had brought him up to date, encouraged him to spend as much time as he could helping out. He told Ted that they were hoping to be home sometime Wednesday.

When Jack contacted Mel, she told him that the American consulate had already been in touch with Helen and Stan. Jack squeezed his eyes shut and massaged his forehead. "Oh, Mel, didn't Tessa call you?"

"Yeah, she did, but when I was talking to her, Mom's number showed up on the caller ID. By then, they knew Gloriann was safe but in police custody and that you had Martin. They were planning to leave for Green Bay, but now they want to go to Thunder Bay. I called my supervisor and requested the next week off so I could go with them. Honestly, I thought Mom was going to have a stroke!" Mel said.

Jack explained more about Gloriann's situation and told Mel it would be best if they just stayed in Tucson until after Gloriann's court hearing. Then they could decide on a plan.

"And Rod is dead," Mel reiterated.

"As a doornail," Jack replied.

"Oh, his poor mother! Does she know?"

"I suppose so. Mel, I'm in a need-to-know position right now. We are in a foreign country, working through the American consulate. I won't know much until tomorrow. I'll call you as soon as I find out anything. Call me if the folks hear things. Don't assume that I know."

Mel agreed, and when they hung up, Jack called Lou to see if she would give him more information. She wouldn't. She offered her concern for Jack and his family and inquired if he intended to come back to work anytime soon. "Yes, that's the plan. I need the money, Lou. I'll finish out my time in St. Louis and then move back to Tucson by Christmas. I'm hoping to leave the kids with my family in Green Bay until I can figure out what to do next. I can't keep pulling them in and out of school. They need some stability right now. They need to be with family."

"And Gloriann?" Lou asked.

"You know more about that than I do, Lou."

Lou nodded, but Jack only heard silence.

"Lou, I'm sorry. I didn't mean to put you in an awkward position; I'm just having a tough time not knowing everything that is happening."

"That's understandable, Jack. If I were in your shoes, I'd pursue all the avenues I could. Don't worry about me. You've got enough on your plate." Lou was sympathetic.

"Well, there is one thing I do hope you can help me with, not as an agent but as a friend. I can't bring Martin home until I get a copy of his birth certificate. I can download the application and fill it out, even get an online notary, but I need someone to go in person to the recorder of deeds office. Maybe during lunch?" Jack was hoping.

"I'll arrange something. You email the completed forms to me, and one of us at the office will get the birth certificate and overnight express it to you."

"On your own time though, right?" Jack was worried.

"Of course, on our own time. All of us know what you are up against, Jack. You have got friends here. We can get it done. If you can email the forms to me as early tomorrow, we should be able to get the certificate on Tuesday. You'd have it Wednesday morning."

"And if you run into problems?" Jack asked.

"I'm sure someone here would officially vouch for the validity and urgency of the transaction if there are problems," Lou assured him. Then she reminded him, "Make sure you get a notarized letter of consent from Gloriann that you have her permission to take Martin across the border."

"Ah, yes. Lou, thank you! I'm so grateful for your help. If there is anything I can ever do for you, just ask."

"Maybe dinner with you and the kids. It would be nice to see you all together again." Lou was smiling.

"OK, it's a deal," Jack said and ended the call.

35

MONDAY, SEPTEMBER 25

Miquel woke to the soft sound of Gregorian chant. He lay in bed for a few minutes listening to it, then reached over and silenced his phone. He arose, shook off the residual turmoil of yesterday, and offered his day to God. Then he picked up his shaving kit and the towel his cousin had given him and headed for the bathroom. Along the way, he stopped at his mother's door and quietly opened it. "Mamá, time to get up." Francesca mumbled something and turned on the bedside light.

It wasn't long before they were walking down the stairs to the kitchen, Miquel carrying their small suitcases, Francesca following, her shoes making clacking noises on the wood.

Francesca's sister, Sofia, was already preparing a light breakfast along with snacks for them to take on the plane. "Good morning! Were you able to get any sleep?" she asked, looking at them and wiping her hands on her apron.

Francesca nodded. "I did. I was just so exhausted."

Miquel added, "I slept a bit fitfully, but all is well. I rested."

Sofia was pleased. "Good. Jorge is up. When you are ready, he will take you to the airport. You can leave your car here. We'll pick you up when you get back."

"Gracias," Miquel and Francesca replied in unison. They hadn't expected Sofia's husband, Jorge, to transport them. Miquel was now visibly relieved that negotiating long-term parking was taken off his to-do list. Francesca had not even considered the logistics; she had so much on her mind.

After breakfast, Miquel walked out into the cool morning air and scanned the horizon. The sky was overcast, the stars hidden. The barking of a dog floated through the quiet; houses were still cloaked in darkness; Queretaro had not yet risen from its slumber.

"Ready?" Jorge asked.

"Yes," Miquel said as he turned and headed for the open doorway. He could see Francesca and Sofia illuminated in the arch of light. They were locked in an embrace, both crying. His heart broke for his mother. He turned and looked at Jorge.

"You get the *maletas*. I'll get Francesca," Jorge said.

The ride to the airport was solemn. "Your flight to Dallas leaves at 6:26 a.m.? How long will it take?" Jorge asked, trying to assuage his discomfort.

"Should be in Dallas around 9:00 a.m., then we have an hour-and-a-half layover."

"And then to Thunder Bay?"

Miquel smiled. "No. There is no direct flight to Thunder Bay. We'll fly to Toronto and should be there about 2:30 p.m. Then we have a long wait. Won't get a flight out until 6:15 p.m., and we'll get in a little after 8:00 p.m. We'll go to the hotel and call it a day, meet with the authorities on Tuesday morning. Ah, I see we are here."

They joined the queue of cars pulling up to the main entrance. Miquel helped Francesca gather her things and get out of the car. Jorge removed the bags from the trunk. Quick hugs were exchanged.

Jorge waved as he drove out, and Miquel and Francesca walked into the bustle of the airport.

They boarded before the other passengers, a new experience for them. Francesca fretted about the first-class seats, but Miquel assured her that all was well. He could afford the tickets. The unspoken truth was that these were the only seats left to purchase on the fully booked flight, and he wanted to get his mother to Thunder Bay as soon as possible.

Once they were in the air, the conversation that Miquel hoped wouldn't come was upon him.

"Miquel, what did I do wrong? Why did Rod choose the wrong path?" His mother's brown eyes searched his.

"Mamá, I don't think you did anything wrong. Rod made his own choices."

"But why? I raised him to be a good man, a kind and truthful man, one who loved God. What happened, Miquel? Why did he choose to do what he did?"

"Mamá, Rod had many influences in his life; we all do. Those influences lead us along various paths. Sometimes the goods of this world, the lure of this world, obscure the goods and the call of God. If that happens, then that's the path one takes."

"I tried to keep those bad influences at bay, but ..."

"Mamá, look. Rod, for whatever reason, lacked *docilitas*, the willingness to learn. You know that. He thought he knew everything, and that made him somewhat unteachable—not because he lacked the capacity but because he thought he was already wise. If you cannot convince someone that others may know better, then there is not much you can do except pray. You've done that; you've kept the door open to him. We both have. We are both grieving him, Mamá. We both grieve."

"Miquel, what do you think happened to his soul?"

Miquel sighed. "Mamá, he is in God's hands."

"But do you think—"

Miquel interrupted her. "I really can't say." In Christian charity, he would not theorize, and in that same charity, Francesca ceased questioning him.

CHAPTER | 36

Gloriann stood at her place behind the rail, and the judge sat in the front of the courtroom behind a large, raised desk. He told her that there would be no charges for crossing the border illegally but that he was imposing an exclusion order against her. Because she misrepresented herself to gain entry, she would be banned from Canada for two years, and after that, she would be subject to additional scrutiny at border crossings. She smiled. She was right! She would not be prosecuted for entering the country illegally. *I can't wait to get out of here*, she thought.

The judge continued to speak, but now Gloriann was only hearing snippets of what he was saying: "A formal extradition request from the United States ... dual criminality ... supporting documentation in the murder case of Reginald Whit III ... authority to proceed issued by the Department of Justice, Canada ... extradition hearing before a judge of the superior court... bail denied due to flight risk," and finally, "you will be immediately remanded to Thunder Bay Correctional Centre."

Gloriann's vision became cloudy, and her knees buckled; she began to pitch forward, but then she grabbed the rail. The spinning room stopped, and her focus returned. A woman in uniform gently took her arm and guided her out of the room. "What just happened?"

Gloriann asked the woman. After the officer explained, Gloriann said, "But there was no murder! They must have made a mistake! I don't know what they are talking about."

"Best thing to do is keep talking to duty counsel and the consular officer from your embassy," the officer told her.

"What happens now?" Gloriann asked her.

"You will spend time at the correctional facility until your extradition hearing."

"How long will that take?" Gloriann asked.

"It depends," replied the officer. "It could take a week or a month. There's paperwork and court schedules. If you don't want to wait, I'm sure you can just tell the consulate that you want to forget the hearing, waive your rights, and go back to the States."

Gloriann had already decided. "That's exactly what I'm going to do. I had nothing to do with a murder! And I'm not spending any more time in Canada. No offense."

"None taken," the officer replied.

CHAPTER | 37

Monday was a whirlwind of paperwork for Jack and Joe. Multiple times, one brother would remark to the other, "It's a good thing we know how to do this. I feel sorry for people who wouldn't know how to even begin to navigate these forms and fees and rules!" To which the other would reply, "Helps you understand what people on the other side go through. Doesn't it?"

They made a good tag team, and by the time their stomachs were signaling lunch, Jack had sent the forms to Lou and talked with the consular officer regarding Gloriann's status. All that was left to do was to download and deliver a letter of consent for Gloriann to sign. The correctional center had a notary on site, and Jack was assured that as long as Gloriann signed it, he could pick it up on Tuesday before 5:00 p.m.

"What if she won't sign it?" Joe asked Jack.

"She will. Heck, she waived her right to an extradition hearing. She wants to get back to the States as soon as she can," Jack said.

"Does she know where she will be going?"

"Yes. She was told that US Marshals would transport her to Minneapolis to be questioned in the murder of Reginald Whit III," Jack replied.

"Do you think she—" Joe did not finish his question.

"No! Gloriann is not a murderer. I'm sure of that. She did awful, stupid things, but murder? No. If she had even thought Rodney murdered someone, she would have been scared, turned tail, and ran."

"Did you talk to her about the murder?" Joe asked.

"No. I wanted her initial reaction to be noted. Her surprise should help her defense. I'll arrange for a lawyer for her in Minneapolis. I doubt they'll have enough to charge her, and if I'm wrong and they do charge, I can't believe she would be convicted."

"So, after we get back to Green Bay, you'll be going to Minneapolis?" Joe changed the subject.

"No, after Green Bay, I'm going to finish my work in St. Louis. Gloriann's folks and Mel can go to Minneapolis. I'll retain the lawyer though."

"You should get some legal advice for yourself, Jack," Joe said, knowing he was on shaky ground. "You need to think about getting sole custody of the kids, at least temporarily."

Jack considered, then nodded.

Joe thought, *in for a dime, in for a dollar.* "Jack, while you are at it, you might want to make sure that an adult is always present when Gloriann visits the kids. Just saying." Joe waited for the explosion, but it didn't come.

Jack just nodded.

Tuesday, September 26

"If I don't get out of here and do something, I'm going to go nuts," Joe said to Jack once breakfast was over. "I mean it. Jack, I'm not used to sitting around and waiting."

"OK, all right. Where do you want to go?" Jack's own nervous energy needed an outlet.

"Well, having read the *Thunder Bay Experience*, I'd say let's go to Kakabeka Falls. It's about a twenty-minute drive. Then we can eat at the Polish Café for lunch. It's right here in Thunder Bay. Lots of good reviews."

They were standing on the bridge over the Kaministiquia River, watching the water crash against the rocks and spew its mist into the air, when Jack's phone rang. It was the consular officer. He wanted to know if he could give Billy's parents Jack's cell phone number. Jack did not hesitate. "Sure, that's fine." They stood for a while longer, silent and content. Even Martin, bundled up and alert, watched happily from his stroller.

A half hour later, Jack's phone rang again. This time, he was seated in the passenger seat as Joe drove. Billy's parents had just come from the hospital. His surgery went well, and he was being released to the correctional infirmary. His parents hired an attorney to assist in the bail hearing. They were calling Jack to express their gratitude for saving Billy's life. "Billy told us that if you had just walked on by, he would not have made it. You took a chance; you saved his life. He is so glad to be alive."

"I'm glad that he is going to be OK." Jack was humble. "Is he cooperating with authorities?"

"Oh, yes! He is taking full responsibility for his part in the Ponzi scheme, and he said Gloriann was not involved. He is sure of it. He also told the police that you knew nothing of his trip here to Canada. However, Billy is adamant that he did not shoot Rod. He swore to me that he did not have his finger on the trigger when the gun went off."

His parents decided they would stay until Billy's bail hearing, and once there was a plan in place, they would go back to Phoenix. Jack asked them if the number from which they called was a good one to use to reach them. They affirmed that it was, and Jack ended the call by asking them to keep him posted.

"Good timing," Joe said to Jack. "The café is just up the street."

There were only a few tables left by the time Jack and Joe got inside. When the waiter brought the menus to the table, he did a double take when he saw Martin. He quickly recovered, but both brothers had noticed his reaction. Jack asked him, "Why did you look at the baby the way you did?'

"Oh, it is nothing." The waiter was uncomfortable.

"No, it was something. What was it?" Jack was curious.

"He looks familiar. There was a baby here last week that looked exactly like him, except it was a girl. She could be his twin sister." The waiter shrugged his shoulders.

Joe asked him, "Can you remember anything about the couple that baby was with?"

The waiter stammered, "I, I am not sure."

Jack jumped in and explained who he was and a bit about his situation. The waiter understood. He said, "Let me seat those women who just came in. Then I'll come back for your order. When we catch up on this lunch rush, I'll sit with you and tell you what I remember."

The waiter was true to his word. He remembered thinking how strange it was that Rodney held the baby the whole time he ate, never giving the baby to Gloriann. Rodney cradled the baby in his left arm and ate with his right, even cutting the sausage with the side of his fork. Gloriann seemed tense, rigid. When the waiter noticed her wiping her eyes, he asked her if she was all right. She said she was, that the food was so delicious it reminded her of her mother's cooking. "'Don't mind me. I cry at the sight of two ripe tomatoes,' she said. I thought, *What an odd saying.*"

Jack asked him if he would talk with the American authorities working the case. The waiter said he would and wrote down his information on a lunch check and handed it to Jack. "And do you have CTV here?" Jack inquired.

"Only in the parking lot. I can get the file if the Americans want it. We keep files for a month before deleting them."

"And the owner will allow it?"

The waiter displayed a broad smile. "I am the owner."

Jack was embarrassed. "Thank you. I'm sorry. I should not have assumed."

"It is fine," said the waiter. "I can see how you might think it."

As they walked to the car, Joe said, "It sure looks like Gloriann couldn't get away from Rodney without endangering Martin."

"I know. That's why I wanted the guy's testimony and the film footage. It should help her case; shows she was under duress, maybe coerced."

"You're not sure how to feel about Gloriann, are you, Jack?" Joe looked at his brother.

"Yes and no."

They stopped at the correctional center before heading back to the hotel. The letter of consent was waiting for them at the information desk. Jack called Lou to check on the status of the birth certificate. She said it was ready for overnight delivery and that he would get it on Wednesday before noon. He told her about his encounter at the café, and she assured him that she would pass the information on to the proper agent.

"What a relief! Everything is falling into place," Jack told his brother.

"Yep! Tomorrow, we can blow the lid off this pop stand and be home before supper."

"You are so corny, Joe," Jack said, shaking his head.

Joe grinned. "I know."

When they were back in the room, Jack's phone rang. It was the consular officer again. This time he wanted to know if the brother, Miquel, could have Jack's cell phone number. "Sure, why not?" a puzzled Jack responded.

Jack turned to Joe. "Well, now I'm awaiting a call from a monk, Brother Miquel, Rodney's brother." Jack busied himself with collecting papers and organizing them. He read notes that he had written to himself, ripped them into small pieces, and dropped them in the wastebasket. He cleaned out his pockets and started to pack Martin's things. Finally, his phone rang.

The man on the other end had a soft but authoritative voice. He told Jack that his name was Miquel and that he had come to town to make final arrangements for Rod. He said that the consular officer had given him a message from Gloriann saying that whoever came to claim Rod's body should call Jack.

Jack had wondered if Gloriann would try to contact Rodney's family. He wasn't sure that she would and was not prepared for the call. Silence was loud on the phone and was not broken until Jack spoke. "Brother Miquel, I have news to share with you."

"Yes, Jack, I am listening."

"I can't tell you over the phone. This news is something we need to discuss in person. Can you come to my hotel this evening? It would be easier if you came here."

"Jack, my mother has accompanied me. We have traveled from San Miguel de Allende. She is fragile in her exhaustion and grief. I am sorry, but I cannot leave her alone. I could meet you in our hotel lobby. That way, I would be accessible to her if she were in need."

"Are you staying in Thunder Bay?" Jack asked.

"Yes, at the Valhalla Inn. Do you know it?"

"Yes," Jack said, "We are staying at the Hampton, not far from you. Would an hour be too soon to meet?"

Miquel discerned Jack's anxiety. "I will look for you in an hour. I'll be in the lobby reading."

38

The Valhalla Inn was less than a mile away. Jack declined Joe's offer to go with him; this was something he wanted to face alone, just he and Martin. He hoped that Martin would stay awake until they could meet Brother Miquel, but the movement of the car, coupled with the baby's full stomach, lulled Martin to sleep. Martin did not wake when Jack lifted him from the car seat. Cradling Martin in his arms, he was overwhelmed with love for him, a love that gave Jack the strength to do what he was about to do. Jack placed one finger in Martin's open palm, and the baby unconsciously wrapped his little fingers around it. Jack sighed and headed to the door.

Inside, Jack was awed by the expanse of the lobby. The towering vaulted wooden ceiling was supported by walls of complementary wood and brick. The tile floor gleamed. The lobby's ambience was one of reverent, comforting calm. He looked around for a monk in a black tunic, but all he saw was a man in civilian clothes, sitting in one of two chairs away from, but in line with, the front desk. The man wore black slacks, black shoes, and a blue plaid, long-sleeved shirt. He had tortoise-shell glasses, a moustache, and thick, black, straight hair, which he parted on the side. He sat with his back straight, his long legs crossed at the knee; he was reading.

Jack approached him. "Brother Miquel?"

The man closed his book and stood. He was about six foot four inches, two inches taller than Jack and lankier. He outstretched his hand. "Jack?"

"Yes," Jack said, completing the handshake.

The man looked at the baby cuddled in Jack's arms, then asked, "Why do you call me Brother Miquel?"

"I was told you were a Benedictine monk."

"Ah, no, I am not. Let me explain how you might have been misinformed. I did spend time at the Monasterio de La Soledad, the Monastery of Solitude in San Miguel, but I left before making the simple profession. I spent a year observing and praying, only to discover that God was calling me elsewhere. And what about you? You are an FBI agent married to Gloriann, yes?"

"Yes." Jack had lost control of the conversation.

Miquel looked again at Martin. "And you are here to tell me something about this baby?"

Jack was dumbfounded. Did Gloriann already tell him? Had Rodney told him? "Yes. How did you know?" Jack asked.

"There is something familiar in his face." Then looking at Jack, Miquel added, "And you were anxious to meet in person. Please sit down."

Jack sat in the only available chair, to the side of Miquel and separated by an end table with fresh flowers. Miquel waited silently, and Jack found himself telling Miquel the whole story of their move to St. Louis, of Gloriann's affair and Martin's birth, of the abduction of Martin, and the abandonment of Emma and Will. He told him that he had suspected that Martin was not his biological son, and that Gloriann confirmed it on Sunday. He finished with the statement, "Martin is my legal son, and more than that, he is a son of my heart."

Miquel's face shone with such kindness that Jack almost expected him to raise his arm and pronounce the words of absolution. Instead, Miquel said, "Thank you, Jack, for your honesty. I do have to ask you though, why is it that you have decided to reveal the circumstances of Martin's birth to us?"

Jack explained that he felt it was the just thing to do. "Your mother has a right to know that she has a grandchild. I thought that he was the only one ..."

"You are correct. He is. Go on," Miquel encouraged.

"I also thought that at some point Martin would find out, that someone would tell him, or he would accidentally overhear it, or enroll in a genetic service. This kind of secret never ends well. It would be easier for Martin if family knew now while he is an infant, easier now rather than later. I don't want him to ever think he lived a lie; there is no trust in that," Jack concluded.

"And Gloriann, is this what she wants?" Miquel asked.

"At first, no, but she must have changed her mind. She did ask you to contact me."

"Yes, I am happy that she did, Jack. Shall we tell my mother the good news?"

"Wait. One thing, Miquel. Do you think you or your mother will want custody of Martin?" Jack shocked himself with his boldness.

"No, Jack, neither one of us would take your son away from you. We would like to be part of his life, yes?"

"Yes! Absolutely. That's why I'm here."

Miquel nodded. "You are a good man, Jack Jurlik. Martin is fortunate that you have accepted him as your son. I hope that one day your family will be made whole again."

"I can't promise that, Miquel. I don't know what is going to happen in the future."

Miquel nodded. "No one does, Jack; no one knows the future."

Miquel led Jack to a seating area in the corner of the lobby. "If you will wait here, I'll go get my mother."

"While you're gone, I'm going to get the diaper bag out of the car," Jack told him. Jack returned to wait alone. The minutes ticked by, and Jack wondered if Miquel was coming back. He looked at his phone. He could call Miquel but decided to give him more time. "Well, Martin, let's walk. Daddy can't sit here anymore." Jack stood and began to pace until he saw Miquel approaching.

Alongside of Miquel was a diminutive woman with long black hair pulled loosely away from her face and fastened with a wide clip behind her neck. She wore brown jeans, a white shirt, and a multicolored rebozo wrapped around her shoulders. As she got closer, Jack could see the hints of white in her hair and the puffiness around her red eyes. She looked at Jack holding Martin, then turned her face up to Miquel's. It was clear to Jack that she did not understand.

"Mamá, this is Jack Jurlik, Gloriann's husband. Jack, meet my mother, Francesca Wilter."

"How do you do, Mrs. Wilter?" Jack said as he looked down at her. She had to be at least a foot shorter than him, and he resisted the urge to bend over as he spoke; he did not want to seem patronizing. "Please sit down," he suggested. When she did, Jack took the chair closest to her and lowered Martin to his lap. She looked at the baby and gasped. Closing her mouth, she shot a glance at Jack, then at Miquel. Miquel nodded.

Jack rose and handed Martin to her. He could not help seeing the light that began dancing in her eyes. She drew Martin to her and grinned, her face shining. She ignored Jack and Miquel— Martin became her world. She began to talk and coo to him, and he rewarded her with a big, gummy smile.

Jack was amazed that he did not have to explain; Martin himself told her all she desired to know. After that, they did talk, not about the past but of the future. Francesca spoke of the beauty of San Miguel de Allende and encouraged Jack to visit, to bring his whole family. Jack promised to send pictures via email. They exchanged contact information and made plans for an early lunch tomorrow.

Francesca noticed that Martin was becoming agitated. "He will need to eat soon, yes?" she asked Jack.

Jack nodded.

"We will not keep you, Jack. We know you must care for your son," Francesca said as she gave Martin another hug and kiss. She brought the baby to Jack, bent to put him in Jack's arms, then kissed Jack's cheek. "Thank you," she said.

"Mamá, I'll meet you back up in the room," Miquel said, picking up the diaper bag. "I'll walk out with Jack."

Jack felt lighter, happier than he had in several weeks. As they walked to the car, he said to Miquel, "I am relieved." And then to his surprise, he shared with this man, a man whom he had just met, a man who was a magnet for his tortured feelings, "I hope my family is as understanding, as accepting. I swear I feel like I'm acting in a soap opera."

Miquel stopped and stood in front of Jack. "Remember, Jack, you perform for an audience of only one—God. Make sure He is the one who gives you good reviews."

CHAPTER | 39

Joe was waiting for Jack when he returned to the room; he wanted to hear the play-by-play of his encounter with the monk. Jack laughed and put a white bag on the desk. "We are eating Chinese tonight," Jack told him. "I stopped on the way back."

"Smart man," Joe said as he peeked inside the bag. "So how did it go?"

"Really well. You'll meet them tomorrow. We are going to the Valhalla Inn for an early lunch. Oh, and by the way, Rodney's brother is not a *brother*; he's not a monk." Jack built up the teaser, then told Joe that he would fill him in when they could sit down and eat. "We're on Martin duty first."

Joe was pleased with Jack's report. "So, are you going to call Mel tonight and talk with her?"

"Nope. I'm taking the night off from the drama. I'm going to pack so we can check out before we go for lunch. I'll give Martin a bath—I have no idea when his last one was—then zone out. Gosh, it is nice to savor the calm."

"Well, do you mind if I tell Tessa? I think it would be better if she knew before you tell the folks and the kids." Joe waited.

"No. Go ahead, call her. I don't want to hear the call, but I would like to know what she says," Jack told his brother.

Joe picked up his phone and left the room. When he came back, he noticed two small garbage bags outside the door. The room was uncluttered except for his clothes draped over a chair. Martin was sitting on Jack's lap, his hair a bit damp; he was wearing a new sleeper. "Gee, he changed colors," Joe said.

"I know. Poor kid. He was pretty dirty. How'd it go?" Jack asked.

"Interesting," Joe answered. "She told me that nothing surprises her anymore. The initial reports of Gloriann's disappearance were a shock, but now she's acclimated. Like when the temperature goes below zero for the first time; that's always a jolt. But when it goes from minus ten to minus fifteen—one just accepts it. She wanted to know what you plan to do."

"What did you tell her?"

"That you didn't know; that things are still up in the air; that you are thinking of looking for a new job but that you are going back to St. Louis because you need to work. You can't afford not to work." Joe saw the worry starting to cloud Jack's sunny mood. "But this should make you happy. She said we are going to take the kids until you get settled. She doesn't want to see them being shuttled around, watched by strangers, pulled out of school. She said they have been through enough."

Jack sat up straight. "And what did you say?"

"Jack, Tessa doesn't pull rank often, but when she does, I snap to attention and say, 'Yes ma'am.' I'm OK with it. Tessa will have it all planned out before we even get home. I know the folks and Ted will help. And maybe this will squash her desire to have just one more baby before her clock stops ticking. I don't think Andy will be too happy, but it'll all work itself out. You'd do the same for me, wouldn't you?"

Jack's eyes got wide, and it took him a moment to respond. "Yeah, I guess so. If I were a single dad, I'd have to find a way to do it. But yeah, I'd do it." Then he let out a sigh and admitted, "Joe, I hope I never have to."

Wednesday, September 27

It was almost 9:00 a.m. when the front desk rang Jack to come down and retrieve an overnight delivery. Jack bolted out of the room, ran down the hall to the exit door, and took the steps two at a time. Within minutes, he was showing his ID and signing the electronic pad held out for him by the driver. He went back to the stairwell, but before ascending, he carefully opened the envelope. He took out Martin's birth certificate and kissed it. "Yes!" he said as he ran up the stairs. "Yes, yes, yes!"

"I got it, Joe!" Jack waved the envelope when he entered the room. "Should I call Miquel and see if we can meet earlier so we can get on the road?"

"Jack, it is going to take us nine hours to get back home anyway. We are scheduled to eat at eleven o'clock? If we leave at noon, we'd be home by ten for sure. Remember, we gain an hour. That way, we won't have to talk to anyone. We can just hit the sack and deal with whatever tomorrow. You should call the consular officer and let him know that we have the paperwork and will be leaving. Also, call Lou. Let her know you got the birth certificate."

Lou was happy to hear Jack's news, especially when he told her that he would be back to work on Monday. The consular officer was equally happy for Jack. "Good for you! Being back in the States will make things easier. I was going to call you and bring you up to date on Gloriann. US Marshals picked her up early this morning. They are driving her to Minneapolis. I've already contacted her parents. Federal agents will keep you informed now. Let me give you the phone number."

As soon as Jack hung up, Mel called. Jack told her that he had just heard that Gloriann was being transported.

"I know. That's why I'm calling," Mel told him. "We'll be in Minneapolis either today or tomorrow. What about a lawyer, Jack?"

"I can't get one today, Mel. We are driving back to Green Bay. I can work on it tomorrow; maybe Elizabeth and Carl can help you sooner. That's a better first step. See if they know anyone. If that doesn't work out, let me know, and then I'll get on it. We need to talk, Mel. Just the two of us, but I can't now."

"OK. I've got things to do here too. I'll call you when I can be alone. Text me Elizabeth's contact info in case the folks don't have it."

"Yeah, I'll send it right now. Thanks, Mel." Jack sent the text, then glanced at the time. "Hey, Joe, we have to get out of here!"

"The trunk is already loaded; I took the keys and checked out. I've got the diaper bag. Grab Martin, and let's go." Joe was eager.

CHAPTER | 40

Before Jack and Joe could even tell the hostess who they were, she approached them with menus and a smile. "Your party is already here." She led them to a square table where Francesca and Miquel were sitting opposite each other; a wooden infant seat cradle was next to Francesca. Joe's hesitancy to meet Rodney's family evaporated with Miquel's handshake and Francesca's warm smile.

Jack positioned Martin's car seat in the cradle holder. The baby was alert and looking around. Francesca stood. "May I hold him? I'll hold him while we eat if that is OK with you." Jack gave his consent, and Francesca unbuckled Martin. She hugged him and kissed him, then turning him to face the others, she sat down. Martin lurched forward. Francesca kept him from hitting his head on the table, but she wasn't fast enough to stop him from grabbing a handful of the tablecloth and pulling. All three men put their hands down on the table to secure the cloth and glasses. Francesca laughed. "I forgot how quick little ones can be, even when they are this little." She moved her chair back a bit and repositioned Martin so he was facing her. She was all smiles; Martin was cooing.

Miquel ordered a sandwich for her and a carryout container. He ordered the soup and sandwich special, as did Joe and Jack. Soon, their easy conversation turned to Rodney. Francesca shared how she met her husband when she came to the United States to visit a relative. There was an immediate attraction, and they were married within a year. She was only nineteen. He was twenty-seven and established in his job as a worker on a train crew. Miquel was born when Francesca was twenty, and Rod came four years later. By the time Francesca was twenty-five, her husband was dead, killed in a yard accident.

"Rod takes after my husband's side of the family with his light skin and dark, curly hair; Miquel takes after mine. It bothered Rod that Miquel and I were darker. Even when he was young, in middle school, he did not want people to know he was related to us. I still don't know why he never took pride in his Hispanic heritage. I'll never know now." Francesca looked down at Martin and smiled, but it was a sad smile.

"Francesca!" Jack jolted her out of her downward spiral. "Martin will know you. He will know your family. We will visit you in San Miguel—not right away, but we will come. There will be no language barrier. I speak Spanish. So does Gloriann."

"You are a good man. And Gloriann? Is she a good woman? Do you think I can meet her while I am here?" Francesca asked.

The color drained from Jack's face. They didn't know. "The US Marshals Service is transporting Gloriann to Minneapolis. They left early this morning."

"Why? Do they think it is because she was involved with the Ponzi scheme? Or is it because she took Martin from you?" Francesca probed.

The sigh that came from Jack originated from deep within. Miquel raised his eyebrows, and Joe decided that it was time to change Martin and get his bottle ready. Jack explained about the fake IDs and the homicide investigation. He told them that the victim was Reginald Whit III and that authorities believe Rodney and Gloriann were near the scene of the crime at the time. Jack tried to be as calm and straightforward as possible.

"They think my son is a murderer?" Francesca went to hug the baby, but Joe had already taken him. Jack watched as she clutched the side of the tablecloth and balled it up. He looked at Miquel, whose face was a tapestry of horror, grief, and restraint. Miquel shook his head, and Jack understood that what Francesca needed now was silence.

"And Gloriann? Could she be a murderer?" Francesca finally asked.

"If Rodney is guilty, I'm sure Gloriann did not know. She would never have gone with him. I can't believe that she would. I don't believe it," Jack answered. "I'm sorry. I assumed you knew about the homicide. I didn't want our meeting to turn out like this. I'm so sorry."

"It is better to know the truth no matter how painful. It is better that we heard it from you, Jack. Now we can be prepared," Miquel said.

"But Martin, how will he take it, knowing his father is a murderer?" Francesca was still wringing the tablecloth.

Jack shot back, "Martin is not Rodney! It is not always true that the apple falls close to the tree." His voice lowered. "Actually, I hate that inference. It is unfair and denies free will. It denies the Resurrection. I don't know how I am going to tell Martin about Rodney." And then his words became muffled. "I can't even think about that now. I've got to deal with telling the kids that Rodney is Martin's father."

Jack's upsettedness dispelled Francesca's; she began comforting him. "Jack, you are right. Martin is not Rodney. He is his own person with his own future. It will be a good future! I know you will do the right thing when the time comes. We each have our sorrows and challenges, but we are strong. We'll help each other."

Joe returned with Martin and the bottle and handed both to Francesca. He sensed the cloud that had formed over the table, sat down, and said to Miquel, "So are you a confirmed bachelor, or do you have a woman in your life?"

Jack was aghast, but both Francesca and Miquel laughed out loud. The mood immediately brightened, and Jack mouthed a "thank you" to Joe.

To Jack's surprise, the reticent Miquel answered, "I do. She is a teacher of English in San Miguel. Right now, we are good friends; someday it may be more." Miquel shared a little about his life in San Miguel, and Joe shared a lot about his in Green Bay. Lunch ended with the exchange of good wishes, blessings, promises, and hugs. Once in the car, Jack and Joe put down the windows, then drove past the entrance to the inn where Francesca and Miquel were standing. As they approached, Francesca and Miquel smiled and waved. Both men responded with vigorous waves of their own. Joe tapped the horn twice before heading for the street. Jack looked back. He saw Francesca crumple in grief, and Miquel wrap her in his arms, almost dropping the take-out container.

"That went well, don't you think?" Joe asked, looking over at his brother.

Jack's mouth dropped open, but no words came out. He closed his eyes and saw Francesca bent over crying.

"OK. I know it wasn't perfect, but it could have been worse. Look at the positives: Francesca and Miquel liked us. They are thrilled with Martin. We parted on good terms, and we made plans to keep in touch. You can't take on the rest of their hurt, Jack."

"Yeah, you're right. We are making progress. Now I'll wait for Mel to call, and then that's one more thing off the list," Jack conceded. He did not have to wait long. Mel called him, and he asked her to just listen to the whole story before saying anything.

When he finished, she broke her silence. "What the heck? You gotta be kidding me! Gloriann was cheating on you? What was she thinking? Oh my gosh! I was feeling sorry for her, and now I could just slap her. I am *so sorry* she did this to you and the kids." When Mel calmed down, she asked, "I'm guessing you want me to tell the folks?"

"Would you?" Jack was pleading.

"You know I will," Mel assured him. "But I doubt they will take this well. Dad will go ballistic. He's already upset that she ran away with Rod, but Mom convinced him that Gloriann had postpartum depression and can't be held responsible."

"And now?" Jack asked.

"I doubt even Mom can come up with an excuse for Gloriann," Mel said.

"I'm sorry to put you in this position, Mel."

"You're sorry? Don't be! It's my sister who put us in this position. She's the one who should be sorry." Mel's voice hit a high pitch. She took a deep breath, then continued, "Don't worry, Jack. I know how to do it. I'll be professional, not emotional; compassionate but not enabling; won't get sucked into old family dynamics. I can do this. I'll approach it like a job assignment."

"Thanks, Mel. Would you mind letting me know how it goes?"

Mel chuckled. "Sure. If I can't call, I'll email a report."

"I don't know if that is wise." Jack was concerned.

"I'm kidding, Jack. I'll call you. Tell Joe I said hi. Good luck with your family," Mel said and signed off.

CHAPTER | # 41

THURSDAY, SEPTEMBER 28

Jack woke up in his old bedroom. Martin was still asleep in the portable crib next to his bed. Jack had gotten up twice last night to feed the baby and hoped he would have time to shower before Martin would eat again. He took small steps to the door, careful not to awaken the one squeaky floorboard. As he padded down the stairs, he could hear Joe talking with his parents in the kitchen.

"Joe, what time did you get here? It's only seven," Jack asked.

"Get here? I've been here. Slept in my room."

"I thought you were going to go home. What happened?"

"I was, but when I called Tessa, she said I should stay here. She'd tell the kids that we would be home right about the time school ends. She said if the kids saw me, they'd want to see Martin, ask questions, and she'd never get them out the door. So here I am," Joe said, smiling and raising his cup of coffee in the air. "That's my Tessa; always one step ahead. She'll stop by after she takes Charlie to preschool."

"Good thinking. I'd like to shower before Martin gets up ..."

"Don't worry, we have him covered. Just leave your door open so we can hear him. And don't take too long. I'm making blueberry pancakes," said his mother.

"And bacon," added his father.

"Take as long as you need, Jack. I'm going to eat as soon as breakfast is ready, so if Martin wakes up, I'll take care of him." Joe looked at Jack, raising his shoulders and eyebrows.

Jack understood. Joe did not want to be around when Jack broke the news about Martin. He didn't blame him. He didn't want to have to do it either. Later, in the middle of Jack's breakfast, Joe excused himself and went upstairs. He brought the baby down to the kitchen and busied himself preparing Martin's bottle. His mother held out her arms for Martin, but Joe pretended not to notice. He knew that if he let her hold the baby, he would get stuck sitting at the table.

His dad watched him, and when Joe left the room, he said, "I know Joe, and he's doing his avoidance dance. What's up, Jack?"

Jack took his opportunity. He told his parents about Martin, Rodney, and Gloriann. To his surprise, they did not say much. They only wanted to know what Jack was going to do. He told them that he was going back to work on Monday; he couldn't afford not to. He explained that Joe and Tessa offered to keep the kids at least until his assignment in St. Louis was finished. "Then I'll have to reevaluate. Leave the kids here to finish the school year or bring them back to Tucson. That's still an unknown," Jack told them.

"And Gloriann? What about her?" they asked.

"That's another unknown. We'll have to see if any charges stick. And I'll be honest with you. I don't know what will happen with our marriage."

"But the children, Jack. You need to think of the children," his mother cautioned.

"I am thinking of the children! I am not going to leave them with Gloriann. I can't trust her to take the kids. No, that's not going to happen—not yet anyway." Jack was firm.

"I think that's wise, Jack. Sophie, this is all going to take time," his father said.

"But you plan to tell them about Martin? Are you sure you want to do that? They are only kids." His mother was worried.

"If not now, *when* Mom? Do you think it is going to get any easier? What if he grows up looking different from anyone in the family? Don't you think they will notice? Don't you think Martin will wonder?"

"Son, you are right—just tell them, help them understand, and close ranks. If you don't tell them, they will find out some other way. The kids are already experiencing blowback from all of this. That's the real reason Tessa didn't want Joe home last night. She didn't want him to see the kids until she could talk to him and you in person. She'll tell you when she gets here," his father said.

Tessa pulled into the drive a little after 9:00 a.m. Joe went out to meet her. Jack watched through the window as they embraced and kissed. The scene warmed his heart but put acid in his stomach and regret in his thoughts. Tessa came in laughing; Joe was right behind her, beaming. She saw Martin lying on his back on the couch, Sophie sitting bent over, entertaining him. "Oh my gosh! He is so cute! Wow, he's a lot bigger than his pictures," Tessa gushed. "I want to hold him. Let me go wash my hands."

After Tessa had her fill of hugging and bouncing and kissing Martin, she handed him back to Sophie, who took him out of the room. "OK, guys. I've got something to tell you," was her opening line. She related how Monday was Emma's and Will's first day at the new school. Everything went well for Will, but Emma had a rough time. "Joe, you know the Casdaks' kid? Virgil? The one in fifth grade? Well, he's in Emma's class. I think you coached him when Andy and he played soccer."

"Yeah, I remember him. He's got three older brothers and knows a little too much for his age. Biggest kid in the class, pushes his weight around. That's the kid, right?" Joe wanted to make sure his memory was correct.

"Yes, that's him," said Tessa.

Jack was alarmed, wondering if Virgil hurt Emma. But then he thought Tessa would have called him. He was impatient. "Go on, Tessa."

"Everything was OK until lunch recess. The fourth and fifth graders were outside together. Andy saw Emma standing by herself but didn't do anything until he saw Virgil and some other kids walk up to her." Tessa stopped and massaged the back of her neck. "OK, so Andy hears Virgil start to tease Emma." She stopped again and looked at Jack.

"Just tell me," Jack said.

"The kid told her that she was a loser and that's why her mother left her. Emma just stood there and stared at him. Then he went on to tell her that her mother must be pretty hot to be doing two guys at once. The other boys started laughing, and some girls were clustered together, snickering. When he repeated, 'loser' to her, well, that's when Andy got to Virgil and pushed him away. Then Virgil pushed Andy to the ground, and when Andy got up, he punched Virgil in the stomach. By the time the teachers broke it up, Andy had a black eye, and Virgil had a black eye along with a bloody nose." Tessa took a breath.

She told them that both sets of parents had been called to the office. When she arrived, Andy and Virgil were already there waiting. Andy was sitting up straight, looking scared. Virgil was slouching, head against the wall, smirk on his face, arms crossed across his chest, his legs stretched out in front of him. When Virgil's mother came in, she made a huge fuss. His father didn't say anything, just shook his head and sat down.

Before Principal Craig could even speak, Virgil's mother threatened to have Andy charged with assault. She said that just because Joe was a cop, his kid shouldn't get special treatment. When Mrs. Casdak calmed down, Mrs. Craig asked Virgil to explain what happened. According to Virgil, Andy went ape on him for no reason. That's when Mrs. Craig said she had witnesses who said otherwise. Then she had Andy give his version of what happened.

Tessa told them that by the time Andy got done with his side of the story, Virgil's mother was deflated, and his father looked embarrassed. They asked what was going to happen to the boys. Principal Craig said that Virgil would receive a detention for teasing Emma, but that Andy would be suspended for starting a fight and that he needed to apologize to Virgil.

"What!" Joe jumped up.

"No, wait. There's more, Joe," Tessa said. Joe sat down. Jack was sitting with his mouth partially opened, his face a portrait of disbelief.

Tessa went on to say that when Andy heard the punishment, he shot up and started shouting, "I'm not sorry I hit him. He's a bully, and he's mean. Picking on my cousin. Not just my cousin but a girl, a girl a lot smaller than him. Mr. Casdak, if your cousin—*a girl*—was being made fun of by a big meany, wouldn't you do something?"

Then Mr. Casdak finally spoke. He told Andy that he was right, he would stick up for his cousin, a girl. He apologized for his son and asked Mrs. Craig to reconsider Andy's suspension. That's when Virgil quit smirking, uncrossed his arms, and sat up. So it was decided that Virgil would get detention and write an apology to Emma. Andy would have to do community service—odd jobs around the church for the next three Saturdays. Then the principal told Andy to apologize to Virgil.

"Did he?" Joe asked.

Tessa nodded her head. "He did, but he said, 'Virgil, I'm sorry that you were so mean that I had to hit you.'"

Joe started to laugh. "Did he get away with that?"

Tessa nodded again. "Yeah, he did. Mrs. Craig started to say something, but Mr. Casdak cut her off and thanked her for explaining what happened. He motioned to his wife to get up, and then they both left the room. The boys went back to class, and that was that."

"I am so sorry," Jack said. "The poor kids."

Tessa sighed. "I didn't think I'd get them to go to school on Tuesday, but they didn't give me any trouble; they both went. I worried about them all day. They came home happy though. The uptake of the whole incident was that Virgil was taken down a few pegs, Andy gained street cred, and several girls asked Emma to be friends. Andy and Emma are now BCFs—best cousins forever, according to Emma."

"Well, so it all worked out," Joe concluded.

"Joe! Not really," Tessa said. "Andy is a bit full of himself right now. You are going to have to talk to him. Dad tried, but Andy got the better of him. First, Andy told him that hitting Virgil was an act of chivalry. When Dad explained why it wasn't, Andy gave him another angle, saying that Grandpa himself had told him about a just war, and hitting Virgil was a just war."

Joe laughed out loud. "See? Andy does listen to Dad's history lessons!"

"Joe!" Tessa stared at him.

"Don't worry. I'll deal with it," Joe said, still chuckling.

CHAPTER | 42

Tessa looked at her watch. "I'm going to have to go soon to pick up Charlie. What's the plan for tonight? Remember, tomorrow is a school day." It was decided to have an early pizza party to celebrate Martin's return. Jack would have time to say whatever it was he was going to say, and the kids would have time for homework if needed.

"Whose house?" Jack asked.

Tessa answered, "It would be easier if you and the folks came over to ours. Then I have more control over baths and bedtimes. We can all help with the little kids. It'll work."

"Should I bring the portable crib?" Jack asked.

"No. Dad already put up the crib in our room. So we are ready to go," Tessa told him. "We still have all the baby stuff from Charlie. Never know when we might need it." Tessa smiled at Joe, who rolled his eyes.

The adults all scattered to attend to chores. Tessa went to pick up Charlie from preschool; Joe stopped in at the station and told them that he would be back to work tomorrow. Pete left for his afternoon classes at the U of W Green Bay. Jack called work and made flight arrangements for Sunday night. Sophie was on Martin duty.

It was in the lull before the hurricane of kids that Jack's phone rang. "Mel? How'd it go?" Jack asked.

Mel told him that she had waited until the ride to the airport to tell her parents. "There's something about a confined space and a set time that makes things easier. We took a nonstop to Minneapolis this morning. By the time we landed, they had calmed down and began to plan. I'm staying at the Hampton near Elizabeth's house, and the folks are staying with Elizabeth and Carl. Carl has friends who are lawyers, and he made a few recommendations. We are meeting with one of them in an hour."

"Are they OK?" Jack asked.

"Yes. Here's the plan. You may not like it, but it is not negotiable." Jack took a breath. "What plan?"

"All right, Jack. You asked me to tell the folks. I did. This is how they want to handle it. There is no use arguing with me or them. It is a done deal. We are retaining a lawyer for Gloriann. You want that; we want that; Gloriann wants that. We are paying his fees though."

"No! Wait a minute." Jack could get no further.

"Not negotiable. This is the only way the folks can assuage their guilt over what Gloriann has done. This is something I can do too; obviously, I am not going to help with the kids. You know I love them, Jack, but kids are not in my wheelhouse. So we are going to work this out on our end and keep you informed about Gloriann, and you're going to handle everything else on your end and keep us informed." There was no arguing with Mel.

"Thank you, Mel, but good lawyers don't come cheap," Jack said.

"I know. But that's not a problem for me, so it won't be for the folks," Mel told him.

"OK, but, Mel, what if it doesn't work out for Gloriann and me in the end? What if we don't stay together? I don't know how this will play out. What are the expectations?" Jack asked, not wanting to be fenced in by assumed reciprocity.

"We talked about that and decided that whatever is going to happen is going to happen. We are not putting any expectations on you or Gloriann. We are helping my sister, their daughter, out of a legal mess. That's it. Plain and simple." Mel was using her take-no-prisoners voice.

"And have you heard anything about Gloriann?"

"She's in custody and will have to stay there until our lawyer gets her out. Look, Jack, I don't mean to be short with you, but I've got to run to pick up the folks so we won't be late meeting the lawyer. I'll let you know more later," Mel said and hung up.

CHAPTER 43

Pete let his last class out early so he would be back in time to go with Sophie and Jack. He did not want to miss seeing the kids' reunion with Martin. He was not disappointed. When Jack pulled into Joe's driveway, the kids spilled out of the house. They ran to the car and surrounded it as children do an ice-cream truck on a hot summer's day. When Jack exited the car, Emma gave him a quick hug, then peered into the back seat. Will gave him a passing hug on his way to the other side of the car to crawl through the open passenger-side door. Emma had already unbuckled Martin and was lifting him out of the car seat when Will got there. "No fair!" Will wailed and grabbed Martin's leg.

Martin began to cry. Will's loud protest and tugging upset him. Pete extricated Will's hand from Martin's leg. "Let him go, Will. You'll get your chance. Let's go inside."

Will wriggled out of his grandfather's grasp, started to cry, and ran after Emma.

Jack intercepted him and lifted him up to hold in his arms. "It's OK, Will. Let's go wash your hands, and then you can sit on the couch and hold Martin," Jack soothed.

"For how long?" Will asked as his crying subsided.

"I'll set a timer. How's that?" Jack knew how to negotiate with a five-year-old.

"OK," Will said. Satisfied, he put his arms around Jack's neck and let Jack carry him to the kitchen sink. When Will was seated, holding the baby, the room's tempo slowed.

The calm was broken later by Joe, who said, "The pizza will be here any minute; I want all you kids to go wash your hands."

Tessa and Emma had already set the table with a potpourri of paper plates, cups, and napkins. Some were from Valentine's Day, a few had shamrocks, and all the others were leftovers from birthday parties. Sophie's fruit salad served as the centerpiece. Name place cards ensured that the adults were strategically placed as separators between the children.

The pizza came, and everyone found their seats. "Dad, would you start grace?" Joe asked. When he did, everyone joined in except three-year-old Charlie, who continued squirming as Tessa held his hands together as if he were praying. Joe served the children first, and the adults started to cut up the slices into smaller pieces for the little ones. Grandma Sophie poured the milk for the kids, making sure the lid to Charlie's sippy cup was secure. Tessa handed Joe, Jack, and Pete a cold bottle of beer each. Emma poured water for her aunt and grandmother.

Everyone was quiet as the first pieces of pizza disappeared. The fruit salad was passed around again and then placed on the counter, putting a stop to Ben and Will leaning over the table to pick out the strawberries. When Andy and Emma were on their second pieces of pizza and Charlie had begged off to go play, Jack said, "I have something to share with you. Something that I told the adults this week. I did not want to tell you on the phone, so that's why I waited until now." Jack stopped and looked around. The adults looked stoic, but the kids were eager to be let in on the secret.

"First, I want to tell you about your mom," Jack said. He told them that she was in Minneapolis and was being questioned about something Rodney did. "Grandma Helen, Grandpa Stan, and Aunt Mel are there to help her. As soon as they know what will happen next, when your mom can come home, they'll call me." No one asked any questions; they were waiting for what he would not tell them on the phone. "OK." Jack took a deep breath. "I have some news about Martin. I am his adopted father, and that makes him your half brother."

"Oh no!" Will yelled. He jumped down from his chair and ran to where Martin was sitting in his infant carrier and began to feel Martin's legs and arms. "What half, Daddy? What half is missing? I want a full brother! What did they do to him?" Will was panicking.

Of all the reactions Jack had envisioned, this was not one of them. Emma got up and went to Will. "He's all there, Will. No one hurt him."

"But Dad said he's only a half brother." Will was confused.

"I know. That just means that Martin has mom for a mother and someone else for a father," Emma said.

Will squinted his eyes and wrinkled his forehead. "I don't get it."

Jack sat back and waited to hear what Emma would say. She continued, "Remember my friend Izzy? She has an older half sister named Madison. Izzy and Madison have the same father but different mothers. It's OK. A lot of people have half brothers and half sisters. It doesn't change anything."

Jack smiled; this was going much better than he had anticipated. Then Emma looked at him and asked, "So is Rodney Martin's father?"

Jack could hear his mother's intake of air and see his father stiffen. Jack's voice was even. "Yes, Emma, he is. If you have more questions about that, you can ask me later. All right?"

"Just one, Dad." And before Jack could tell her to wait, she asked, "Is Rodney going to take Martin?"

Relieved that the question was not the one he was dreading, Jack told her that Rodney was dead, that he had gotten into a fight with another man, and a gun went off. Both men were shot. One was injured, and the other was killed.

"Good! He was a shithead anyway!" Andy exclaimed.

"Andrew!" Joe said. "What did we talk about?" Joe's hand slipped up to hold the back of Andy's neck.

Jack studied Andy, who had summed up Jack's feelings rather succinctly. Andy would be lectured for voicing what the adults were fighting internally—the relief that Rodney was out of the picture and the knowledge that such a thought should not be allowed to blossom. Jack glanced at Will. He could see that little cogs were at work in Will's brain. Before Will could open his mouth, Jack commanded, "Will, come sit back down. Next to me. Right now."

The tension passed. Jack continued telling the kids that he had to go back to work in St. Louis and that he was flying out Sunday night. "You can call me anytime; we can FaceTime; and I'll come back here as often as I can. I want you to help Aunt Tessa and Uncle Joe with Martin. If all goes well, I should be done in St. Louis by the end of the year."

"When will Mommy come home?" Will asked.

"I don't know, Will. We will wait and see what happens. OK, buddy?" Jack was gentle.

Emma was staring at him. He met her stare. She understood that whatever she was going to say should wait. Jack let the silence stand. Then he clapped his hands. "OK, let's get going. You have school tomorrow!"

Friday, September 29

Cheese—it was a staple on Fridays at his house. He could smell it when he walked in, the familiar aroma of homemade macaroni and cheese. Gracing the supper table, too, was a lettuce and tomato salad, leftover cheese pizza, and the fruit salad from the night before. Smiling faces looked up to greet him.

"Cheese! What a surprise!" Joe exclaimed.

Tessa, Jack, and the little kids laughed. "Daddy, you always say that," Ben said.

"Well, we live in the cheese state. How much cheese did Wisconsin produce last year?" Joe queried.

"Three billion pounds," Andy said, making a sour face. "Almost twenty-seven percent of the nation's cheese production."

"Cheer up, Andy. Life's not that bad. You won't be at church all day tomorrow. I talked with Fr. Roch today. Let's pray, and then I'll tell you about it."

When grace was finished and everyone was eating, Joe got back to Andy. He told him that Fr. Roch wanted him to be in the sacristy right after the 8:00 a.m. Mass. "He asked me to come with you so that he can show you where the cleaning supplies are. You'll be washing the pews from eight thirty to nine fifteen. That includes setup and cleanup time. He explained to me how to do it so I can get you started, because he will be hearing confessions. The church cleaners will also be there working. So maybe start putting things away about five after nine. One of us will either stay or pick you up when you are done," Joe said, looking at Tessa.

"I'll never finish all those pews!" Andy protested.

"Father Roch knows that. He said to just remember where you stopped, and you can pick up again the next Saturday. He just wants you to do a good job. However far you get in three weeks is fine," Joe explained.

"I can do that." Andy felt his body relax. The gush of relief surprised and elated him. The adults, however, observing Andy's reaction, felt the pain of his multi-day anguish. They looked at one another but remained silent. None of them knew what to say.

When supper was over, Joe said, "OK, kids, let's help Mom clean up," to which Tessa responded, "Why don't you take the boys outside? I'll tackle the kitchen."

Emma looked at Jack. "Dad, could we take Martin for a walk?"

"Sure. I'll get him ready. The stroller is in the garage. I'll meet you there."

Andy turned to Emma. "Do you want company?"

"No, thanks, Andy. I want to talk to Dad alone."

"I got it," Andy said and headed for the backyard.

Tessa started to clear the table and load the dishwasher. She looked out the window and watched the boys playing home run derby with Joe. He was the pitcher. Andy used a regular bat; the others took turns using the plastic jumbo bat. Joe adjusted his pitches according to each boy's ability so that no one struck out. A wiffle ball that made it past the maple tree was a home run. She could hear cheers erupt as well as the occasional wail, "It's *my* turn!"

Tessa relished the momentary peace of the kitchen, but she also knew that she enjoyed the energy of the children, even the occasional chaos. She would be at a loss without them. She was happy to have Emma, Will, and Martin if only for a short time and knew she would miss them when they left.

CHAPTER 44

"Dad, I have questions," Emma stated as she and Jack walked down the street.

"I figured. Go ahead and ask me. Emma, you know you can tell me whatever is on your mind."

"I have questions about Mom," Emma said, then waited for Jack to respond.

"Go ahead, ask."

"So, Mom had sex with Rodney even though she's married to you? I mean, that's how Rodney ended up being Martin's father. Is that right?" Emma had stopped walking and was looking up at Jack.

Jack's voice was even. "Yes, Emma, that's why Rodney is Martin's father." As he waited for her next question, Jack was wondering just how much Emma knew about sex. They had talked about it in general terms, but as far as he knew, they had never discussed the specifics.

"Daddy, she left me and Will! *She left us!* Why didn't she just share? April's parents are divorced, and she takes turns staying with her mom and then her dad. We could have all stayed together, and she could have shared Martin. Why did she leave us? Was she mad at us? Did we do something wrong?" Emma started to cry.

Jack put his arm around her. "No, honey, you didn't do anything wrong. Will didn't do anything wrong. Mom made a bad choice. She should not have done what she did. She should not have left you, but we have to forgive her, Emma."

"No! I can't forgive her! She didn't want me, and now I don't want her. I know Will wants her, but I don't! I don't ever want to see her again!" Emma's face was red, and her hands were balled into fists.

Jack sighed. They walked along silently for another block, and then Jack said, "Emma, I understand how you feel. I'm feeling hurt too. I'm upset with what happened. And, yes, I'm upset with your mother. But I've chosen to look at it this way. I've known your mother for a long time, and she has never done anything like this before. She has been a good wife, and you know she has been a good mother to you and Will. She's done all the things good mothers do. She's taken care of you when you were sick. She cooked, made birthday cakes, played with you, made sure you had clean clothes, drove you where you needed to go. She's helped you with your homework. She's always been there for you. A lot of kids don't have that, Emma. Yes, it's true, she's made a mistake."

"She's made a big, huge mistake," Emma insisted.

"Yes, but before this mistake, she was a good wife. She was a good mother. Can you agree with that?" Jack asked.

"Yeah, I guess so," Emma struggled to say.

"Well, that's good enough for now, Emma. We need to keep trying our best, and someday, all will be well," Jack assured her.

"Do you really think so, Daddy?"

"I know it, Emma. Try not to worry. I know that is hard but try to just leave it to me. My job is to handle this mess; your job is to do well in school, help around the house, make friends, and enjoy your time here. Can you do that for me?"

Emma said, "Yes, I can do that, Dad."

"That's my girl," Jack said, and they headed back to the house.

Jack helped get the kids settled in for the night, then headed back to his parents' house. It was about 9:00 p.m. when Mel's number displayed on his cell phone. Jack answered, "What's up, Mel?"

"Jack, I've got a lot to tell you. Is this a good time?"

"Yes. Go ahead," he told her.

"Gloriann is out!" Mel exclaimed.

"What? That's great! How? Can I talk with her?"

"Ah, no. She's in the hotel room with my dad. I'm sitting in the car in the parking lot. I had to get out of there. Listen, we are flying to Phoenix tomorrow. Talk to her when we get back to Tucson—later tomorrow or even Sunday. She needs time to process. We all do."

"Can you tell me what happened?" Jack asked.

"Sure. That's why I'm out here, so I can have some privacy and, well, to save my sanity." Mel told Jack that Gloriann met with the lawyer, Eric Edison Evers, on Thursday evening. "Everyone calls him 'Three-E'; the guy moved quickly. Minnesota has a thirty-six-hour and a forty-eight-hour hold period before a person must be brought before a judge. Each of those times have different rules. Gloriann was under the thirty-six-hour rule. Since she was transported to Minnesota on Wednesday, her thirty-six hours began at 12:01 a.m. on Thursday. She was scheduled to see a judge before noon today."

Mel continued, "Minneapolis did not have enough evidence to charge her with aiding and abetting murder. Three-E said that they wouldn't even have had enough to charge Rod. Everything they have is circumstantial. They can place Rod's car in the area during the time of the murder, but there are no forensics indicating he murdered Reginald Whit III. They don't even have video of Rodney going into the grain elevator. In fact, the camera showing the entrance to the grain elevator wasn't working, so anyone could have gone in after Rod. It's a hot spot for urban explorers. They can prove that Rod was in phone and internet contact with the kid, but so were a lot of other people looking for fake IDs.

"They questioned Gloriann, but she knew nothing about a murder. She knew Rod bought fake IDs, and she admitted using them. They charged her with a misdemeanor for possessing the false IDs, imposed a five-hundred-dollar fine, and let her go. There is always the possibility that they can come back and charge her in the future if they can gather enough evidence against both Rod and her. Three-E thinks that will never happen."

"Well, that's a relief," Jack said. "Gloriann must be happy. The folks must be pleased."

"They were, but the joy was short-lived. Right after lunch, Gloriann was arraigned in federal court and charged with international kidnapping. You know that's a felony, Jack! The judge set bail at fifty thousand dollars. Three-E tried to get it lowered, but the judge wouldn't budge. She said that evidence suggests that Gloriann helped plan Martin's abduction and used false legal documents to accomplish it. I guess the judge didn't see her as a coerced victim. She attached conditions to the bail. Gloriann can have no unsupervised contact with Martin. Not even with Emma or Will! She also must surrender her passport, which, by the way, she doesn't even have because she gave it to Rod. She is allowed to go back to Tucson to await trial." Mel stopped to take a breath.

"Who posted bail?" Jack asked.

"Mom and Dad. They got a bail bond—put down five thousand dollars and used their house as collateral. If she skips the trial, the folks will have to sell their house or take the money out of their retirement account. At any rate, they are out the five thousand."

"She won't skip town!" Jack was surprised that Mel even considered it.

"No. I doubt Dad will let her out of his sight. She will be living with them since your house is still being rented. The renters are out at the end of December, right?"

"Yes. We will have the house back the first of the year. I think she would be brought to trial before that. At least I hope she will," answered Jack.

"So do I. Three-E said that the maximum sentence she could get is three years. He believes he can plea bargain and get it down to six months because of Rod's influence, Gloriann's clean record, and the fact that Martin was returned unharmed. He doesn't think she'll get off with no jail time. The prosecution has a strong case, and the fact that she left the country, even if she was in Canada for a brief time, does not bode well. With luck, Gloriann will be out by June, and life can get back to normal. Whatever normal is going to be."

"Wow. OK. So you are all at the Hampton for tonight?" Jack asked.

"No. I am now sharing my room with Dad and Gloriann; Mom is still at Elizabeth's and Carl's. They offered a room to Gloriann, but she refused. She told Mom that she doesn't want to ever see Elizabeth again. She's too embarrassed. I tell you, Jack, she doesn't want to apologize to Elizabeth; she doesn't want to own what happened; she just wants it all to go away." Mel sighed.

Jack ignored Mel's last statements. "I've got two more questions, and then I'll let you go. It sounds like Three-E is going to represent her in Arizona. Is he licensed there?"

Mel chuckled. "He is. He can practice law in Minnesota, Arizona, and Florida. He says he's a full-service lawyer for the snowbirds."

"What about the Ponzi scheme?"

"That's not even an issue. Gloriann is willing to talk to the FBI about it, but she was not involved. I think the feds know that. It's all good. It is just the kidnapping."

Just the kidnapping, Jack thought. *Just the kidnapping.* If it were only just that, but it wasn't. There was the betrayal, the lies, the abandonment, the crimes, the emotional and financial burden, the shattering of all they knew—if only it could be all wished away.

CHAPTER 45

SATURDAY, SEPTEMBER 30

Jack slept fitfully but woke up feeling more awake than he had in the past two weeks. He felt settled. The race to save his family from harm was over; the tension gone. It was as if a veil of dread had been removed, and now he could be confident in his path forward. He drew up a list of all the things he wanted to get done before his flight out on Sunday. The main points: spend the day with the kids, work out arrangements with Joe and Tessa, touch base with Billy's parents, go to Mass with the family, and talk with Gloriann.

When he joined his parents for breakfast, his dad commented, "You must have slept well last night, Jack. You look better."

"So, what, I looked bad before?"

"No, I meant …" his father stammered.

"I'm teasing, Dad. I am better," Jack said.

"Is there a reason?" His dad was cautious now.

"Yes. I got the monkey off my back." Before they could respond, Jack told them about Mel's call and detailed Gloriann's status. Afterward, he went into his plans for the day and finished by announcing that he was going to call Billy's parents first. "I thought we'd all get together later for Mass and dinner. Dinner is on me.

Mom, would you call whatever restaurant would be best and make reservations?" When she assented, he said, "Thanks, Mom," and headed up the stairs.

Billy's parents were glad he called. They told him that Billy was charged and pleaded guilty to illegally transporting a prohibited handgun into Canada and pointing a firearm at Rod. He was sentenced to one year in jail and a $5,000 fine.

"There might be some charge in Rod's death, but that has not yet been determined. The prosecutors have time now to build a case for murder or manslaughter, and the defense is working on self-defense. Billy swears that he did not shoot Rod, that Rod pulled the trigger. So we'll just have to wait and see. We're pretty sure our lawyer will get a deposition from you soon, while it is still fresh in your mind," Billy's dad said.

"Yes, I'm prepared for that. I'm prepared to be a witness for the defense. From what I saw, Billy did not intend to kill Rodney, but his actions did lead to Rodney's death," Jack said. "What about the Ponzi scheme?"

Again, it was Billy's dad who spoke. "Compared to a murder charge, the Ponzi scheme doesn't seem like much. Billy is cooperating with the FBI. If the United States is going to put him in jail for it, they'll have to wait until Canada gets done with him."

"And what about you? How are you holding up?" Jack's voice was full of concern.

"Well, what are we going to do? This wasn't the future we had hoped for our son, but it is the one we got. We are going back to Phoenix. The lawyer will keep us informed, and we'll stay in contact with Billy. He's our son. We will support him. I do have to say that I am proud of him in a way. Not proud of his involvement in the Ponzi scheme but proud that he is doing all he can to make it right. And I believe him when he says he didn't kill Rod. That's something.

That's something that we hold onto. Maybe we could meet you back in Arizona and talk about all this."

"I have to be honest," Jack said. "I called because I said I would, but I don't think it wise for us to meet. I am not trying to be mean. I do not want the prosecution to think that we are friends and that my testimony is biased. Best to keep things on a professional level; best to communicate only through your lawyer."

"I understand. I hadn't even thought of the implications." Billy's father was disappointed.

Jack continued, "I wish all of you the best. If you find yourself needing help or support, contact your local social work office or even law enforcement. Don't be shy about that. They can direct you to resources. There are also support groups for parents dealing with incarcerated children." Jack ended the call and drew a line through "call Billy's folks." He put the list back in his pocket and headed out to see Emma, Will, and Martin.

CHAPTER | 46

Gloriann slept on the flight back to Arizona, an early morning nonstop from Minneapolis to Phoenix. She looked out at the city as they began their descent. How often she had seen this view, but now it looked foreign to her. Even her parents and sister seemed foreign. The comfortable silence that she once enjoyed with them was gone. They did not treat her any differently than before, but now she was an outsider peering through the windows of someone else's home.

As they walked across the airport to where the PHX Sky Train would pick them up to take them to long-term parking, Gloriann wondered if anyone would recognize her as the woman who left the country with Rod. She was relieved that no one seemed to notice her. But soon her relief turned into a deep feeling of loneliness. People were going about their daily lives as if nothing had happened. There were families with happy, skipping children and ones with crabby, crying ones. There were people walking alone and couples clinging together, pulling their suitcases behind them. Gloriann mourned for the life she once had, and she bristled at the unfairness of it all.

It was less than a two-hour drive from Phoenix to Tucson, and as they approached Tucson's city limits, Gloriann felt as if she would be sick. Her throat tightened, her intestines cramped, and her stomach felt as if she were on a roller coaster. She wondered if she would ever feel normal again. "Mel, drive by my house, would you?" Gloriann said.

"Are you sure you want to do that?" Mel asked.

"Would you just do it?" Gloriann's voice was clipped.

Mel slowed the car as they drove past the house. Gloriann observed it. At one time, she thought that she and Jack would never move. They would grow old together, and their grandchildren would play with the toys she had stored away. Now the house was just a reminder of her mistake. She did not want to live there anymore. She did not want to know the people she once knew. She wanted to start again where no one would know her or Jack.

The thought of being a stranger in new surroundings pleased her. This time, however, she would not have to change her name; she would not need a fake ID; she would not have to hide. She would still be Gloriann, and she would still have her family. She would just revise her historical narrative. That's all she needed to do—change her story. Her mood brightened. "Thanks, Mel. I can't wait to get to the folks and call Jack."

Mel was disbelieving but turned and smiled at Gloriann. Her mother squeezed Gloriann's hand. "I'm so glad to hear that, honey. I knew coming back home would be good for you." Stan sat up straighter in the front seat but gave no other indication that he had heard Gloriann's comment.

Jack was in the backyard playing home run derby when his phone rang. He looked at the caller ID and saw it was Stan's and Helen's landline. "Time out!" he shouted. "Joe, you pitch, I've got to take this," Jack said as he walked closer to the house.

"Jack?" It was Gloriann's voice.

"You're home. That's great. How are you feeling?" Jack felt awkward. He wished he could think of something better to say.

Gloriann commandeered the conversation. She began to tell him of her plans to sell the house and move to a different state. "I was thinking of Georgia. Atlanta might be good. We could start all over again, Jack. It would be like nothing happened. I'm sure there's a big FBI office there."

"Like nothing happened? But something did happen, and we are going to have to face it. You want to move? Well, I've been thinking about moving too, maybe back to Green Bay," Jack said.

"I don't want to go to Green Bay. People know us there. I want to go where no one knows us," Gloriann insisted.

"Look, Gloriann, that is not going to work. Even if we were to go where no one knows us, people will question why Martin doesn't look like one of the family. What are you going to tell them?" Jack asked. He decided to see how far Gloriann was willing to take her fantasy.

"I have thought about that. At first, I thought we could say he was adopted, but realized that probably wouldn't work. But what we could say is that you, or I, have Hispanic blood in our genetic makeup. What do you think?" Gloriann was eager.

Jack's voice was gentle. "Gloriann, you are still on the run. Right now, you are a fugitive from reality, from yourself. The only way you will have peace, the only way you will find happiness again, is if you own your part in this tragedy. You are going to have to work through it. There is no other way."

"Oh, and like you had no part in this, Jack?" Gloriann shot back.

"I'm owning my part, Gloriann. I'm going to look for a new job, one that allows me more family time. But we have different degrees of culpability, and I'm certainly not taking yours on my shoulders. You are going to have to deal with your part yourself," Jack said. His voice was strong; he had taken the gloves off.

"So what? Do you want me to walk around with a big red A on my chest? Is that what you want? Is that going to make you feel better?"

"No! I just know we can't run away. We can't pretend this didn't happen. We can't abandon our family and friends to live some happy lie," Jack said, trying to make her see the truth of the situation.

"Jack, I want to talk with the kids. Is that all right with you?" Gloriann changed the subject.

"Yes. I'll put you on speaker so I can hear your conversation," Jack told her.

"Really, Jack? Do you think that's necessary?" Her irritation resounded in his ear.

"Gloriann, you are not to have unsupervised contact with the children. That's a court order. I'll get them," Jack said and took a few steps to get closer to the derby game.

"Emma, Will, Mom's on the phone. She'd like to talk with you," Jack said as he waved the phone in the air. Will came bounding like a gazelle. Emma put the bat on the ground and slowly walked toward Jack. "Let's go inside," Jack said. "It'll be easier to hear."

Will took the phone first. "Hi, Mommy! I miss you!"

Gloriann said, "I miss you too, Will."

Upon hearing her voice, Will's demeanor changed. He looked at the phone like it was a grenade that just had its pin pulled. He handed the phone back to his father and ran outside. Jack said, "Here, Emma," as he handed her the phone.

"I'm not talking to her," Emma said, then turned on her heel and left.

"Gloriann, I'm sorry. The kids …" Jack tried to smooth things over.

"Why won't they talk to me? Have you been badmouthing me?" Gloriann asked.

Now Jack was angry, "No, Gloriann. I haven't badmouthed you—no one has. Everyone has been more than supportive. The kids are hurt, and they are angry. Remember, you left them. They have a lot to work out, Gloriann. It is going to take time."

"Whatever. Are you bringing them back to Tucson? They could stay with us. That might help," Gloriann suggested.

"No, I am not bringing them back to Tucson. They are staying with Joe and Tessa for the rest of the school year. They need the stability. I'm going to St. Louis tomorrow to get back to work. When I have a couple of days free, I'll come visit them, or I'll come visit you."

"I want them back here, Jack. You have no right to make these decisions on your own." Gloriann was miffed.

"I do have the right, Gloriann. I am also seeking sole custody of the children until a time that I feel it would be safe to reunite our family." Jack spoke as if he were talking to a crime suspect.

"No judge will agree with you. Custody usually goes to the mother," Gloriann said.

"Not a mother who abandoned her children; not a mother who is being charged with international kidnapping; and not a mother who will be incarcerated in a federal prison. Look, Gloriann, this isn't just miraculously going away. You need to get counseling and do the work. Then *maybe* we have a chance. I'll go to counseling; the kids will go to counseling; and we'll see how this all shakes out. We are not the only couple in the world facing difficult challenges. People get themselves into all sorts of situations every day. They can lie about it; they can pretend it never happened; or they can accept it and fix it. Life does go on." Jack's heart was pounding.

"Yeah, you have everybody, but I'm alone, Jack. I'm all alone." Gloriann sounded despondent.

"You are not alone. No one has abandoned you. Your family and your friends have not abandoned you. Reach out to your friends, Gloriann. Don't hide from them," Jack said. "First free time I get, I'll come to Tucson. Until then, we'll talk by phone. Take one step at a time, Gloriann. That's what I'm doing. That's what the kids are doing—one foot in front of the other. Listen, I'm grateful that you are safe, and the kids are safe, and that our families are so supportive. You should be grateful too," Jack told her.

Gloriann nodded, a response that Jack could not see, and then she disconnected the call.

He sighed, put the phone back in his pocket, and went outside to rejoin the game.

"Everything OK?" Joe asked.

"Yeah, peachy." Jack picked up the ball, took his place on the make-believe mound, looked at his family encircling him, then called out, "OK, I'm pitching now. Batter up!"